INTO

the

BRIGHT

UNKNOWN

RAE CARSON

Greenwillow Books
An Imprint of HarperCollins*Publishers*

Into the Bright Unknown
Copyright © 2017 by Rae Carson

All rights reserved. No part of this book may be used or reproduced in any manner whatsoever without written permission except in the case of brief quotations embodied in critical articles and reviews. Printed in the United States of America. For information address HarperCollins Children's Books, a division of HarperCollins Publishers, 195 Broadway, New York, NY 10007.
www.epicreads.com

The text of this book is set in 11-point Hoefler.
Book design by Paul Zakris

Library of Congress Control Number: 2017951925

ISBN 978-0-06-224297-6 (trade ed.)

17 18 19 20 21 PC/LSCH 10 9 8 7 6 5 4 3 2 1
First Edition

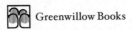 Greenwillow Books

For my husband,
who came with me on this long journey

Dramatis Personae

Leah "Lee" Westfall, a sixteen-year-old girl

Jefferson Kingfisher, Lee's fiancé

The Joyners

Rebekah "Becky" Joyner, a widow from Tennessee

Olive Joyner, her seven-year-old daughter

Andrew Joyner Jr., her five-year-old son

Baby Girl Joyner, an infant

The Glory, California Crew

"Major" Wally Craven, former wagon train leader

Hampton Freeman, formerly Bledsoe

Mary, Lee's friend

Old Tug and the Buckeyes, miners from Ohio

Wilhelm, a hired thug turned blacksmith

The Illinois College Men

Jasper Clapp, a doctor

Thomas Bigler, a lawyer

Henry Meek, currently seeking employment

Others, in San Francisco

James Henry Hardwick, a wealthy businessman

Miss Helena Russell, an associate of Hardwick's

Jim Boisclair, a former store owner from Dahlonega, Georgia

"Mr. Keys," Hardwick's accountant

Frank Dilley, a hired gun

Sheriff Purcell

Sonia, a pickpocket

Billy, a young orphan and thief

Melancthon Jones, a ship's carpenter and cook

LATE JANUARY 1850

Chapter One

The log cabin I share with the Joyner family is murky and dank, with a packed dirt floor that moistens to near mud at the base of the walls. But it has a solid roof, a cozy box stove, and—best of all—a single bright east-facing window with a real glass pane. Real glass! It's such a rarity since coming west to California, but our claims have proved out so well that we can afford a few luxuries.

I work hard each day and fall into my bedroll exhausted but happy. Usually, I'm awakened by Zeus, Becky Joyner's proud rooster, who trumpets every single dawn like it's going to be the best day of his life. Sometimes I don't wake until the first light of morning shines through that window, warming my cheeks and eyelids.

And every great once in a while, I'm so late abed that Becky or one of the children must intervene.

"Miss Leah Westfall, you get up right this minute, or I'm going to pour the wash bucket onto your face."

A skirted shape looms over me, backlit by the light of the window. Her hands are on her hips, her head cocked to the side. I groan and rub my eyes. "Becky?"

"Pull on your boots and a coat and come help me. Quick."

Obeying Becky is such a habit that I'm sitting up and reaching for my boots before her words sink in. "Something wrong?" I ask.

"Just got news the peddler is coming. Any miner within fifty miles square is showing up this morning, and a few Indians besides. Every seat is full. We'll probably run out of food, but we can keep everyone full up on coffee."

Becky is a terrible cook, but that hasn't stopped her tavern business from booming. People come from all over to experience the "bad food, bad service" of the Worst Tavern in California. Or so they say. I expect the real reason they travel so far and spend so much gold is that our town of Glory now boasts a few female residents. Becky suffers at least one marriage proposal per day. Mary, her hired waitress, gets several per week. Even I get my fair share, in spite of the fact that I'm already affianced to the best fellow in all of California.

Thinking of Mary puts a puts a nervous hitch in my breath. I've been meaning to talk to her about something important—about the *real* reason for Glory's prosperity—but I keep finding excuses to delay: Knowing the truth might put Mary in danger. Knowing the truth might chase her away. Knowing the truth might make her stay, but for all the wrong reasons.

I've been putting if off for weeks, ever since we escaped

Uncle Hiram's mine together. I just need to gather my gumption and get it done.

"I'll see you outside," Becky says, and she leaves.

I lace up my boots, splash icy water on my face, and wrap a scarf around my neck. I'm still wearing yesterday's skirt of soft yellow calico, a parting gift from a friend who left for Oregon territory. If Mama were alive, she'd box my ears to see me wearing my everyday skirt to bed.

My hand goes to the golden locket dangling at my throat, like it does every morning. It's my last keepsake from Mama; I took it from her still-warm body right after she was murdered, and it traveled all the way across the continent with me.

And as I clutch the locket in my palm, letting the precious metal invade *all* my senses, I realize that Mama would have been fine about the skirt. She was smart and practical, and she would have understood that things are different in California.

I pull on my coat, push open the door, and step into the brisk morning.

It's a clear, bright day, perfect for prospecting. Frost surrounds the stoop, covers the canvas roofs of the nearby shanties, even edges our big muddy pond at the end of town. The sun is just now peeking over the oak and pines, turning all that frost into glittering diamonds. Shanties and lean-tos and tents hug the slope of our hill, all the way down to the muddy field and paddock. The structures don't look like much from the outside, but one tent houses Jasper, a doctor; another has Wilhelm, a blacksmith; and still another a leather worker.

Glory is a right and proper town now, as fine a town as any I've lived in, with even finer people.

To my left is the Worst Tavern, full up on folks sitting at long tables beneath an enormous, thrice-patched awning. Mostly miners, a few Indians. Two woodstoves keep everyone in steady biscuits and provide extra warmth—the seats nearest the stoves are always first to fill. Becky works a griddle, flipping flapjacks and bacon. Her daughter, seven-year-old Olive, is at the other stove, using tongs to lift biscuits into a basket. Mary, Glory's only current Chinese resident, is scurrying back and forth between the stoves and the tables, delivering food, filling coffee cups, growling at customers.

When she sees me, she gives me a relieved smile.

"What can I do?" I ask.

"Coffee. Here, take this." She shoves the pot into my hands. "Olive's got a second pot brewing on the stove for when that's empty. Sure hope that peddler brings another one. We'll need three pots going at once by the end of the month."

I start at the nearest table and fill all the cups to three quarters full. Mary grabs dirty plates and heads toward the wash station. One of the miners, a grizzled fellow with a big bald spot dead center on his scalp, reaches up with grasping fingers for Mary's backside.

Mary whirls and—quick as a viper—whips out a handkerchief and snaps it at him.

The grizzled man snatches his hand back. "I was just being friendly!"

"Be friendly without using your hands," Mary says.

The man frowns. "You ask me, this tavern ought to be called Uppity Women."

Mary grins. "Thank you for the compliment, sir."

He squints. Before he can suss it out, I step forward with my pot. "Hot coffee, sir?"

"Don't mind if I do!" he says, Mary forgotten.

This is how it is most days at the Worst Tavern. Becky and Olive and Mary work themselves ragged to feed hungry miners, making mountains of biscuits, flapjacks, scrambled eggs, and bacon, cleaning dish after dish, all while avoiding the wandering hands of fellows who think coming to California means they no longer have to act like gentlemen. Sometimes I help out, but most days I'm out in the goldfields, working my own claim or helping my friends with theirs.

I return to the stove for more coffee, just as Mary comes back for more biscuits. "I need to talk to you," I whisper to her. "Just as soon as the morning rush is over."

She hefts the plate of biscuits with one hand and wipes her brow with the other. "Sure, Lee," she says, and she's off.

Becky leans over. "You're going to tell her?" she whispers.

"Yep."

Becky's brow furrows. "You sure you can trust the girl? She's young and . . ." Her voice trails off.

And Chinese? And foreign? I'm not sure what it is Becky won't say, and I keep my face smooth with some effort.

"She deserves the truth, Becky," I say firmly.

Becky turns away, scrambling her eggs a little too violently.

"She helped me destroy Hiram's Gulch, remember? We

wouldn't have escaped without her. I can't begin to guess how many lives she saved. Besides, she's been working here for a month. In all that time, she's earned for you three times what you pay her, without once complaining. I trust her, and so should you."

I'm preaching to myself as much as Becky, I suppose. I trust Mary. I do. It's just that my secret is such a big one, and so many people have been hurt because of it.

"What does Jefferson say?" Becky says. "He's going to be your husband; it's only proper you consult him."

"Jeff trusts her. He says it's up to me whether I tell her or not."

She shovels eggs onto a plate just in time for Mary to dash by and sweep it up. "If you think it's best," Becky says.

The morning passes quickly. Miners only linger if they had too much to drink the night before; otherwise, they're up and away to their claims as soon as possible. Everyone knows the easy diggings will be gone soon, and there's no time to spare.

A final wave of hungry miners heads our way, and I look up, hoping to see Jefferson, but it's just Old Tug and his Buckeyes from Ohio. Jefferson must be at his claim already. With our wedding coming up, he's keen to build his stake.

"Morning, gentlemen," I call out as Tug and his men find seats. "Coffee?"

Tug wipes at bleary eyes. "Please, Miss Leah."

"Hard night, huh?" I ask, filling his cup.

He grins through wiry whiskers, showing all two of his teeth. "Won two gold eagles playing cards," he says.

"Congratulations."

"Two gold eagles makes me mighty eligible, don't you think? High time I found a Mrs. Tuggle."

Not this again.

"It's a pity I'm already affianced," I tell him solemnly.

"Oh, not you," he says with a wave of his hand. "Got my eye on that little China girl." And sure enough, his gaze follows Mary as she heaps bacon onto plates and wipes up spills with her handkerchief.

I sigh. Poor Mary.

"You think she'll have me?" he asks.

"I doubt it," I say.

His eye widen with affront. "Ain't nothing wrong with me!"

"Course not. But Mary is one of the handsomest girls I ever saw. Also, she's a woman of intelligence and learning. Did you know she speaks three languages?"

He shakes his head.

"So, I suggest that instead of proposing straight out, you court her. Woo her. Show her what a fine gentleman you are."

"You think so?"

"I do." That will give me time to warn my friend. Old Tug has asked every woman he's met to marry him, starting with Becky Joyner and then me.

"I reckon you might be right," he concedes. "I don't want to mess this one up."

I give his shoulder a pat and move on to the next table.

The Buckeyes eat quickly, but unlike most customers, they scoot their chairs and benches in and take their dishes to the wash station themselves. They tip their hats at Mary, who is elbow deep in the washtub. Old Tug lingers. "Have a fine day, Miss Mary," he says, with the most earnest, hopeful gaze I ever saw on a fellow.

She looks up from her dishwashing and smiles. "Thank you, Mr. Tuggle. You too."

After they leave, Mary turns to Becky. "All right if I steal away with Lee for a spell? She needs me. I'll be back to finish the dishes; I won't shirk."

Becky stops scraping the griddle just long enough to give a wave of permission.

Mary grabs my hand and pulls me away from the stoves and the giant awning and into the sunshine. "I'm so glad you wanted to talk," she says. "I needed a break."

"Is it awful, working for Becky?"

"No, not exactly," Mary says. We head toward the creek and then turn upstream. The path is rocky and steep, but well traveled now that so many Glory residents have claims in this direction. "But after the miners leave, it's just me and Becky and Olive, working in silence. Olive is a sweet thing, but I don't think Becky cares for me much."

I'm not sure she's wrong. "Becky is distrustful of all things unfamiliar," I tell her. "But she'll come around."

Mary shrugs like it's no big deal, but Mary is not one to share her thoughts easily, and the fact that she did is a sure sign that she is vexed.

"Becky hasn't been unkind to you, has she?" I ask

"No. But she hasn't been kind either. Anyway, what did you want to talk about?"

"Not yet. Once we're out of earshot of town."

Mary raises her eyebrows but doesn't protest.

We continue uphill until we reach a spot where the creek stairsteps down a series of boulders, creating frothing rapids. The sound of the rushing water ought to mask our voices.

I glance around to make sure no stray miners are passing by. "So," I say. "I have a secret."

"I'm listening," Mary says, and she has that unreadable look again, the one I used to find so daunting.

I take a deep breath. Why does this never get easier? "You see . . . I . . . You know Old Tug?" Silently I curse myself for cowardice.

"Yes."

"He's sweet on you. He might ask you to marry him. Didn't want you to be caught by surprise."

Her face brightens. "Maybe I ought to encourage him."

Not the answer I expected. "Mary! He's vile!"

She nods. "Yes. All men are vile."

"No, they're—"

"Lee, I know a lot more about men than you do, and trust me, they're all gross, disgusting creatures. But Tug is nice. Maybe the nicest man in Glory. He never grabs me or threatens me or treats me like I'm not a person. He could stand to bathe more, but he always picks up his dishes, and he leaves me generous tips."

"Huh." I consider defending Jefferson, who is the opposite of vile, but I decide I'd rather not argue. "I hadn't pegged you for the marrying kind."

She gives me a look that would curdle cream. "Because of my previous occupation?"

"No! You're just . . . I guess I don't know."

"Well, I haven't decided if I want to marry or not. But if I do, it will be to a kindhearted fellow like Tug. Is that what you needed all this secrecy for? To tell me about him?"

"No."

Mary crosses her arms. "Out with it, Lee."

I sigh. A breeze sends a gust of waterfall spray, and as I wipe my wet face with the end of my scarf, I say, "So . . . remember my uncle? How he kidnapped me? Forced me to help with his mining operation?"

"I was there, remember?"

"Right. Of course." The end of the scarf twists in my hands. *Twist, twist, twist.* "Before that, he killed my parents. Took over the homestead. And after I escaped, he chased me across the continent."

Mary peers into my face. "I always thought his obsession with you was mighty peculiar. I mean, you're his niece, but still."

"It was more than that. And Mary, you have to swear up and down and sideways that you won't tell another soul what I'm about to tell you."

"I'll swear no such thing. You either trust me or you don't."

I glare at her. She is determined to make this difficult. "Fine. Here it is. I can find gold. Not like a miner. Like a witch. I have a . . . power."

Her black eyes fly wide as she blurts something in Chinese.

"What? I don't know what you just said—"

"Something my mother would have whipped me for saying. Are you serious, Lee? You _are_ serious, aren't you. You're not funning me at all."

"I'm not funning you."

Her sudden smile could light up all of California. "Show me!"

"Wait. You believe me?"

"Of course. You may be daft sometimes, naive in the ways of men, but you're not a liar. And it makes sense. All those rumors about the Golden Goddess . . ."

"Yeah. Those."

"Show me," she says again.

I've had to prove myself before, so I know just what to do. I reach behind my neck and unclasp my locket. I hand it to her, chain and all.

"I'm going to turn around and close my eyes. Hide the locket somewhere, and I'll tell you where it is."

"All right."

I turn my back to her, extending my gold sense. The locket shines like a beacon in my mind, a spot of warmth and light. Only a few seconds pass before I say, "Don't put in your pocket, Mary. That's too easy." Mary gasps. "Hide it somewhere more interesting."

A moment later, I hear scuffling, scraping of rocks, a bootheel digging into the ground.

"Okay, find it," Mary says breathlessly.

My back is still to her, but I can sense the locket just fine. I roll my eyes. "It was clever of you to make all that racket, but the locket is still in your pocket."

"No, it's not," she lies.

In answer, I imagine invisible fingers wrapping themselves around the locket. I picture them clenching into a fist, lifting the trinket into the air.

Mary blurts something in Chinese again. I turn around to find her gaping at the locket, a shiny bit of gold floating in the air before her, chain dangling.

But this is a new trick for me, and I can't keep hold of it for long. My mental grip weakens fast, and the locket plummets to the ground. Slowly, almost reverently, Mary crouches to retrieve it, brushes off dirt and pine needles, and offers it to me.

I put it back around my neck, where it belongs.

"Who else knows?" she asks.

"Jefferson, of course. The Major. Becky and the children. The college men. Hampton."

"Even the children?"

"They've seen some hard things since leaving Tennessee. They understand consequences, and they know to keep quiet."

"Well." Mary gazes into the distance. The damp air is chilly here by the rapids, making me shiver. A raptor screeches from far away, and I look up, expecting to see one of California's giant condors, but the sky is a bright blue bowl of emptiness. "Thank you for telling me," Mary says finally. "For trusting me."

"You should understand, Mary, that being my friend is

dangerous. My uncle murdered to get his hands on me, to control what I can do. You have a right to know what you're in for."

Mary waves it off. "California is nothing but danger. I expect being your friend might also be . . . useful . . ." Her mouth forms a little *O*. "That's why Hampton's claim is doing so well! And Jefferson's. And *yours*. Lee, you're going to be rich. If you're not already . . ."

I know that gleam in her eye. I've seen the fever take people a thousand times.

"Don't worry," she adds, as if reading my thoughts. "I won't tell anyone. And you don't have to help me get rich. Though . . ." She waggles her eyebrows. "It wouldn't hurt if you put in a good word for me with Becky. She should pay me more."

I laugh. "I'll see what I can do."

"I'd better get back to the dishes before Becky—"

"Lee! Mary!" comes a high little-girl voice. It's Olive, running toward us, skirts in her hands to keep them out of the mud. "Ma needs you again."

"What's wrong?" I ask, just as Mary says, "Everything all right?"

"It's the peddler," Olive says, gasping for breath. "He's here. And Ma got a letter."

"From the Robichauds?" I say excitedly. "The Hoffmans?"

Olive shakes her head. "From a stranger. In San Francisco."

I have no idea what that means, and my excitement slips away like water through a sieve. Letters ought to be exciting. Joyful, even. But as Mary and I follow Olive back to town at a jog, an uneasy feeling tingles the back of my neck.

By the time we reach the Worst Tavern, several of our friends have already gathered. The Major is there, bouncing the unnamed Joyner baby on his knee. The college men—Jasper, Tom, and Henry—have their heads together at the other end of the table, reading Becky's letter. Jefferson and Hampton arrive just as Mary and I do, little towheaded Andy at their heels, followed by the dogs, Nugget and Coney.

Everyone else must be out perusing the peddler's wares, because we have the tavern all to ourselves.

Jefferson grins when he sees me. Already, a smudge of mud sweeps across his brow, and his temples are slick with the sweat of hard work. The sight makes me happier than a lark in a meadow. I grin right back.

"We'll have to move fast," Tom tells Becky from his place at the table. "Seems as though the letter took a while to find you, and your cargo won't be stored much longer."

"What do you mean?" I say. "What's going on?"

"It's my house," Becky says. "The one my late husband had disassembled and shipped across the Panama Isthmus. It arrived in San Francisco some time ago, and a letter to Andrew asking him to claim the cargo just now reached us."

Jefferson sidles over so he can put an arm around my shoulders. I lean into him. My head barely reaches his jaw now, and I decide I like that just fine.

"So what are you going to do?" Mary asks.

Becky raises her chin. "I'm going to get what's mine, of course."

"You sure it's worth the trouble?" the Major asks gently. "You earn so much each day with your restaurant, and you have a sound cabin already."

Becky's eyes soften. "I do. And I'm grateful for all of it. But that house has sentimental value. And it comes with other items of worth—some furniture, a few heirlooms. It would be a final courtesy to Mr. Joyner to lay hold of it all and pass it along to his children someday."

"Well, that's good enough reason for me," the Major says.

"Ba!" says the baby girl in his lap.

"I would dearly love to see San Francisco," Henry says. "My claim has done fine. I could take my stake to the city. Get a job as a tutor."

"Maybe this is a good time to set up my law practice," Tom says.

Jasper says, "I'd love the opportunity to study with a city doctor for a while."

I stare at the college men, my heart sinking. "So . . . you want to leave Glory?" We traveled across a whole continent together, and I can't imagine the place without them.

"Maybe," Henry says.

"Just temporarily," Jasper says, with a pointed look at his friends. "I'm not giving up *my* claim."

But Tom grasps Henry's hand with his own, and some kind of understanding passes between them.

Hampton reaches down to scritch Coney behind his long ears. "I wouldn't mind heading to San Francisco, see if there's any word of my wife, Adelaide." With Tom's help, Hampton arranged to buy his wife's freedom. We're hoping to hear the sale has gone through and she's on her way. It's probably way too soon—it takes months for letters to find their way back east—but you can't blame a fellow for being optimistic.

Becky turns to Jefferson and me. "What about you two? Any interest in a trip to San Francisco?"

"I don't want to give up my claim," Jefferson says. "I'm about to be a married man!"

"Tug and the Buckeyes could work your claims while you're gone," Tom suggests. "In exchange for keeping a percentage of what they find. They've proven themselves hardworking and trustworthy. I could even draw up some quick contracts."

"I suppose that would work," Jeff says. "Lee, what do you think?"

"I think . . ." I take a deep breath. Mama and Daddy were originally from Boston. They used to tell me about the sea, about water that stretched farther than a body could gander, a color that's the most perfect deep blue in the world. "I think I want to see the ocean."

"Then it's settled," Jasper says.

"Wait, Becky, what about your restaurant?" I ask. "You have so many customers that—"

"I'll do it," Mary says, and we all look at her. "I can do it," she insists.

Becky taps a finger to her lips, considering, sizing up the girl.

"I might need to hire a little help," Mary adds, "but I can keep the place running."

"Very well," Becky says at last, and Mary grins from ear to ear.

"We should leave soon," Tom says. "Maybe even tomorrow. I don't know what they do with unclaimed property, but if Becky doesn't act fast, it could get dumped into the bay. Or even stolen."

We work out a few more details, but it's settled in no time. The Joyners, the college men, Hampton, the Major, and Jefferson and I are all headed to San Francisco. The Buckeyes and Mary will stay behind to keep things running smoothly.

When our meeting comes to an end, Jefferson and I head out toward our adjacent claims, walking hand in hand, the dogs at our heels. I'm already rich. My stash of gold pieces and nuggets and dust is fit for a king. Still, I want to find as much gold as I can today, because who knows what our journey will bring?

"There's another reason I want to go to San Francisco," Jefferson says after a stretch of silence.

"Oh? Something you didn't want to say in front of everyone else?"

"That James Henry Hardwick fellow. Doesn't he have holdings there?"

We had some business with him over Christmas. We paid him a tidy sum for his services, and while he made good on his word to get rid of my uncle once and for all, he still hasn't fulfilled *all* the terms of our agreement. "You're thinking of the town charter he owes us."

"Yep. If we don't get that straightened out soon, the people of Glory have no protection. The town could just . . . go away."

Together we leap over a small rivulet, onto a rocky embankment that marks the boundary of Jeff's claim. "I thought you didn't care about owning land and all that fuss."

"I don't. But Glory is bigger than me. It's a safe place for a lot of folks now."

"A sanctuary."

"Exactly. A sanctuary. So maybe we can find Hardwick, remind him he still owes us that charter."

I frown. "He gives me a bad feeling."

"Oh? Why?"

"He uses tricky words and fancy deals and shiftiness. Like my uncle. I prefer a straight-up fight."

Jefferson laughs. "Well, maybe we'll learn to fight differently. Anyway, going is the right thing. It's fitting."

"What do you mean?"

"Once we get to San Francisco, once we see the ocean, we'll have really gone all the way across the continent. I mean, it'd be a pity to come all this way and not finish the journey."

I squeeze his hand. "Then let's do it. Let's finish the journey."

Chapter Two

On a cold, cloudless morning, after weeks of hard travel, we reach the busy San Francisco docks. The Major and the college men depart right after breakfast to pursue their own errands, so it's just me, Jefferson, Hampton, and the Joyners.

The huge bay is a wonder, so crowded with ships it looks like another city spread out across the water. Masts rise like steeples of a hundred churches, each one a temple to the love of gold. Seagulls dive between ships, or settle on abandoned masts, or swirl in the air. Beyond the ships, choppy gray-green waves froth into white peaks.

The air is breezy and wet, and it smells of salt and fish. To our left, out of sight beyond the golden hills of the peninsula, the Pacific Ocean supposedly stretches as far as the eye can see. We caught glimpses of it on our way here—smudges of blue shining through the creases of the hills—but I've never seen an ocean up close, and there's no way I'll allow us to do our business and be on our way without setting eyes on such a marvel.

I turn to say as much to Jefferson. He's riding Sorry, the sulky sorrel mare that carried him all the way from Dahlonega, Georgia, to the goldfields of California, the same way my palomino girl, Peony, carried me.

Jefferson's hat is tipped back, his dark hair spilling out around the edges. His eyes are alight beneath raised brows. An odd thing happens every time I look at his face, ever since I asked him to marry me and he said yes: my heart beats faster and everything else in the world—the crowds, the noise, even the smell of fish gone sour—disappears like a puff in the wind.

A grin plays at the corner of his mouth.

"What?" I wipe the back of my hand across my cheek, thinking of the crumbly sweet bread we had for breakfast at Mission Dolores.

"That look!" he says. "Miss Leah Westfall has seen all the wonders of the continent, and she still turns into a slack jaw at something new."

I clamp my mouth shut and glare at him.

"It's one of the things I like most about you," he admits.

"Well, can you blame me?" The wide sweep of my arm encompasses the city, the ships, and the bay. "They say it's one of the most perfect harbors in the world. Canyon deep all the way through the Golden Gate, but shallow in the shelter of the bay."

He turns his head toward the water, which is fine by me, because I like his profile as much as any other part of his face.

Peony shifts beneath me. We've all stopped to take in the view, but the folks around us are starting to glare, like we're taking up too much space.

The muddy street overflows with people bustling by foot and cart and horse, with faces and fabrics from all over the world. A brand-new warehouse goes up before our eyes as workmen scamper up and down the scaffolds. Beyond the warehouse rise the hills of the San Francisco peninsula, the slopes covered with every manner of building, house, and tent. The air resounds with voices shouting in a hundred languages, hammers pounding, wagons creaking.

Jefferson says in a soft voice, as if we're all alone, "Those ships look like the woods after a wildfire. No leaves, no branches, nothing left but barren trunks standing up against the sky."

I see it through his eyes. A forest of abandonment. "What will happen to them all, do you think?"

"They'll get scavenged. Used for building up on land. Some might be turned into prisons, like the one we saw on the Sacramento River."

The one holding my uncle Hiram, is what he doesn't say. We've been through a lot together, Jeff and me. I reach out and clasp his fingers with mine.

"Will the two of you stop mooning over each other?" Becky Joyner asks, from the wagon behind us. "You'd think nobody in the world ever fell in love before the two of you invented it."

"Becky!" Heat fills my cheeks, and I drop Jefferson's hand. She grins at me.

Becky sits with Hampton on the wagon bench, holding the reins of a team of cart horses we bought at Mormon Island. The one on the right, a chestnut with a wide white blaze, tosses his head in impatience.

"I don't care if the two of you make eyes at each other all day like lovebirds in a cage," she says, "but can you carry on with it _after_ we get my house? If we don't run into any snags, we can shop for your wedding dress and then head home as early as tomorrow."

I frown. This is not the first time we've had this discussion. "Jeff and I don't need a fancy wedding, and I don't need a fancy dress."

"Nonsense. We're family now, and your family wants to see this done right."

"Jefferson?" I plead.

The traitor holds up his hands in mute surrender.

Hampton quickly schools his grin. "We might even have time to get a proper suit for the groom," he suggests with a perfectly straight face.

Jefferson and I glare at him.

"All right, folks," Becky says. "Let's go get my house."

I urge Peony toward the docks, and the wagon rattles behind. We carefully make our way down the slippery, muddy slope until we reach the dock described in the letter.

"That's it!" Becky calls out.

I swing a leg over Peony's back to dismount, but as soon as my feet touch the ground, my legs turn to jelly, and I stumble.

Becky jumps down from the wagon, and Jefferson leaps off

Sorry, so that within seconds I have someone at each elbow, steadying me.

"You all right?" Jefferson asks.

"Just need get my bearings," I say, suddenly breathless. There's no need to explain the problem—they all know my secret.

Gold has been singing a muted song for our entire journey here, sometimes from far away, sometimes buzzing in my throat. But this, when my feet touch ground here . . . *this* is like hearing a chorus of a thousand voices.

Softly, so only Jefferson and Becky can hear, I say, "I think it's all the practice I've been doing, learning how to control the gold when I call it to me. It's made things . . . sensitive."

"How bad?" Jeff asks.

"It's everywhere—like trying to sip water from a flood."

"What do you mean, everywhere?" says Becky, looking around in consternation. "I don't see—"

"Everywhere," I whisper.

My gold sense is always strongest when I touch the earth. Men are digging a hole in the street outside the warehouse to sift gold flakes from the dirt—there are two ounces to be found if they've half an eye. A block farther, a couple of children sit outside a tavern, where they lick the heads of pins and use the wet tips to pick gold dust out of the sweepings, speck by speck. They won't get much for their labor, but each mote of gold burns like a tiny ember. Buttons and watches and brooches and hairpins flare all around me. Gold is in almost every purse and pocket. My own significant store of gold, in Peony's saddlebag, brought along for an emergency. The locket dangling at my throat. A half-dozen nuggets in Jefferson's right trouser pocket—he's been carrying them for months, ever since we escaped from my uncle's camp. And, in a little velvet clutch tied to her waist, Becky has more than a dozen gold coins—

A group of laughing, dirty-faced children plows into us, setting the horses to bellyaching. They are no older than Olive or Andy. A few apologize with "Sorry, ma'am!" and "Sorry, sir!" while others shout "Tag!" and "You're it!" before dashing away.

Becky brushes dirt off her skirt, as if the children's behavior might be contagious. "So rude. I have to wonder where their mothers are."

"Becky, where is your—?"

I sense her purse, or rather the particularly shaped pile of gold coins in her purse, moving away. I scan the crowded street ahead.

There—a towheaded little scamp, rapidly disappearing among taller bodies. Without taking my eyes off him, I hand Peony's reins to Jeff. "Hold this," I say, and I start running.

The boy is small and quick as a rodent, disappearing behind people and barrels and wagons. I'm not really pursuing him, only what he carries, and all the other gold around me is a distraction, like trying to follow the buzz of a single bee in a hive. But my practice pays off. With focus, I hear the unique melody of Becky's gold, not quite overwhelmed by a cacophony of overlapping songs.

I have him in my sights. "Hey! Stop!"

He glances over his shoulder, sees me gaining, and pumps his legs even faster, dodging carts and barrels. His head is cranked around, eyes wide with fear, when he careens into a young woman, maybe even younger than me. Her hair is dirty blond, her skin is darkened by the sun, and her secondhand calico dress—too loose on her by half—is dimmed by dust and wear. She clutches a small cloth bag to her waist like it contains all her possessions in the world. The boy bounces away and falls down.

She snatches him by the collar, smacks him on the back of his head, and scolds him. He's almost in my grasp when he tears free and darts around the corner into a warren of smaller streets and shanties. The young woman continues calmly toward the docks as if nothing has happened, clutching that bag tight.

I tear after the boy. I'm around the corner and halfway down the street when I catch myself.

The melody of Becky's gold is moving in the other direction now. Away from me.

The bump was a handoff.

It was done so smoothly that I didn't suspect a thing. Without my witchy powers, I'd have missed it, for sure and certain.

I dust myself off and turn around as if I've reluctantly given up pursuit. My performance is wasted. The boy is long gone, and the young woman is headed away, oblivious to me.

She walks at a normal pace, like a woman with nothing to fear, so it's easy to extend my stride and catch up. Seeing as how she's leading me right back to Becky and Jefferson and Hampton, I'm in no rush.

I steadily close the distance and listen for the gold. The shape of it tells a story. She has a secret pocket sewn in the waist of her dress, which she hides by clutching the mostly empty bag in front of her. The pocket holds Becky's purse and two others, plus several large nuggets of varying shapes and a few loose coins, including a half coin with a sheared edge.

That last one's call feels sad, like a song in minor key. The shape of it is so distinct and specific that it's easy to single out from the rest. It becomes my beacon.

As I approach her from behind, I focus all on my attention on that broken coin.

When I first learned to call the gold to me, it was all or nothing. Every nugget, every flake, every piece of dust in range came flying and left me standing there like a statue covered in gold leaf. The first time, it happened when a few folks happened to be watching.

It was dark and rainy, and no one knows for sure what they saw. Still, in the months since, the story spread faster than a summer wildfire. Even some of the miners in Glory have been telling tall tales of a Golden Goddess. They say she's lucky. That if you catch a glimpse of her in the hills, you'll be blessed by a straight week of pure color.

There's no stopping tall tales from spreading, but letting those stories get connected to me will draw a deadly kind of attention. So with Jefferson's help, I've been figuring out how to control my power.

Only a few steps behind the young woman now. The waist of her dress is cinched as tight as it can go, and it still hangs loose. In spite of the cool air, sweat curls the dirty blond strands at the nape of her neck.

I think hard about that broken coin. Then I hold my hand out in front of me and close my fist.

The jagged edge surges toward me, straining against the pocket seams.

I unfold my hand and push the broken coin away.

The gesture is unnecessary—I can control the gold just fine without it—but I've found it makes things a little easier, acting like a focus for my thoughts. So my fist clenches and releases, clenches and releases, as we walk down the street. I probably seem daft to anyone looking, but San Francisco is a busy place, and no one pays me any mind.

My friends are waiting just ahead. Hampton has climbed down from the wagon. Jefferson stares at me with a worried frown. Becky seems distressed.

I ignore my friends for the moment and work harder, pulling and pushing the rough edge of that coin like a saw against the seam of the hidden pocket. The young woman's steps quicken; surely she has noticed something odd by now.

She's making her way around our wagon, and my friends are stepping toward me, when the seam breaks and the coin comes flying out of the dress.

I mentally grab everything else in the pocket—the other purses, the nuggets, the coins—and imagine a sharp tug downward, just like milking a cow.

A small fortune in gold tumbles from her dress and plops into the mud. She gasps, falling to her knees, ruining her skirt.

"Ma'am," I say, rushing forward before she can gather it all up herself. "Ma'am, you dropped something."

She faces me. Up close, she's even younger than I expected. In spite of her light hair, her eyes are as brown and hard as acorns. An awful lot of thinking is going on in those hard brown eyes.

"I reckon this is yours." I pick up the broken coin and put it in her hand. It gleams like a half moon. Her palms are calloused, her fingernails ragged as if trimmed by teeth. She did hard labor before turning to thievery.

Her fingers close around the coin, and she slips it quickly into the cheap cloth bag she carries. I squat beside her.

"I don't know what happened," she says, quickly gathering nuggets and loose coins into her bag. "I must have tipped my bag when I wasn't paying attention."

"Just an accident, I'm sure," I tell her. "My name's Lee."

"Thank you, Lee. I'm Sonia. I can't tell you how much your kindness means to me."

She reaches for Becky's coin purse. I pin her wrist with one hand and snatch up the purse with the other.

"Sonia, I'm afraid this one belongs to my friend. There's an engraving on the inside of the clasp that says R.J., and I can tell you exactly how many coins are in it and what their weight comes to."

Her brows knit, and she stares at me with those hard eyes. She tries to jerk her hand free, but I'm not about to let go—I've spent my life doing hard labor too, on the farm at home, on the wagon train west, in the goldfields.

Becky, Jefferson, and Hampton surround us. "What's going on here?" Jefferson asks, genuinely mystified.

"My new friend Sonia here dropped some things, and I'm helping her pick up," I explain. I hand Becky's purse to her. There's a firm set to Becky's mouth, and unlike Jeff, she knows exactly what we're about.

Sonia jerks her hand away, and this time I let go. Her face shows relief as she shoves the remaining items into her bag and stands. No one will be turning her in today.

"Thank you for your help, Lee. Not everyone in this town would've been so kindly."

"That little blond-haired boy—is he your brother?" I ask.

"Billy? No, ain't many left as still got family. Just a few friends."

Maybe I'd be in her place, if I didn't have Jefferson and Becky and Hampton and everyone else. "It's important to have friends."

She holds my gaze. "Thanks again. Be careful here in San Francisco—this city is full of thieves." She pauses, her stare unwavering. Then, carefully: "The biggest thieves, the _real_ ones, will take everything you have, even the clothes off your back."

She rushes off before I can respond. Jefferson removes his hat and scratches his head. "What just happened here?"

Hampton laughs, a deep rumbly sound. "That little slip of a girl just tried to rob Mrs. Joyner. Thought she had a sunfish on the line, but it turned out to be a shark."

I glare. "*I'm* the shark?"

"Meant it as a flattery."

I turn to Jefferson, the question in my eyes, and yes, I'm not ashamed to admit I'm fishing for a compliment.

"Well, you do have a dangerous smile." Before I can follow up, he says, "But seriously, what just happened here?"

I say, "She's working with that group of children who bumped into us. I bet she walks down the street and identifies the targets—"

"Marks," says Becky. "Mr. Joyner always called them marks. Gullible gamblers. Different situation, same principle."

"So she walks down the street and identifies the *marks*—"

"Probably while the two of you were staring all googly-eyed at one another," Becky interrupts again. She's clutching her purse tight in both hands, knuckles white as she comes to grips with the fact that she nearly got robbed.

"And then she sends the little urchins out to play in the street and pick pockets. They bump into her coming back the other direction, but it's really a handoff. That way, if anyone catches the children, they don't have any evidence."

"Anything *incriminating*," suggests Becky, who never heard a fancy word she didn't want to flaunt. "There was a pack of orphan children back in Chattanooga that functioned much the same."

Maybe that's what my life would have been like if my uncle Hiram had murdered Mama and Daddy and left me an orphan when I was five instead of when I was fifteen.

"She almost got away with it," Jefferson says.

"Well, she didn't," Hampton says, climbing back onto the wagon bench. "Let's get on with it. I want to check the post office when we're done, see if there's any word of my Adelaide."

Hampton started out his journey on the California Trail as a slave. When his master died, he followed the wagon train west, secretly aided by the Illinois college men. Once we got to California and found gold, he bought his own freedom, with Tom's help.

"What ship are we looking for?" Jefferson asks.

"It's supposed to be right here at Washington Pier," Becky says. "It's called the *Charlotte*."

"Then let's have a look around."

Chapter Three

Calling it Washington *Pier* is being optimistic. A long, muddy street winds down the marshy hill until it meets the bay. Toward the end, where the mud gets so bad it's almost impossible to walk, a boardwalk begins, jutting well into the water. To either side of the boardwalk are abandoned ships run hard aground. People dump wheelbarrows of dirt into the soupy muck, turning it into land and trapping the ships right where they sit. On our right, a crew swarms over one of the hulks, stripping the wood like a pack of termites devouring a pine shack. On our left, a lonely twin seems to await a similar fate.

At the end of the dock, men swing precariously over the water, hammering boards into an empty framework. An anchored ship waits to tie alongside, just as soon as the dock is ready. A foreman hollers at us to step aside as a group of workmen rumble past, carrying a huge log smeared with pitch on their shoulders—another pile to drive into the water and extend the dock even farther. The whole structure sways precariously from side to side as they go.

"I think I'd rather stay here," Hampton says, eyeing the dock with distrust.

"Sure," I reply.

"I'm not sure those fellows know a single lick about building piers."

The workmen drop the new pile, and the dock shakes so hard one of the boards pops loose and falls into the water. "We need someone to watch that wagon and the horses anyway," I assure him.

Jefferson and Becky and I step onto the rickety dock, which feels more solid under my feet than I expect. I can't help gawking at the ships as we go. Jefferson, never one for shyness, cups his hands to his mouth. "The _Charlotte!_" he hollers. "We're looking for the _Charlotte!_"

Sailors shake their heads. One rakish fellow leans over the side of his ship and shouts in an Australian accent. "Oi! If you find Charlotte, tell her I'm looking for her, too!"

"Rude humor is a mark of low character," Becky shouts back.

"Of course I've got low character," the sailor responds. "I come from down under!"

His crewmates laugh. Jefferson looks to me as if to share a grin, but I shake my head. Becky Joyner is on a mission, and this is no time to cross her.

The sailor wisely returns to work. We pass another ship and reach the end of the dock. Still no _Charlotte_.

"Maybe this is the wrong place," Jefferson says.

"I'm sure this is it," Becky says. "I reread the letter and checked the directions with people at the mission before we came down to the waterfront."

If Becky says she's sure, she's sure. "Maybe they left already?"

"I made inquiries," Becky says. "The *Charlotte* was expected to remain in port."

Her knowledge doesn't surprise me one bit. Thanks to her restaurant regulars, Becky now has more connections and better information than anyone I know.

"We must have missed it," I say. "We just need to head back and start over."

We return to Hampton and the wagon. "Things got mighty precarious," Jefferson tells him solemnly. "But the dock didn't fall into the bay."

"But you didn't find anything either, so I was better off waiting here, wasn't I?" Hampton says.

"I think this is the ship right here," Becky says.

"What?"

She's staring up at the abandoned hulk, the one that's never setting sail again because the bay's been filled in right around it. The faint outline of weathered letters appears on the bow, obscured by soot and mud. They *might* have once read the *Charlotte*. I'm almost certain of the A and the R.

There's no way to climb aboard, so I pound on the side, which I recognize for the long-shot hope it is. The hull echoes back at me like a giant kettledrum. "Hey! Anyone aboard?"

A thump, like a body falling out of a hammock, then an

apple-shaped face pops up over the side, surrounded by a rat's nest of gray-black hair.

"Whaddayawant?" he says.

It comes out as one angry, messy word, but I reckon that's a natural state of things, rather than any specific anger being directed at us. I've heard the same New York accent from other miners we've met.

"We're looking for the _Charlotte_," Becky says. "It sailed out of Panama, carrying cargo that came across the isthmus, including my disassembled house."

As the stylish Southern lady addresses him, the New Yorker stands straighter and combs fingers through his hair, though without noticeable effect. "I have some good news and some bad news," he says.

He bends, and with a grunt and heave, he slides a gangplank down to the dock. It lands hard and sets the dock to swaying. The man puts hands to hips and says, "Well, come aboard. I'm not gonna shout at you from way up here."

I look to Hampton. "I volunteer to watch the horses," he says.

The gangplank is sturdier than it looks. Becky, Jefferson, and I make the steep climb single file and step onto the deck. It's an old ship, and because of the faded paint and soot marks on the hull, I expect it to be in disrepair, perhaps even in the process of being scavenged. But everything is tidy and well stowed, the deck clean of debris and dirt.

"Name's Melancthon Jones," the sailor says. "What can I do for you?"

We introduce ourselves. "I have to ask," I say. "What happened to . . . ?" I glance over the side at the faded lettering.

He shrugs. "We made port, and the captain and the rest of the crew jumped ship to go find themselves a fortune."

"But not you?" I say.

He shrugs. "I dug ditches to help build the Erie Canal. So much digging. A *lifetime* of digging. If I never touch another shovel in my life, it'll be too soon."

"So you're just . . ." Jefferson glances around the deck. "Here?"

"I'm no sluggard, if that's your implication," Melancthon says with a glare. "Hoping for a chance to catch passage back east, but no one's hiring. The ships keep coming in, but most never leave. The few that do leave don't need crew."

Becky steps forward. "You said there was good news and bad news?"

He slips his thumbs beneath his suspenders. "Good news first. This ship here is—or was—the *Charlotte*, and we had your cargo aboard. Loaded it myself down in Panama. I was the ship's carpenter, and I admired the way everything had been taken apart, labeled, and stored. A fine bit of work."

Becky nods. "My husband supervised everything himself. He was very particular. What's the bad news?"

"Because the ship has been abandoned, the Custom House holds claim to any cargo left behind. You'll have to get permission from them to collect it, and you'll need to hurry before they auction it off."

"They can't do that!" Becky says.

"Oh, they can and they will," Melancthon says. "They're going to auction off the ship, too—sell it right out from under me."

"Will they let you stay?" Jefferson asks.

"Seems unlikely. Too much money to be had. If you have the means, you can buy a piece of property here for ten thousand dollars, then turn around two months later and sell it for twenty." Jeff and I exchange a look of consternation. Back east, a body can just about buy a whole town for ten thousand dollars.

"Where will you go?" I ask Jones.

"Don't know," he says. "Been nice having a free roof over my head. Better quality than any boarding house in the city, too. Good thing, because the captain took off without paying my wages. I might have to look for work ashore soon."

Becky smoothes the front of her dress, adjusting the pleats. "So my cargo can be found at the Custom House?"

"No, ma'am, I'm sure it's stored in one of the warehouses. The folks at the Custom House are just the ones in charge." A seagull lands on the railing, but Melancthon shoos it away.

Jefferson is stiff in the space beside me, and I can practically sense his frown.

"What's wrong?"

"This whole state," he grumbles, "no, this whole *country*—is based on stealing things from people, starting with their land. And if you don't have land, they'll take whatever you do have."

"I reckon you're right."

He's been dwelling on this a long time. Jefferson is the son of a poor white man and a Cherokee woman. His whole family on his mama's side was forced to march west after their land was stolen out from under them. Jefferson was left behind with his good-for-nothing daddy; legally, his mama didn't have options on that account. He hasn't seen her since she left, and he doesn't even know if she's alive. Now the same thing is happening to the Indians here in California. We've watched their land get taken, watched them forced into slavery, even watched them die.

"And where will I find the Custom House?" Becky persists.

"A block up the street, at Portsmouth Square," Melanchthon says, pointing. "Follow the sound of hammers. The city burned near to the ground on Christmas Eve."

"That was barely two months ago!" I say. No wonder there's soot on the hull.

"That why they're in such a hurry to rebuild."

We were headed toward Portsmouth Square anyway, since the best hotels are found there. We thank Melancthon for his help and wish him well, then make our way back to Hampton and the wagon.

"Was the good news good enough, or was the bad news worse?" he asks, giving Peony a pat on her nose.

"Not sure yet," I say.

"Our next stop is the Custom House," Becky adds. "We have to clear some things up."

Jefferson says, "Hampton, if you want to go check the post office, I'll lead the horses and the wagon. Meet up at Portsmouth Square?"

Hampton brightens. "I'd be obliged."

As he hands the reins over and takes off, Becky says, "Don't you worry, Lee. We still have plenty of time to get this straightened out *and* shop for the wedding."

I look to Jefferson for rescue, but he is wholly focused on tying up the horses to the back of the wagon. "Please, let's not hurry," I say. "All I need is Jefferson at my side, and my friends there to witness."

She waves this off with a flutter of her hand. "Yours is going to be the first wedding in Glory, California. Ever. Not only will it set a precedent for a proper wedding to everyone that follows, but it'll become part of the town's history, and that will make it part of the history of the new state. Your betrothal was a bit . . . unconventional." That's a kind way to put it—I was the one who did the proposing, during the Christmas ball in Sacramento. "I wish I could have been there to guide you. But as your friend and bridesmaid, I have a responsibility to make sure everything *else* is done properly."

I definitely consider Becky my friend. But she used to be my employer, and I will always remember the Mrs. Joyner who, on the wagon-train journey, served her husband's every meal on a fancy table set with a perfect tablecloth and fine, fragile china. I sigh. "Yes, ma'am."

It's a short walk to Portsmouth Square, just as Melancthon promised. The Custom House is a long, low adobe building stretching the full length of the square. An American flag whips from a high pole out front—thirteen red and white stripes, and thirty stars in a block of five by six. They'll have to figure out how to add another star once California officially becomes a state.

Along a wide veranda are three evenly spaced doors. The nearest is marked OWEN AND SON, BANKERS, the door in the middle has a sign for law offices with a much longer list of names, and the entrance at the far end is the Custom House. Jefferson offers to watch the wagon, and Becky and I line up behind a dozen others waiting to get inside.

The orderly, colorful crowd represents every corner of the globe—Peruvians and Chinese and a whole family of Kanakas from the Hawaiian Islands. It makes me feel like I'm part of something bigger than myself, something that involves the whole world.

The door opens onto a room with a long counter made from ship planking. Facing us from the other side is a small line of white men in starched shirts and perfectly barbered hair. Becky and I listen as, one after another, the people ahead of us receive answers to their problems.

The men in starched shirts are very sorry.

It isn't their fault.

The claimant will have to take it up with the original ship owner.

No, they can't help find the original ship owner.

The claimant might wish to go to a bank to solve that problem. They can recommend the one two doors down, the oldest and finest bank in San Francisco.

Unfortunately, the claimant will need to acquire legal advice to solve that particular problem. There are law offices all over the city, but perhaps they might care to try the services of the office next door.

Tears do not bring different answers.

Becky and I exchange a dark look. I'm starting to get a bad feeling.

Outrage doesn't help the Chinese man in line ahead of us, although it does tend to quickly mobilize a couple of rough-looking men who stand at the ready in case of trouble.

The cheerful and helpful-sounding men in starched white shirts have an answer to every question, but no one leaves satisfied.

The line moves efficiently, and soon Becky and I reach the front. My view has darkened, as though I'm in a state of about-to-be-angry, but Becky stands patiently and confidently, with all the assurance of a person who is used to having things work out for her.

"Next!"

We step up to a clerk with a face as angular as a wedge of cheese, framed by a pair of bushy sideburns. Small wire spectacles sit on the end of his nose. When he looks up from his ledger and sees us—or, rather, sees Becky, who is a fine lady in California, and therefore dearer than gold—a delighted grin spreads across his face. He reaches up and straightens his collar.

"How can I help you, ma'am?" He eyes me over the top of his glasses and amends: "Ma'ams." I'm still wearing my travel trousers, sure, but my hair has grown long enough to put up in a proper bun, and I'm no longer binding my chest with

Mama's old shawl, so the fact that I'm of the feminine persuasion is obvious to anyone paying attention.

Becky smiles at the clerk like he's a perfect piece of cake. "I believe that a house, disassembled for shipping, was delivered aboard the *Charlotte* out of Panama, and before that from New Orleans, and originally Chattanooga. Mr. Melancthon Jones, formerly the ship's carpenter aboard the *Charlotte*, reports that unfortunately, due to the irresponsible behavior of the captain, who, I understand, also neglected his duty to compensate his crew, the cargo of the ship has now been entrusted to your authority for rightful delivery to its proper owners. Here is the letter we received stating that the cargo was ready for collection."

She hands the letter over, and I want to whistle my appreciation. That was a mouthful to be sure, but Becky made it flow like fresh cream over strawberries.

The clerk appreciates it also, to judge from his childlike grin. "That's an excellent summary, Miss . . ."

"Mrs. Joyner."

His face falls a little. "Of course, *Mrs.* Joyner. You have to understand that very few people come prepared with all the appropriate information." He reads the letter and hands it back to her. "So the house is in the name of . . ."

"My husband, Mr. Andrew Joyner Senior."

She doesn't mention that he's dead. She may be scrupulously honest, but I notice that doesn't extend to volunteering information that hasn't been requested.

"Of course," the clerk replies. He rises from his seat and

goes to a stack of record books on another table behind the counter.

"I'll be so glad when this is resolved," Becky says.

"I thought we'd have more trouble."

"I did, too. But these are clearly very capable, competent men doing their best in difficult circumstances."

I gape at her. Becky sees men with authority as associates. I see them as adversaries. It might be the biggest difference between us. Rather than explain, I say, "You must have really missed that house, sleeping in the wagon for months."

The corners of her eyes crinkle. "It was our honeymoon cottage, on Andrew's father's plantation. I was seventeen when we got married—just a little older than you and Jefferson."

"You must have a lot of happy memories of it."

"Oh, goodness, no. We were far too young to marry, even Andrew, who was eight years older. It's one thing to be in love at that age, but it's another entirely to go live with someone."

I stare at her. Becky has never been forthcoming about her marriage.

"Don't act so surprised. Men are difficult and uncouth. And it didn't help that Andrew's father didn't approve of me, and he didn't want us living in the big house with them. Andrew was wild then—always a gambler. I suppose I was a bit wild, too."

I'm not sure what Becky considers "wild." Daring to go without a hat or bonnet on occasion? Using the dessert fork first? Before I can ask, she says, "I had several miscarriages before I became pregnant with Olive. That's when I finally began to settle, I think. After she was born, Andrew's mother put her foot down, and we moved into the mansion. And finally, after I bore a male child, we were set up with an inheritance and a place of our—"

She doesn't finish because the clerk returns, his thumb marking the spot in an open ledger.

"Found it," he says. "So many people have unsolvable problems. It's a pleasure to help somebody with an easy solution."

Becky smiles at me as if to say "I told you so."

"Now if you'll just have Mr. Joyner come in and sign this release form . . ."

Becky reaches for the pen on the counter. "I'll sign on his behalf."

The clerk jerks the ledger away, and his smile falters. "I'm sorry, but I can't allow that."

"But I'm his _wife_."

The clerk's smile fades a little more. "Have you heard of coverture, ma'am?"

Becky's answer has a strong streak of vinegar. "Are you a lawyer, sir? Do you presume to lecture me on the law?"

"If you know the law, you know that a wife has no legal standing. All her rights are covered by, and thus represented by, the rights of her husband. Thus, coverture. It's the law everywhere in the United States, and California will soon be confirmed as part of the United States." He slams the ledger shut. "Mr. Joyner's signature is absolutely required."

"But—" Becky says.

I squeeze her hand, hard, and she falls silent. "But what if her husband is up in the hills protecting their gold claim and working the land?" I say. "He can't be in two places at once."

I'm careful to phrase it as a possibility, because I don't want to lie direct and offend Becky's sense of propriety. She squeezes my hand in response.

"He'll just have to make the trip down here," he says.

"When is the auction scheduled?" Becky asks.

The clerk peers at the calendar on the wall and says, "A week from Tuesday, at the Hardwick Warehouse on Montgomery Street."

A little chill goes through me at the mention of the name Hardwick—most likely the very same fellow Jefferson is hoping we'll run into. James Henry Hardwick funded my uncle Hiram when Hiram kidnapped me. Then Hardwick took every penny we could raise in Glory in exchange for a promise to charter our town . . . a promise that hasn't yet been delivered. It seemed like a good idea at the time, but I've worried ever since that Hardwick may be no better than my uncle.

"There's no way we can retrieve Mr. Joyner in Glory and return by then, not with this weather," Becky says. "The winter roads are terrible—you know this to be true." I clear my throat, hoping she'll understand my message: "Stop talking." Becky is smart, but she's accustomed to getting her way. She has no idea how, as a woman with no husband and no property, the world is not on her side anymore.

The clerk rubs his cheese-wedge chin thoughtfully. "You could always buy the house at auction."

I was already thinking the same thing. It would attract more attention than we want, but I can afford it. Thanks to my gold-witching ways, I can afford to do a lot of things for my friends right now. "That's a good idea," I say.

"Where will we get the money to do that?" she asks tightly.

He says, "If you need a loan, you might go to a bank to solve that problem. I can recommend the one two doors down."

"And how am I supposed to get a loan without my husband's signature?" Her voice is sharp enough to shave with, and I imagine it taking the fellow's whiskers clean off.

"I see the problem," he says. "But the law's the law. Perhaps you might wish to consult with an attorney. I can recommend you to the gentlemen in the office next door."

"But—"

"I'm sorry. I've done everything I can here to help you." He looks past us to the next group in line, a Chinese family trying to speak through an interpreter who's dressed in black like a missionary. "Next!"

I'm willing to stand our ground and keep arguing, but Becky, ever conscious of protocol, turns and leaves. I follow her outside to the cold shade of the veranda, where Jefferson waits.

"So, how did it go?" he asks.

Becky's glare is so withering that he takes a step back.

"Not well," I say. "They'll accept Mr. Joyner's signature only, and no substitutes."

"Coverture is a barbaric doctrine," Becky says. "What am I, a piece of property to be handed around from one man to the next like a gambling chit? Now that Andrew's passed on, I suppose I'm covered by my father-in-law, a man who still despises me. Given half a chance, he'll take Andrew Junior to raise as his heir and send me off to a convent or something."

Jefferson and I exchange a surprised glance. We've heard more and more of Becky's opinions since the death of her husband, enough to know she's been thinking them in the quiet privacy of her own mind for a long time, maybe years. But this is one of the strongest we've heard pass her lips.

"We could always buy the house at auction," I suggest.

"Or have a man buy it for me, you mean," Becky says.

"Or that."

"No. I won't pay again for something that's rightfully mine."

"If the law's involved, we should talk to Tom about it," Jefferson suggests, and I could kiss him, because that's the perfect next step. Actually, I could kiss him anyway. "You should have let him come with you."

"He had his own worries," Becky says.

"Not sure it matters now," I say. "He's out looking for space to rent, which means he could be anywhere."

"Just saw him," Jefferson says. "Went next door. Said he was having trouble finding a place in his price range. He's rethinking his plan to go independent."

"Fine," Becky fumes, stomping away. "Let's go see Tom."

Chapter Four

If anyone can help us, it's Tom, and Becky holds her head high and marches into the law office, me following behind.

It's the same size as the Custom House, with comparable furniture and decor, but that's where the similarities end.

Instead of orderly lines, calm voices, and every nationality, I see only well-dressed white men, smoking cigars while talking over one another. The song of gold is loud—the main chorus comes from the bank next door, but notes of it sing from fine pockets around the room. Voices suddenly crescendo to threatening shouts, and I tense, ready to grab Becky and run, but laughter follows a split second later, accompanied by hearty slaps on shoulders.

"There's Tom," Becky says. He's been tromping around the city half the day, but I don't see a speck of mud on him. Though he dresses plain, it always seems he rolls out of bed in the morning with his hair and clothes as neat and ordered as his arguments.

We walk over to join him, and he acknowledges us with a slight, perfectly controlled nod.

He's one of the college men, three confirmed bachelors who left Illinois College to join our wagon train west. Compared to the other two, Tom Bigler is a bit of a closed book—one of those big books with tiny print you use as a doorstop or for smashing bugs. And he's been closing up tighter and tighter since we blew up Uncle Hiram's gold mine, when Tom negotiated with James Henry Hardwick to get us out of that mess.

"How goes the hunt for an office?" I ask.

"Not good," Tom says. "I found one place—only one place—and it's a cellar halfway up the side of one those mountains." Being from Illinois, which I gather is flat as a griddle, Tom still thinks anything taller than a tree is a mountain. "Maybe eight foot square, no windows and a dirt floor, and they want a thousand dollars a month for it."

"Is it the cost or the lack of windows that bothers you?"

He pauses. Sighs. "Believe it or not, that's a reasonable price. Everything else I've found is worse—five thousand a month for the basement of the Ward Hotel, ten thousand a month for a whole house. The land here is more valuable than anything on it, even gold. I've never seen so many people trying to cram themselves into such a small area."

"So it's the lack of windows."

He gives me a side-eyed glance. "I came to California to make a fortune, but it appears a fortune is required just to get started. I may have to take up employment with an existing firm, like this one." Peering at us more closely, he says, "I thought you were going acquire the Joyner house? I mean, I'm glad to see you, but it seems things have gone poorly?"

"They've gone terribly," Becky says.

"They haven't gone at all," I add.

"They'll only release it to Mr. Joyner," Becky says.

Tom's eyebrows rise slightly. "I did mention that this could be a problem, remember?"

"Only a slight one," I say with more hope than conviction.

"Without Mr. Joyner's signature," Becky explains, "they'll sell my wedding cottage at auction. Our options are to buy back what's ours, which I don't want to do, or sue to recover it, which is why I've come to find you."

If I didn't know Tom so well, I might miss the slight frown turning his lips. He says, "There's no legal standing to sue. Andrew Junior is of insufficient age, and both his and Mr. Joyner's closest male relative would be the family patriarch back in Tennessee. You see, it's a matter of cov—"

"Coverture!" says Becky fiercely. "I know. So what can I do?"

"There's always robbery."

I'm glad I'm not drinking anything, because I'm pretty sure I'd spit it over everyone in range.

"Tom!" Becky says. "Are you seriously suggesting—?"

"I'm merely outlining your full range of options. You don't want to buy it back. You have no legal standing to sue for it. That leaves stealing it or letting it go."

This is the Tom we've started to see recently. A little angry, maybe a little dangerous. I haven't made up my mind if I like the change or not.

"I'm not letting it go," Becky says. "Just because a bunch of men pass laws so other men who look just like them can legally steal? Doesn't mean they should get away with it."

We've been noticed; some of the men in the office are eyeing us curiously. "How would *you* go about stealing it back, Tom?" I ask in a low voice, partly to needle him and partly to find out what he really thinks.

He glances around, brows knitting. "I suppose I would get a bunch of men who look like me to pass some laws in my favor and then take it back through legal means."

I laugh in spite of myself.

"You're no help at all," Becky says.

He holds up his hands as if in surrender. "I'll give it some thought, make some inquiries. There may be options I haven't considered."

The front door bangs open; conversations stop.

"Miss Leah Westfall!"

My hackles go up as a tall man strides into the room. His white hair and bushy sideburns frame ax-sharp cheekbones and a wide, smug mouth. He's dressed immaculately, with gold buttons on his dark jacket, a gold pocket-watch chain, and a gold-knobbed cane in his left hand. His right hand clutches a cigar, which he puffs with obvious pleasure.

James Henry Hardwick. Though he's only a councilman in Sacramento, some say he's the richest man in California at the moment, and the power behind the powers.

An entourage follows him into the room. The first is a small, mousy fellow with the tiniest nub of a chin, who stands so close to Hardwick you'd think they were tied together. A ring heavy with keys hangs from his belt loop, tugging down his pants. He carries a large leather bag, which he shifts from arm to arm. A fortune in gold is piled inside that bag; it knocks on my skull like an undeterred suitor.

A beautiful auburn-haired woman follows. She steps around the fellow with the keys, and slips her hand through Hardwick's elbow. She wears a green dress—a full crinoline skirt with flounces, a bodice that makes her waist look unbreathably narrow, and a low-cut neckline that makes you forget about her waist. She smiles on the room like a queen bestowing graces, and I can tell from the gazes of most of the men in the law office that Becky and I have all but disappeared.

Hardwick's two bodyguards follow last, and that's when I discover my stomach can sink even further, right through the floor.

Frank Dilley.

My uncle's right-hand man. Former right-hand man. The no-good snake who kidnapped me last fall. I'd heard that Frank had died during the insurrection at the mining camp a couple months past. In fact, it was Hardwick himself who told me as much, that lying Cain.

The right side of Frank Dilley's face looks like melted wax— likely he'll never grow hair there again. When he sees me, his left hand drifts to the revolver at his waist.

"Frank," I say, trying not to let my voice quaver. "I heard you died."

"Still alive and kicking," he says. "No thanks to you."

And because sometimes I can't control the meanness in my heart, I say, "You're looking better than ever."

Hardwick laughs. "Well, isn't this almost a family reunion?"

I glance around, half afraid I'll see Uncle Hiram. If Hardwick lied about Dilley, maybe he lied about my uncle being gone, too. Maybe I ought to run like blazes.

Hardwick steps toward me, and his associates trail in his wake like a school of fish. "I was on my way to the bank when I recognized Mr. Kingfisher outside, and I knew you wouldn't be far away. Of course I had to divert my path to join yours. It's not everyone who gets the better of me in a deal!"

He says it condescendingly, like me dealing with him was adorable and sweet . . . but there's a fire in his eyes that makes my belly squirm. A moment ago, I had been invisible to the men in this office. Now every eye is turned toward me. A few are merely curious, but not one of them is kindly.

Hardwick takes a puff on his cigar and blows a huge cloud of smoke in our direction. His breath is wet and sickly sweet with tobacco.

"Mr. Hardwick," I say, more as an acknowledgment, and falling just short of a greeting. "I didn't expect to see you with Dilley. You told me he died."

"Well, we thought he had! His men hauled him to the mission, where, with care and prayers, he made a miraculous recovery."

"Praise the Lord," Frank Dilley says.

"You still working for my uncle?" I ask Dilley flat out.

"You didn't know?" he says. "Westfall is halfway to Australia by now."

No reason for him to lie about that, and the relief almost buckles my knees.

Becky is bristling beside me. "We were about to be on our way."

"No need to hurry," Hardwick says. "What brings you all the way down from—what was the name of that little camp of yours—Charity?"

"Glory," I answer, and I regret it as soon as the word slips my mouth.

"Glory be!" Hardwick chuckles. "That's right, Glory. What brings you all the way down from Glory?"

The beautiful auburn-haired woman leans over and whispers in Hardwick's ear.

"Excuse me, I don't believe I've had the pleasure," Becky says, and I know she cannot bear to have anything whispered around her. "I'm Mrs. Andrew Joyner, lately from Glory, but before that from Chattanooga, Tennessee."

"Mr. James Henry Hardwick, at your service, Mrs. Joyner. Allow me to introduce my newest associate, Miss Helena Russell."

He makes "associate" sound like a fancy word for something I don't quite understand.

"At your service," Miss Helena Russell says, with a tinge of the mountains in her voice. Nothing about her is the least bit servile, but up close, I can see how the makeup and fine clothes cover a life of labor. Her skin is weathered and freckled. The wide sleeves of her dress fail to conceal forearms corded with the kind of muscle that comes from carrying milk pails and swinging axes. She may be dressed as stylishly as Becky Joyner, but she has more in common with me.

We pass introductions all around, and I'm still looking for a convenient way out that doesn't include fighting past Frank Dilley when Hardwick doggedly returns to his original question. "You never did say what brings you to San Francisco, Miss Westfall."

"No, I didn't," I reply. "What brings you?"

He laughs, and I wonder what puts a man like him in a good mood. Maybe it's the lady standing at his elbow. "I'm here for the same reason you are," he answers.

"You lost your home and family and had nowhere else to go?"

"I came to make my fortune."

He's already taken thousands from us, which seemed like a fortune at the time, but now, sensing all the gold of San Francisco—even just in this room—I know he has bigger ambitions. "And how are you going to do that?"

"Any and every way I can," he says, nodding to himself. "Any and every way I can."

"And that includes taking advantage of men like my uncle."

Another puff on his cigar, while he considers this. "I didn't know you cared about him. In fact, our agreement led me to believe that all you cared about was being free of him."

"I care about the people he robbed to pay you. I care about the people he hurt trying to get rich, in order to make you richer."

"You didn't come out of the affair too badly. You somehow ended up with enough money to pay all his debts."

My hands start to tremble, and tears well up in my eyes. I was kidnapped and force-fed laudanum. Dressed up like a doll for my uncle's amusement. The Indians had it worse; I watched them beaten, starved, murdered. "We still haven't received the charter for the town of Glory," I blurt, just to get the images out of my head.

That was the key part of my agreement with Hardwick at Christmas. We'd pay off my uncle's debts, and Hardwick would use his influence to get us a town charter so we could govern ourselves.

"California isn't a state yet, my dear, and the wheels of politics grind slowly." His grin is slow and satisfied. "And sometimes those wheels require additional amounts of grease to keep turning."

Additional grease? "You're saying you'll need more gold."

He scowls, and he glances around the room at the assemblage of lawyers. "This isn't something we should haggle over in public."

My whole body is tense, like a bent spring. "That's not fair."

He puffs himself up like a cock ready to cry doodle-do. "Sweet girl, you'll learn. Life's not fair."

"Then we're honor bound to make it fair," I snap.

He laughs at that, a genuine belly laugh, and it's like a slap in my face. My cheeks flush hot, and I look toward the door, hoping for a swift, easy exit, but the doorway is blocked. It's Hampton, striding inside.

I gasp. Because right behind Hampton is someone I thought to never see again: Jim Boisclair.

He made it to California after all. He's really here.

Jim was a good friend of my daddy's back in Dahlonega, a free Negro and store owner who helped me run away from my uncle the first time. I'm so happy and relieved to see him that I barely keep myself from giving him the hug of his life. In fact, I'm so overcome that it takes a moment to realize the whole room is as silent as the grave, and every single person in it is now staring at Hampton and Jim.

"I didn't know you were in San Francisco," I say cautiously.

He gives me an unsmiling nod, and there's an awful lot in that nod I'm not sure I understand. His eyes sweep the room warily, like he just stepped into a snake pit. "Glad to see you safe and hale, Miss Leah," he says, but his eyes are on everyone but me.

Jim had been a free man in Georgia, and he found enough gold in the rush there to set up a general store. There's a lot more to his story than I know, but I trust him with my life, and if he's wary in this place, then I am, too.

"Found him at the post office," Hampton says, waving an envelope. "Needed someone to read my letter to me."

"Good news?" I ask with false cheer.

"My freedom papers!" Hampton says, with another flourish of the envelope. "It's all official, but still no word on Adelaide." His voice is tight, and I know exactly why. It's tempting fate for two Negroes to walk into an office like this, even free ones. We need to leave, and fast.

"I don't want to intrude on another happy reunion," Hardwick interrupts, sounding bored. "So I'll take my leave. It was a pleasure to see you again, Miss Westfall."

The pleasure is all his. "Until we meet again, Mr. Hardwick." And as soon as I say it, I know I'll be seeing him again as surely as water fills the Pacific Ocean.

The conversation officially over, I take Becky's arm and start walking toward the door, herding Hampton and Jim before me. The air in the room feels like a clothesline about to snap.

Tom follows behind me. As we pass Hardwick, Miss Russell leans over to whisper in his ear again. He replies, "Are you certain?"

We're only a few feet from the door and escape when Hardwick calls out. "Mr. Bigler—a moment of your time."

We freeze. "Tom," I whisper, meaning to follow it up with a *don't*.

Tom turns, his face expressionless. "Mr. Hardwick?" he says.

"My lawyers tell me that they've never seen a tighter, cleverer contract than the one you wrote for Miss Westfall at Christmas. I would like to discuss the temporary application of your considerable talents to a venture of my own."

I don't want Tom to do it. I'm shaking. Surely he can tell? As surely as I sense his stature swelling huge with pride? All the attorneys in the room are now evaluating Tom, trying to determine if he is a potential ally or a new rival. Strange how all that scrutiny directed at me moments ago made *me* feel small.

At least no one is staring at Hampton and Jim anymore. Becky leans in and whispers. "Go on, Tom. It can't hurt to listen. Maybe you can find a way to do something about my house."

"Perhaps I can," he says quietly. "I'll rejoin you later at the hotel." And then, louder, "I'm delighted to see what I can do, Mr. Hardwick. Perhaps some of the gentlemen here can lend us some chairs to talk."

Chairs scrape across the wood floor, and a dozen voices compete to invite the conversation into their own space.

Hampton, Jim, Becky, and I go to leave, but Frank steps in our way and blocks the door. "I would have saved myself a heap of hurt if I just let you die in the desert," he says.

"The way I recall," I say, "you did leave us to die in the desert, and Therese Hoffman paid the price."

Becky adds, "And then one of your men killed Martin." Her voice quakes with the effort to hold back tears. "You know what would have saved you a heap of hurt? Not fighting against us every time. Choosing to join us even once."

He doesn't have an answer for that, and the rest of Hardwick's school of fish is moving toward a desk at the far corner of the office. Frank sneers at me. Or maybe he smiles. The burn on his face makes his expressions hard to parse. Finally he lets us be and hurries off after his new boss.

We flee out the door and out into the cold winter light, and it feels like emerging from my uncle Hiram's mine all over again. I breathe deep, as if the sea salt air can cleanse my soul, but I can't stop shaking.

Chapter Five

"Lee! Are you all right?" Jefferson is blocked by two men with revolvers. Panic surges in my throat, and I bolt toward him, hands balled into fists.

The men step out of the way at once, guns lowered. Up close, I recognize their faces. I don't remember their names, but I'm certain they used to work for my uncle. "We were just trying to keep him out of trouble, Miss Westfall," says one. "He tried to follow Frank inside, and I thought someone might come to harm. Thought it might be the fellow without a gun."

"Don't do us any favors," I say. I throw my arms around Jeff, not caring that everyone is watching, and he wraps me up in his. After a moment, I stop trembling.

When I step away, the men with guns are gone. Jefferson says, "There were two of them, or I would have forced my way inside."

"I know. Are you all right?"

"They didn't give me trouble, really. That one fellow was

just trying to calm things down; he didn't want anyone getting hurt. Did Frank—?"

"Frank Dilley is still a bully and a coward, but I'm fine." As I say it, I know it to be true. Trouble is brewing, for sure and certain. But I'm breathing easier, more clearheaded. Jeff and I have been through so many troubles together, and I know we'll find a way through the next one, even if haven't quite put my finger on what it is yet.

"It was Jim's idea to go in and check on you," Jefferson says, with a nod toward Jim and Hampton. "When those fellows trained their pistols on me, he thought you might be in a pickle."

So that's why they dared the lion's den. I turn and clasp Jim's hand. It's large and rough, warm and steady, like the man himself. "Thanks, Jim. I'm real glad to see you."

Finally, he smiles, and the genuine warmth and welcome in that smile go straight to my heart. "Goes both ways, Miss Leah. It's good for the soul to see you and Jefferson arrived safe. Also . . ." Jim clamps Hampton's shoulder. "I enjoyed meeting your friend here. He told me a bit about his situation, coming west."

"He's done well for himself," I say. "We're still hoping to bring his wife out, though."

"We can't wait to meet Adelaide," Becky adds.

"I have to know," Jim says, eyes full of concern. "Your uncle Hiram . . . did he . . . is he—"

"He's no longer a problem," I say firmly.

"Well, that's a blessing."

"Where's Tom?" says Jefferson, indicating the law office. "Did he help you with the house?"

"Not yet." Becky says. "Nothing's gone quite as expected."

I glance toward the door we just exited, feeling an overwhelming urge to flee. Next time I encounter Dilley or Hardwick, I plan to be armed. All our guns are stashed in the wagon, unloaded for the journey. "Let's discuss it elsewhere," I say.

Becky nods. "My mother always said it's not wise to go shopping after such an upsetting encounter, especially not for something important like a wedding dress. We'll catch up with the others for now."

I don't know how that woman can think of shopping at a time like this.

"Miss Leah," Jim says, suddenly formal. "I have a little surprise for you. I was planning to track you down in the spring, but since I've found you, I'll fetch it and bring it around tomorrow."

I'm not one for surprises, but I say, "We'd surely love to see more of you. Call on us at the Parker House hotel."

We take our leave of Jim, promising to chat more soon.

"Can you believe it?" Jefferson says, staring after our friend. "Seeing Jim is like having a little piece of home."

"Sure is." If Mama and Daddy are looking down on me now, they're smiling to see that Jim and I found each other.

We climb into the wagon for a short ride across the plaza to the Parker House. It's the largest hotel I've ever seen, so wide it fills the street front from corner to corner, with a row of dormer windows all the way across the second floor. It is also, the proprietor informs us, completely full.

Becky's big blue eyes somehow grow bigger and bluer as she tells the innkeeper about her "sweet children who are desperate for a roof over their heads after a harrowing journey through the wilderness." He is helpless under her gaze, and he suddenly recalls that our friends stopped by earlier. He gestures through the window toward the City Hotel, a smaller structure with a garret, where he assures us we will find rooms and our friends.

The innkeep at the City Hotel is gambling in the smoky parlor with some of his customers. When we ask after our friends, he grunts in the direction of the stairway. Jefferson is taking care of the horses and wagon, so Becky, Hampton, and I tromp up the narrow staircase to the garret, following after the sound of laughing children.

Becky dashes down the hall to an open door. There's little space in the tiny room, so Hampton and I hover in the doorway. Olive, seven years old and a hundred years curious, peppers her mother with questions, while Andy plays on the floor with clever wooden animals carved by the Major. Major Wally Craven sits on one of two canvas cots in the room, feeding something mushy and unidentifiable to Becky's baby girl.

We met the Major on the wagon train west, and he's been a good friend ever since Jasper amputated his leg to save his life. He's a large, strong fellow, clever with his hands, who wears a wooden leg of his own design. Becky won't travel anywhere without her children, and she doesn't trust anyone but the Major to watch over them.

"The room's barely larger than a wardrobe," Becky says, hunching over to avoid the bare rafters. "But the children have endured worse."

The Major shifts the baby to his shoulder and pats her on the back to burp her. "There were only two rooms available. Twenty-five dollars each per week, rent paid in advance. I took them both. Apparently a fire took out a lot of buildings last month." He points up to the bare rafters. "They barely finished this place before they moved on to the next. We'll have to sleep in shifts."

"Oh, dear," says Becky, in a tone that I'm pretty sure means *This won't do.* "San Francisco has not been kind to us so far. At least Hampton got his freedom papers!"

Hampton waves them triumphantly.

I sense someone approach and turn to see Henry, clean-shaven and hair slicked neat as you please. A silk cravat hangs around his neck, a brighter blue than fashionable.

I say, "I thought you'd be out looking for a teaching job."

"The new state constitution requires public schools," Henry says, "but it seems no one has gotten around to building them. I was told the first school will be built in Monterey."

"So what are you going to do?" I ask.

"Some wealthy white and Mexican families hire tutors, so I've set up a few meetings."

"Poor Henry," I say. "Sounds like you'll have to get up early for a change."

"No. I'll meet them tonight." His eyes sparkle. "In gambling dens."

"Oh, dear," Becky says again.

"You're a terrible gambler," I point out. "Even I can tell when you have a good hand."

Henry blinks. "I'm only doing it to make connections, of course."

Jefferson, having stabled the horses and wagon, makes his way down the hall with our bags. He drops my saddlebag on the floor with a heavy thump. "What did you pack, Lee, a bunch of rocks? Oh, hello, Henry."

"Have you seen Tom?" Henry asks. "I hope he had better luck than I did."

I say, "He's interviewing for a post with Hardwick. And I have a bad feeling." I explain everything that happened.

"You don't have to worry about Tom," Henry assures me.

"I wish I could be sure. He's . . . different."

"Working in your uncle's mine was hard for him. He . . ." Henry hesitates, considering. "Well, he gets wound up at night and can't sleep because of it."

"I can understand that," I admit.

"Tom has been hard to read lately, it's true," Jefferson says.

"He's the one who should be a gambler," the Major points out. "He has such a poker face."

"*No one* should be a gambler," Becky says.

Henry squeezes my arm. "Give Tom some time. I know he's intently focused right now. He thinks we've got a better chance to practice our professions here, and the sooner we get to work, the more of a head start we'll have on everyone else."

I can't help the little sigh that escapes. "Sometimes I just wish things could go back to the way they were, when it was just us, relying on each other. Looking to stake our claims and make a better life for ourselves."

"That's exactly what we're doing," Henry says. "We're just staking a different set of claims now."

"But if the three of you stay in San Francisco, I'm going to miss you."

"Me too," says little Andy from the floor. I should have realized he was listening carefully to every word. "I'll miss you the most."

"Then you must continue to work on your letters," Henry says. "So we can write to each other every week."

The stairs creak, and Jefferson says, "Hey, Tom. We were just talking about you."

"Speculating on my prospects of future employment?" Tom asks as he strides toward us.

"Praising your immaculate presentation and good looks," Henry says.

"Don't let me interrupt you then," he says dryly.

"Did Hardwick offer you a job?" I ask.

"He did."

"Did you take it?" My voice is a lot louder than I intend.

Tom pauses. "I asked for time to consider his generous offer."

I want to follow up, demand to know why he didn't reject it outright, but a door to another room slams open. A large man reeking of booze and wearing only an undershirt, thrusts his bald head into the hall. "If you all want to have a confab, that's why God invented parlors. Get yourselves downstairs and use one—some of us are trying to sleep!"

He slams the door shut again.

After a brief pause, Henry whispers. "Anyone else tempted to start a rousing chorus of 'Used Up Man'?"

Becky can't hide her grin as she waves us all into the tiny room, then closes the door behind us. We take seats on the cots, the two small chairs, the floor. I grab a spot beneath the single window. The rough wood of the unfinished wall makes my back itch. Jefferson squeezes in beside me, and Andrew comes over to show off his wooden animals. Jeff agrees that they are very fine animals and makes an appropriate variety of barnyard and woodland sounds, which somehow makes me want to kiss him even more than usual.

Becky drags one of the room's two chairs to the center of the floor and sits like a queen on her throne, hands folded in her lap. "Our original plan to come to the city, get the house, and depart directly isn't going to work," she begins.

"I've got my freedom papers, but I don't have any word on Adelaide," Hampton adds. "The postmaster says it could be a few days or a few months until the mail comes next. It all depends on when the ships arrive. So I might have to stick around."

"Hardwick's going to break our agreement and cheat Glory out of its charter if he can," I add.

This is news to some, including the Major, who frowns. "People could lose their homes," he says.

"Once word gets out that our charter's not coming," Becky points out, "we'll start having trouble with claim jumpers again. The promise of a proper town has given us a lot of protection."

"Once California is declared a state," Tom says, "we'll have legal recourse. Until then, the contract gives him a loophole."

"By then it might be too late," I say.

Becky says, "But one thing at a time. Right now the problem I care about is my house. Tom, did you think of something?"

He shakes his head. "Hardwick wants my help with his auctions—many involving properties of dubious provenance—and he needs legal assistance managing the contracts and bills of sale to alleviate questions of legal ownership. Your house is currently stored in one of his warehouses. Working for him might give us another option for recovering it."

Maybe that's why Tom was so eager to hear Hardwick out—so he could help us. Henry was right; Tom would never betray us.

"What if we buy it?" I suggest. I reach out with my gold sense, assuring myself that all the money we need is right there. In my mind, my saddlebag shines brighter than a full moon.

"The auction is a week from Tuesday," Becky says. "Staying almost two weeks in this city will cost a mother lode. And there's no guarantee we'll be the highest bidder."

"Almost every item has a 'buy now' price," Tom says. "I could find out the price for your house. It's likely to cost twice as much as you'd pay for it at auction."

"Let's do it," I say. "I'll chip in. Let's just buy it and get out of town." And away from Hardwick and Frank Dilley and everything else that's making me feel as tangled up as a squirrel's nest. The wind blows outside, shaking the roof tiles. "There's something bad here," I say. "It's like . . . it's like a snake's rattle, warning us to back off. Let's buy the house, however much it costs, and get on our way."

It's a reasonable request. Everyone can see that, I'm sure.

But Becky's frown deepens, and she raises one finger in the air.

"So let me get this straight," she says. "My dear late husband, Mr. Joyner, already paid once in full to ship this house to California for me. Now the petty self-appointed bureaucrats of this territory want me to pay a second time to reacquire my property. And if I want it in a hurry, without the disadvantage of bidding against strangers after a costly stay away from home, then I have to pay for it a third time."

"That's about the size of it," the Major grumbles.

"No!" She jabs her finger at him. "It's wrong, and it won't stand."

"So what are we going to do about it?" he asks. The baby is nearly asleep on his shoulder. She has recently discovered the wonder that is her thumb, and her tiny cheek pulses with drowsy sucking.

"Have you decided to steal it back?" Tom asks, brightening.

"I can't steal back what's already mine," she says. Olive, sensing the tension in the room, scoots over to lean against her mother. Becky strokes her daughter's bright blond hair and says, "But I have a plan."

"Sounds intriguing," Henry says.

"Henry Meek," she says. "How would you like to be my husband?"

"What?" Henry gulps.

"What?" the Major adds.

"She just wants someone to pose as her husband," I say gently. "Remember? We discussed the possibility last fall in Glory."

"I can do that," the Major says, a little too eagerly.

Becky shakes her head. "The Joyner family is well known back in Tennessee, and it's possible there are a few folks right here in San Francisco who are familiar with my late husband, at least distantly. Henry can pass for Andrew at a glance. But you, Wally, you're . . ." A little smile plays at the corners of her mouth. "You're as different as can be."

Henry straightens. "I was quite the thespian in college," he says. "And I would be honored to pose as your fine gentleman spouse."

The Major does not seem convinced, but Becky brightens, saying, "Then this is what we're going to do."

Chapter Six

Noon the following day finds me and Jefferson sitting on the wagon bench in front of our hotel, keeping an eye on the Custom House across the plaza. Jeff's arm is settled across my shoulders, and I lean into him, loving how easy it is now that we're affianced. When I want to hold his hand, all I have to do is reach for it. When he wants to press his lips to the top of my head, he doesn't hesitate.

Hampton has gone off in search of his supper. Wisps of fog still dally with the hilltops, and the air is thick with chilled wetness. I wear a floppy straw hat, in part against the cold, in part to cover my face.

The clerk who helped Becky and me yesterday entered the office right when it opened this morning, and he hasn't yet emerged. For Becky's plan to work, he needs to take a break. Then, we'll approach one of the other clerks, who won't remember our failed attempt to acquire the house once already.

Becky strides toward us from across the square, accompanied by a tall gentleman in a fine suit. For a split second, I wonder where Henry is, even though he was supposed to accompany her, preparing for today's adventure.

Of course, the finely dressed gentleman *is* Henry, and I let out an appreciative whistle. "Hello, Mr. Joyner."

He preens, but Becky scowls, and Henry slips into a dour expression that reminds me so much of the late Andrew Joyner that's it's almost a punch in the gut.

"What do you think?" Becky asks.

The resemblance is uncanny. "How?"

"We visited a variety of shops," Henry says in a perfect Southern drawl, turning so I can see him from every angle. "Until I found the perfect suit. You'd be surprised at the items that have made their way out here. Why, I could dress myself like anyone—from a Japanese samurai to a French countess."

He extends his arms so we can admire the flashy cufflinks on his shirt. They're exactly the sort of thing Mr. Joyner would have bought.

"You even sound like him!"

"He used to imitate my husband," Becky says. "To amuse the other bachelors when he thought no one else was listening." She scowls up at him. "But *I* was listening."

"The lesson is that someone's always listening," Henry says without breaking character, though he does manage a small amount of shame. Mr. Joyner was an uppity ne'er-do-well and few cared for him at all. But he *was* Becky's husband, and I hope Henry's imitations haven't pained her.

Jefferson says, "I swear you've aged a decade since yesterday."

"Sleeping on the hard floor of a garret, with six people in a room meant for two, will do that to a soul," Henry says.

"Stop bellyaching," Becky tells him. "We all slept in much worse conditions while crossing the continent."

"But if you recall, *I* always slept on a feather mattress!" Henry says, fully into his character.

It's the worst thing he could say. Mr. Joyner packed a whole household's worth of fine furniture for their journey west, including a full-sized bed that filled most of their wagon. It was the furniture that killed him, in an accident high in the Rocky Mountains. He sacrificed his life trying to save a huge oak dresser, and I can still picture him smashed and bloody in the dust, broken pieces of wood scattered all around him.

Henry sees the expression on my face and says, "I'm . . . I'm sorry."

"No, that's good," Becky says, and maybe I've overestimated her heartache. "That's exactly the kind of thoughtless thing he'd say. You stay in character until we have my house."

Henry gives her a small bow. "Your wish is my dearest desire." He turns to Jefferson. "We stopped at a ladies' store to sample some of the maquillage. It makes a lady look younger, but a gentleman much older."

"It's astonishing," I tell him, because it is.

Becky nods toward the shaded veranda of the Custom House. "Has our helpful friend from yesterday taken a break from his duties yet?"

"Not yet," I say.

"And we're sure no one is using the back door?" she asks.

Jefferson shrugs. "I circled the whole building. Nothing back there but trash."

"A flaw in our plan, perhaps," Henry says.

"I'm optimistic he'll leave through the front, just like the others," Becky says firmly.

As I settle back into the crook of Jefferson's arm, our friend Jim appears around the corner and heads for the front of the hotel. He carries a large rolled blanket. I shout hello to him, and he changes course, waving to us.

Jefferson tips his hat. "Free Jim," he acknowledges.

"Just Jim now," Jim and I say in unison.

"Well, all right then," Jefferson says, with a hint of a smile. "Jim it is."

"Glad I caught you," Jim says to me. "Was afraid you'd be out and about, and I'd miss seeing the look on your face when you opened this."

He hands the long package up to me, and I lay it across my lap. It's a heavy weight. A familiar weight. I know what it is; I'm sure of it. My hands shake as I peel the blanket away, because now I've gotten my hopes up, and what if I'm wrong?

Polished wood and steel glint up at me.

"Lee?" Jefferson says. "That's a dead ringer for your daddy's Hawken rifle."

"It *is* my daddy's Hawken." I examine the stock and find familiar scratches, plus a few more. I hold it up and sight along the barrel. "Jim—where . . . ? How . . . ?"

He smiles like the cat that ate the canary. "Remember

when we saw each other last? In Independence? It was on a rack in that general store, and I recognized it right away. I figure somebody carried it west, and then traded it for a pan and shovel. That, or you were so desperate for money you had to pawn it yourself. I snapped it up right before I left, but then I couldn't find you again."

A laugh bursts out of my chest, a pure clean feeling of delight. I jump down from the bench and throw my arms around him and give him the tightest hug, and I don't care what anybody thinks.

Jefferson climbs down and shakes his hand. "We appreciate this a great deal, Jim," he says as I take a step back and admire the rifle all over again.

"Reuben Westfall bought that gun in my store when you were barely toddling around," Jim says.

I can't stop staring at the rifle. Three brothers robbed me of it last year, when I was barely out of Georgia. I never thought I'd see it again. "This is the last thing I have to remember Daddy by," I tell Jim.

"Aren't those his boots you're wearing?"

I look down at the boots and scuff them in the dirt. They aren't the same, no matter how much they look like Daddy's boots, but I'm grateful to have them. "Nah. The Major made these for me. They fit me a lot better. I'd have had fewer blisters had I hiked west in these." I hold up the rifle again, just to admire it. "But Jim! This gift—it's . . . it's . . ."

"Too much?" suggests Jefferson.

"A surprise?" asks Jim, suppressing his grin.

It's the best thing to happen to me since Jefferson agreed to marry me. "You have to let me pay you for—"

"There he is!" shouts Becky. She's pointing at the Custom House. "There he goes!"

Sure enough, yesterday's clerk is strolling along the veranda with one of his fellows. I grab the blanket, rewrap the rifle, and stuff it under the bench. "Let's go," I say.

While Jefferson catches Jim up on what's going on, Becky, Henry, and I set off across the plaza at a brisk pace. "So, you'll stand watch?" Becky asks me.

She must be nervous, because we've been over it a thousand times. "If I see the clerk coming back, I'll come inside and signal so you can slip out," I assure her.

Henry jumps in with, "Then I'll take the letter and continue to wait in line by myself. If you still have concerns, I can go in alone."

"No, no," Becky says. "I'll feel better if I see it through myself. And though we've done our best to anticipate questions, the situation might still require a woman's touch."

Because that worked so well for us yesterday. But I refrain from saying as much.

Becky and her false husband step into line. Across the plaza, Hampton has returned to the wagon, and my stomach rumbles when he offers something to Jefferson and Jim.

Everyone is in place now, so I lean against the wall between the Custom House and the law offices, like I'm waiting impatiently for someone inside, which will be my excuse should anyone bother me. I pull the brim of my hat down over my face so I don't have to make eye contact with anyone. I pull my sweater down over my hands because I'm cold. I cross my arms with what I hope is a strong signal to leave me alone.

From the corner of my eye, I catch sight of a woman approaching, and for a split second, I think it's Helena Russell, the woman who was keeping company with Hardwick. I'm like a deer about to bolt, until a closer look reveals the truth: it's the pickpocket from the previous morning.

"Hello, Sonia," I say without warmth. She must frequent Portsmouth Square often. A lot of miners here with gold to spend. After they've had a few drinks, it's probably easy to part them from their fortunes.

"Oh. Miss Lee," she says, eyes widening, feet faltering. She turns and dashes away.

I'm almost sad to see her go, because two generously whiskered fellows come along and lean against the wall beside me. They pretend like they're talking to each other—about the empty lot one just purchased, and the lucky card streak the other is on—but I'd bet my boots they're bragging to get my attention. I pretend they don't exist. It's a damp, chilly day, and my attitude is even chillier. Eventually they move on.

Becky and Henry make it inside. The line isn't long compared to yesterday. After about twenty minutes, I notice that everything has gone peculiarly silent, and people are leaving the Custom House—folks who made it inside *after* Becky and Henry. They all seem anxious and hurried.

I start to worry a little.

Then our helpful clerk from yesterday saunters back with

one of his fellows, and I start to worry a lot.

I peel off from the wall and stick my head in the door, about to wave the signal for Becky to cover her face and slip away.

I freeze.

Frank Dilley stands just inside, Colt revolver trained on Becky and Henry. They are seated in chairs, guarded by two impeccably groomed men in suits. One of the guards is very large, and the other is larger. Frank grins when he sees me. He motions with the gun for me to stand beside the chairs.

Henry is hunched over on himself, looking defeated. Becky is like a stray cat cornered in the barn—I can't tell if she's about to bolt or attack with her claws.

"This won't take but a minute," Frank says. The burn on his face is smeared with glycerin, giving it a red shine. The scar pulls the corner of his mouth back into a joyless smile. It looks painful. I hope it's painful.

"Just play by the rules and nobody will get hurt," Frank says. "I know that goes against your nature, but do it this once, for the sake of your friends. Then we'll all be on our way."

I walk slowly to Becky's side, hands up, eyes on that gun. The clerk comes through the door and skids to a stop. "Oh," he says. "Oh, my."

The other clerks peer at us from across the counter, like this is a show they've been waiting to see.

"Mr. Brumble," Frank says.

Yesterday's clerk bobs his head. "Yes, sir. Present, sir."

"Are these two . . . well, I don't know what to call the two of them together, but for the sake of argument, we'll say *ladies*.

Are these two ladies the ones who came in yesterday and tried to collect property belonging to one Mr. Andrew Joyner?"

"Yes, sir. Yes, sir, they are."

"And this gentleman here presented himself today as Mr. Andrew Joyner. You can confirm this, correct?" Frank waves his hand in the direction of another man in a starched white shirt, who immediately provides assent.

"This time last year," Frank says, drawing the words out with obvious pleasure, "I was wagon master on the train that brought this sorry group of deceivers and reprobates west to California. Mr. Andrew Joyner was a member of our party, but he got himself killed crossing the Rocky Mountains. That boy there with the fancy suit is Henry Meeks, fresh out of college and completely ignorant of honest work. He is not Andrew Joyner. Do all of you recognize their faces now?"

The line of clerks nods, solemn as a jury.

"If any of these troublemakers makes another attempt to claim property belonging to the late Mr. Joyner—or anyone else, for that matter—you are authorized to seize them for fraud, and hold them until they can be arrested by the sheriff or his deputies."

"Does that come from the sheriff?" asks a small, balding clerk. It's not much defiance, but it's _some_ defiance, and I appreciate him for it.

But Frank says, "That comes from _Mr. Hardwick_," and the clerks nod, even the balding one. We have no champions here.

Frank twirls his gun and slips it into his holster—a fancy trick I'll have to teach myself if I get the chance. He pulls out a pocket watch and checks the time, then nods to the large gentleman guards. "I've got an appointment with Mr. Hardwick. Hold these folks for a couple minutes and then send them packing. Catch up to us later."

He slips out the door, and the clerks try their best to look busy. The two guards continue to hold guns on us. Maybe we should just walk out. Would they really shoot us if we did? The fact that Dilley wants us to stay put for a spell is interesting. It means he's a little afraid of us, of what we might do, and he wants to get away clean.

Becky is furious, but she makes no motion as if to leave. Henry is pale under his maquillage.

"You didn't see Dilley come in this morning?" Becky asks me.

"No," I admit. "I'm sorry."

"Wouldn't have made a difference," says Large.

"We were all here before sunup, since we weren't sure when you'd show," adds Larger.

"Was about ready to give up, myself," says Large.

"Frank was too, but the boss told him to wait."

"So we waited."

A hard knot settles in my gut. "You *knew* we were coming," I say as Becky and Henry exchange an alarmed glance. "How?"

The only people who knew of our plan were in that room last night. I'll go out on a limb and assume that neither the Major, nor any of Becky's three children gave us away. And either Becky and Henry are the finest actors in the whole wide west, or they're just as shocked as I am. Jefferson would never do it. That leaves only Hampton and Tom, and I can't imagine either of them would be betray us either. Maybe the drunk in the other room eavesdropped through the walls, but we kept our voices low after his outburst.

"I never know how the boss knows what he knows," says Large.

"He's Mr. Hardwick," says Larger with a shrug. "You just assume he knows everybody and everything."

Large holsters his gun and waves toward the door. "Shoo. Get out of here. Don't misbehave."

Larger follows suit. "Go, and sin no more."

Becky rises slowly and primly. Henry bolts out the door before I can say boo. We catch up to him outside beneath the veranda, where he paces in a tight circle with his hands deep in his pockets.

"Frank wasn't going to hurt us," Becky assures him. "He just wanted to scare us."

"Well, he sure did *that* like an expert," Henry says.

"He's an expert bully," I tell him. "He has loads of practice. He knows that house belongs to Becky morally, if not legally. Sometimes people are inclined to do the moral thing regardless, and a different clerk might have let us sign those papers." I'm pretty sure the small balding fellow would have helped us if we'd been lucky enough to get him yesterday instead. "This was meant to scare all the clerks too."

That changes Henry's perspective a bit, and he stops circling like an anxious dog on a short leash. "So what do we do next?"

"We can still go buy the house," I say.

Becky shakes her head. "Now that they know how much I want it, they'll charge five times the price."

"Or ten," I say. "But it might be worth it just to be done with all this."

"No," she says firmly. "We'll wait until the auction and take our chances then. New houses go up so fast here, there's no reason for someone to overpay for one tiny, disassembled cottage shipped from Tennessee."

Which is an excellent point. "But I can afford it. Even at ten times the price."

My words ring hollow, even to myself. Spending that much money at a public auction will attract attention we don't want. Besides, it feels like giving in. Hardwick has already hinted at shaking us down for more money. The last thing we need is to let him get started at it.

Becky looks offended that I would even suggest such a thing. Her mouth is shaping a reply, but a commotion reaches us from across the plaza—shouts, the sound of a hammer smacking wood, the whinny of a frightened horse. San Francisco is a boisterous place, and I've already grown accustomed to ignoring its daily clamor, but Henry says, "That's Jefferson and Hampton. Looks like they're in trouble."

Chapter Seven

$\mathcal{I}$ spot Jim first. He sits in the mud in front of the wagon. Blood flows down his scalp and fills one eye. I sprint across the plaza, dodging delivery wagons and shoving my way through clusters of people as Jim tries to stand, slips, falls again.

Beside him, Jefferson is trying to manage the horses, who dance nervously from side to side. A fierce-looking man in a bearskin coat swings a bully club at Jefferson. He dodges in the nick of time, but the man winds up for another swing.

"Hey!" I yell, and the man hesitates.

Three other thugs have Hampton pinned facedown on the ground. Hampton thrashes as one tries to pull a burlap sack over his head. A second straddles his waist as he binds Hampton's hands with rope, and the third struggles to pin his legs. Mud flies everywhere.

I lower my shoulder and ram the man pinning Hampton's legs. We both sprawl in the muck.

Hampton kicks out, knocking loose the second man, but

not soon enough to keep his hands from being tied. He rolls over onto his knees and tries to rise just as the first man cinches the bag around his neck.

I lunge forward, intending to yank the sack away, but one of the men swings a fist. I dodge left. My feet slip out from under me, and my backside splats into the muck again.

"Lee! Duck!"

Jefferson's voice. I cover my head and roll. A club glances off my shoulder, scraping a chunk of skin with it.

I come up with a handful of mud and fling it blindly in the direction of my attacker. A splat sound tells me I've hit something, so I grab and fling again while struggling to my feet.

A hand grabs my elbow and pulls at me, so I lash out. My fist connects with something solid and I hear an *oof* from Jefferson.

"Sorry!" I wipe the mud from my face with the back of my forearm. Jefferson grabs my waist and yanks me back just in time to avoid a swing from Bearcoat's club.

"Let's go!" someone yells to Bearcoat before he can try again.

Hampton is now in the back of an empty dung cart, ropes binding his wrists and ankles. The man in the cart seat gestures at Bearcoat to follow.

But Bearcoat and his friends won't be budged. They're frontiersmen. Bullies for hire. I recognize the type from the hills back home.

"That one's a girl," says one, like it's the worst thing a person can be.

"She rung my bell," says another, picking up a coonskin cap

from the mud. He's the one I knocked off Hampton. "She should pay, girl or not."

Bearcoat still holds the club out in front of him, daring Jefferson or me to take a step. "That's up to them."

Becky and Henry arrive at that moment. "I demand to know what's going on here," Becky says. "Why have you attacked my companions?"

"This ain't no business of yours," Bearcoat says, jabbing the club in her direction.

"The hell it isn't," I say, taking a step forward. Jefferson grabs at me, but I shrug him off. "You're kidnapping our friend."

"Ain't no kidnapping," says Bearcoat. "Got a notice from an Arkansas paper saying he's a runaway slave. Perfectly legal for us to catch him, return him to his proper owner."

"He's a free man," Jim says, and I cast a glace over my shoulder to see him rising to his feet and wicking mud from his trousers. His gaze is unfocused, and he teeters when he moves.

"The Bledsoe family says otherwise. Says he ran away last summer."

Hampton's cart is rolling out of sight, beyond the Parker House.

"You are mistaken," Becky tells the three roughnecks. "He has his freedom papers. In any case, California is going to be a free state. There's no slavery here."

Buckskin snarls at her. "Where you from?"

"Tennessee, but—"

"I thought I could hear God's country in your voice, ma'am, but you are on the wrong side here."

"I'm on the side of my friends. I'm on the side of doing the right thing. Where are you taking Hampton?"

"Don't answer that," Bearcoat says. He checks over his shoulder and confirms that the cart is long gone. "Let's collect our bounty and be done. It's already been more trouble than it's worth."

The three men back away slowly, then turn and hurry.

I spin around. "Jim! Are you all right?"

He's standing, leaning against the wagon, hand pressed against his temple, while Henry calms the horses.

"I'll be fine as soon as my head clears," he says.

I reach under the seat and peel the blanket off my daddy's Hawken rifle.

"What are you doing?" asks Jefferson.

"I'm going to find out where they're taking Hampton. He might be hurt."

"I'm not sure that's a smart—"

I don't hear the rest, because I'm already off and running.

A mood's taken hold of me, the same way fire takes hold of grease. First came all the reminders of my uncle and the horrible things done in his mine. Then Frank Dilley and his bullies held guns to our heads to scare Becky and keep her from what's rightfully hers. Now this. It's gone too far. I'm not sure what I aim to do about it yet, but it's not fair. And I can't lose another friend like I lost Martin and Therese.

Girl, you'll learn. Life's not fair, Hardwick said.

Well, maybe I aim to make it fairer.

I turn the corner onto Clay Street and head downslope

toward the bay. The coonskin cap bobs up and down a block or so ahead. Beside him is Bearcoat. They're walking fast, but by the time they turn right on Battery Street, I'm less than half a block behind.

Slave catchers look the same whether they're in the woods of Georgia or the hills of San Francisco—covered in fur, well armed, mean as snakes. To them, a person is just another animal to hunt. Well, I can hunt too.

Battery Street is one of those waterfronts being filled in. To my left, a ship has been grounded and transformed into a saloon. An awning flaps at the entrance, and above it, the ship's masts have been replaced by a second story, built right on top of the deck. Across from the saloon to my right is an old brig still moored in water, but who knows for how long.

A sign hangs on the side of the brig: SAN FRANCISCO JAIL.

The empty cart is parked at the water's edge. Hampton kneels on the ground beside it, the driver looming over him. A small cluster of familiar figures surrounds them, and my steps falter.

Hardwick and Frank Dilley are conferring with the slave catchers. Miss Russell, Hardwick's "associate" from the law offices, presides over them all, wearing a dress of deep violet and fine lace.

Dilley searches Hampton's pockets and removes his precious letter, while Hardwick counts out gold coins to the roughnecks.

The driver shoves Hampton into a waiting boat and starts rowing him out to the brig.

I'm all alone with no plan. But somehow I have to get that letter. It's the only proof we have that Hampton is a free man.

I take a deep breath and stride forward, hefting my rifle, trying to appear more certain of myself than I feel. My gun isn't loaded, but no one needs to know that.

Helena Russell is the first to notice me. She leans over and whispers to Hardwick, who pulls out his pocket watch and checks the time. He nods, raising an eyebrow as if impressed. Somewhere in the city, church bells ring out the hour. Frank Dilley gives me a side-eye, then sticks a cheap cigar in his mouth and strikes a match to light it.

I stop about twenty feet away. Jefferson runs up behind me, out of breath. Part of me wishes he hadn't followed, because I have no idea what I'm about to get myself into, but I'm glad to have him at my side just the same.

"What do you think you're doing, Mr. Hardwick?" I shout.

"I might ask you the same thing, Miss Westfall."

"I'm checking on the welfare of a friend."

"That's very gentlewomanly of you. I'm upholding the laws of the land by paying professionals with a specific set of skills to locate and apprehend a runaway slave. I'll arrange for his transportation back to Arkansas and collect a hefty fee. The law and profit go hand in hand."

"He's no runaway, and you know it. You were there when he showed us his freedom papers."

"These papers?" says Frank Dilley. He waves the envelope he just took from Hampton, lifts it toward the glowing end of his cigar.

I whip up my rifle and aim it at his head. Dilley's free hand reaches for the gun at his holster.

"I don't miss," I tell him. "Especially not at this range, which you well know. You want to bet your life that you can draw faster than I can pull a trigger, you just go ahead."

Dilley's face goes white, but he doesn't draw.

"Do you want us to take care of this?" Bearcoat offers, tapping Hardwick on the arm. The other two roughnecks look like they're itching for a fight as well.

"There's no need for violence," Hardwick tells them. "You've been paid. The Apollo saloon is just across the street. I suggest you repair to that location, acquire something refreshing, and enjoy the show."

Bearskin shrugs, and the three men peel off to the saloon. They join the crowd of drinkers who have come outside to watch the commotion.

"It's wrong to make a show out of someone's freedom," I say. "You still there, Jefferson?"

"Yeah," he says behind me. His voice is quiet and very controlled.

"Would you please walk over to Mr. Dilley and take that letter from him? And make sure it's Hampton's letter."

"Glad to," he says.

"Frank?"

Frank glares. His gun hand twitches at his side.

"You hold that letter way out to your side—the other side. Away from everybody else. I want to see your gun hand the whole time. Jeff?"

"Lee?"

"Best stay well out of my line of fire. I don't want anything coming between this rifle and that varmint."

Jefferson closes the distance like a man approaching a nest of angry hornets. Hardwick whispers something to Miss Russell, and she moves behind him. I get the impression he's protecting her, using his own body as a shield. What makes a man like him do something so selfless?

Jefferson snatches the envelope from Dilley's outstretched hand and pauses just long enough to glance inside. "This is it."

"Good. Get back behind me."

He returns a whole lot faster than he went, keeping his eye on Dilley the whole way.

"Mr. Hardwick," I say, enunciating carefully. "Release Hampton."

"Can't do that. It would be breaking the law. But someone going through the proper channels could arrange to purchase his bounty from me before I sell it to the owner in Arkansas. Arkansas is an awful distance."

"This letter proves he's a free man."

"And I have a bounty that proves he's a runaway. Who is the law going to believe? A runaway Negro and a runaway girl? Or an upstanding man of industry?"

I think I might hate Hardwick. "Release him anyway."

"Ah, no," Hardwick says, smiling. "You'll have to take that up with the sheriff, since the runaway has been remanded to the authority of the jail."

"So, let's talk to the sheriff."

Hardwick just grins.

"Let me guess—the sheriff isn't here right now."

"He's a man with many duties."

Part of me wants to storm over and free Hampton by force. But there's just me and Jefferson with two unloaded guns between us. "This isn't over," I say fiercely.

Hardwick's smile widens. "I would be disappointed if it was."

I back away slowly without lowering the gun. Before I've taken a dozen steps, Hardwick puts his arms around Dilley and Helena Russell, herding them toward the Apollo saloon. The last thing I hear him say is, "A round of drinks for everyone, on me."

I lower the rifle. My arms are shaking.

"Let's go," Jefferson says. "Before they change their minds."

We hurry around the corner and trudge up the hill, toward Portsmouth Square. The first block passes in silence. Partway up the second block, he says, "You know that rifle isn't loaded, right?"

"Frank didn't know that," I say.

"What were you going to do if he called your bluff and drew on you?"

"My plan didn't account for him making that choice."

"Lee!"

"What?"

"Sometimes you need a better plan."

"But Hampton's letter was as stake! What if Dilley burned it or threw it into the bay before we could get it back?"

"I don't know if the letter mattered one whit. Like Hardwick said, who's the law going to side with? The white man, of course."

I'm silent a long while. We've reached the square before I can admit it. "You have a point."

"Thank you. I don't mind going along with whatever you want to do, but I'd appreciate it if you didn't put me in the line of fire without a better way of backing me up. And running off half-cocked isn't the kind of thing that hurts you and me; it's usually the people we're trying to help who get themselves killed. We learned that at your uncle's mine."

"I'm sorry. It was the heat of the moment." He's right. It's always the most vulnerable who suffer most. I'm lucky Hardwick didn't take it out on Hampton. Yet.

"Well, give me a warning if there's more heat coming."

"I . . . I'll be more careful."

Jefferson leans over and plants a kiss on the top of my head.

When we get back to the wagon, Becky, Henry, and Jim are waiting for us. Jim sits on the bench, looking shaken but much better than he did before I ran off. Henry tends to Jim's wound, wiping the blood from his face. Becky paces on the boardwalk. When she sees me and Jefferson, she demands, "Where's Hampton? Is he safe?"

"For the moment, but maybe not for long," I say. I offer a quick accounting of what happened, leaving out the bit about me threatening to shoot Frank Dilley with an empty gun. "At least we got his freedom papers back before Frank burned them."

"Let me see those," Jim says, hopping down from the wagon.

Jefferson hands them over, and Jim opens the envelope, checks the letter, then folds it right back up. He slips it into the pocket of his trousers.

"Maybe we should give the freedom papers to Tom?" Becky says. "He's a lawyer, and he—"

"We have more than a hundred years' experience with this sort of thing," Jim says. "But Tom is welcome to take a gander at them anytime."

"We *have* to get Hampton back," Henry asks. "And we have to do it soon. There's not a prison in the world that keeps a man hale."

"We'll find the sheriff and pay Hampton's bounty," Jefferson says.

"I've got some money—" I begin.

"Hold on to it," Jim says.

"Why?"

"You're acting like this is the first time a free Negro has been kidnapped and locked up until he pays a fine," Jim says. "When the law can't take our freedom, it takes all our money instead. Takes both when it gets the chance."

"We can't leave Hampton in jail," Becky says.

"We won't. But it's important for us to solve this, because it affects all of us."

"We *are* trying to solve it," I say.

"Don't get me wrong; we can definitely use your help. But freeing Hampton is taking the easy way out. We can do that part just fine ourselves. And when I say *us,* I mean free

Negroes. This is our problem. It was our problem before Hampton got arrested. It's gonna be our problem long after he gets free again. "

My heart aches. The fire that was burning inside me just a little while ago has about gone out, leaving me cold.

"What do you want us to do?" I say.

"We want to help," Becky adds.

"Hampton is our friend," Henry insists.

Jefferson stands beside Jim. He doesn't say a thing, but he doesn't need to.

"You can't barge in and try to fix Hampton's situation like it's something unusual, like it's a one-of-a-kind circumstance," Jim says. "That's what white people do. They fix one tiny thing and think they're heroes."

He stares right at me as he says it, and my gut churns in response. When I met Jim in Independence, I mouthed off to the store clerk for treating Jim poorly. I thought I was doing the right thing then, but maybe I was just making things worse.

"What happened to Hampton happens to free men all the time, all over this country," he continues. "*We* will take care of him, but then you gotta take care of Hardwick. It ain't enough to rescue a man in trouble, if you don't stop the man who put him there. Hardwick'll just do it again to someone else."

Life isn't fair.

Then it's our job to make it fairer.

Oh, I realize. *This* is what that means.

"Jim's right," I say. "My uncle took everything from me.

Then . . . remember how Dilley treated the Indians we met crossing the continent? Hardwick funded my uncle's mine, and we know what happened to the Indians and the Chinese there."

Henry adds, "Then Hardwick took all the money we raised in Glory and promised us a town charter, only now he's holding the charter ransom for even more money."

I nod. "He's stealing Becky's house, and he's going to sell it to somebody else. Now he's stealing Hampton's freedom. Over the last year, we've been treating all these things like separate problems, but they're not. They're all one problem."

"What's the one problem?" Jefferson asks. "Hardwick's an evil cur?"

"No, there are lots of bad men. I mean, yes, he is, but the real problem is the way he's got the law all tied up with money. He uses the law to rob people. Then he uses his money to change the laws and to buy lawmakers so he can rob even more people. It's a vicious circle, and it won't stop until he's not able to do whatever he wants to anyone."

"So what are we going to do?" Becky asks.

"We're going to stop him."

Jefferson steps forward, puts his hands on my shoulders, and looks at me dead-on. "You know I'm with you, right, Lee? Always, no matter what. But this time, we need a plan. No more going off half-cocked."

"A plan," Becky agrees.

"Something foolproof," Henry adds.

"Easy," I say. "Right?"

Chapter Eight

*T*wo mornings later, we take leave of the City Hotel, long before our full week is up—paid in advance, both rooms, all four cots—and form a small parade with all our possessions to walk down to the docks.

The Major has the baby tucked in one arm and holds Andy's hand with the other. I'm afraid he's going to topple over on his wooden leg, but he stomps along like a man who's been doing it his whole life and not just a few months.

Olive flits like a hummingbird. She runs ahead half a dozen steps, notices something new, and then immediately dashes back to tell us about it. "Ma, the sign on that big house says it's an oh-per-uh. Ma, what's an oh-per-uh?"

"An opera is a form of musical entertainment—"

"Jasper, is that man sick? He's sitting against the wall and his skin is *blanched*. You said that when a man's skin is—"

"Hush, dear," says Becky. "It's not polite to point out such things."

The three bachelors walk together. It's the first time they've all seen each other in days, because Jasper has been volunteering at doctors' offices throughout the city.

"I'm trying to find someone I can learn from," Jasper tells his friends, "but when a man with a crushed hand needed two fingers amputated, I was the one teaching the doctor how to do it instead of him teaching me."

"That's still better than my search," Tom says. "Plenty of law offices, but none willing to give me a job unless I bring in my own clients. If I had my own clients, I could afford rent, and I wouldn't need a job."

Henry rubs his eyes. I suspect he was up all night again. I don't think he gambles as much as he says, else he'd be broke by now, but he sure loves dressing fine and being sociable.

Jefferson and I bring up the rear, leading the wagon, which is loaded with our bags, and Peony and Sorry, who seem relieved to be let out of the stable. It's our first private moment together since the walk back to Portsmouth Square the other day.

"I think Becky's forgotten about the wedding dress," I tell him. Softly, so there's no chance of Becky overhearing.

"Not a chance," he says.

"How can you be sure?"

"Well, this is Becky we're talking about."

"Good point."

"Also, she asked Henry if he'd be willing to help me find a proper suit."

"Really?"

"I tried to dissuade him, but without luck. He knows just the place. And he's certain he knows just the color for me."

"What color is that?"

"I'm pretty sure he said plum."

"Plum?"

"Plum. Which, until that moment, I could have sworn was a fruit."

I want to ask if any other colors were mentioned, but it's a very short parade route and we have arrived at our destination, which is the *Charlotte*. I don't see Melancthon anywhere about the deck, so I bang on the side.

"Whaddyawant?" comes from somewhere inside the cabin.

I hammer the side of the ship again. "Prepare to be boarded!"

His rat's nest of hair bobs to the surface of the ship, and Melancthon Jones squints over the side at us. "Oh, it's you," he says, frowning. "I already told you, the house we loaded in Panama isn't here anymore. You'll have to go up to the customs office in Portsmouth Square."

"We've been and gone," I say. "That situation isn't resolving as quickly as we would prefer. In the meantime, we've bought this ship."

Major Craven reaches into my saddlebags, which are a lot lighter than they were a couple days ago, much to Peony's delight. And much to mine. Carrying around all that gold was worrisome.

The Major holds up a deed for the ship and the land underneath, and waves it at the sailor.

Melancthon straightens like a man called to attention. After a moment's pause, he hurries to the side of the ship and drops the gangplank.

"Come aboard," he says, but he eyes us with mistrust. As far as he knows, we've just bought his house out from under him.

The children are the first to rush aboard. Andrew jumps up and down, cheering. "We have a ship! We have a ship!"

"A _land_ ship," Olive clarifies.

The Major pauses at the top of the gangplank and allows Melancthon to inspect the bill of sale.

"This is unexpected," Melancthon says, combing his hair with his fingers, once again with no noticeable effect. "I didn't plan to vacate until next Tuesday, but it'll only be a few minutes' work to gather my things."

"Don't be in such a hurry," I tell him. "You said you were a carpenter?"

"That's correct, ma'am. Started out as a carpenter's mate nigh on twenty years ago. Been ship's carpenter for seven years, the last three aboard the _Charlotte_."

I like the way he squares his shoulders when he speaks, like a man who takes pride in his work.

"I need a carpenter," I tell him. "Are you familiar with the Apollo saloon?"

"Formerly the _Apollo_? Now sadly run aground, down on Battery Street. I may have had a nip or two there on occasion."

"I noticed they added a door at street level, along with an awning, and a second story above the deck."

"Yes, ma'am. And they've got a very nice saloon inside—a

long bar running the length of the lower deck, with booths and tables beside. Do you mean to turn the *Charlotte* into a saloon, ma'am?"

"Would that be a problem?" I ask.

"It's just you don't look . . . old enough to be the proprietor of a saloon. No offense intended."

"None taken," I assure him. "What can you tell me about this ship?"

"She's one hundred fifteen feet in length, with a beam of twenty-eight, and a depth of sixteen—"

"I meant, more generally, what can you tell me about the ship?"

"We were a whaler, came sailing around Cape Horn, where we put in at Paita in Peru. The captain received an urgent letter from the American consulate there, enjoining him to pick up passengers and cargo at Panama and bring them to San Francisco. We sold off or unloaded all our stores right there, and converted the ship as well as we might en route to Panama. Once we got here, the captain decided to run the ship aground at high tide. . . ."

Again, not exactly what I need to know. "Maybe it would just be better to take us on a tour."

"I can do that," he says.

"Olive! Andrew!" calls out Becky. "Gather around. We're going to take a tour of the ship."

Our group, which had been wandering and inspecting independently, converges at the center of the deck. Melancthon points to the front of the ship. "That's the foaksul . . ."

"Pardon me, the what?" asks Tom. "Could you spell that please?"

"F-O-R-E-C-A-S-T-L-E."

"Ah," says Tom, as if this makes perfect sense.

"Forecastle?" I ask.

"That's what I said!" Melancthon points in the other direction. "And that's the quarter deck, and there in the rear, that's the poop deck."

Olive turns to her mother. "Ma, did he just say *poop* deck?"

"I'm certain you misheard," Becky says.

"It's from *la poupe*, the French word for the stern of the ship," Henry explains. "Which, in turn, is derived from the Latin word *puppis*."

"La poop, la poop, la poop," Andrew says. His mother turns scarlet.

This is all going terribly off track. "Maybe I can just tell you what I want, and you can tell me if it can be done, and, if so, how fast you can do it."

"Yes, ma'am," Melancthon says.

"I'd like separate rooms for us to sleep in, and a larger room where we can meet."

"We already did the first part, turning the crew deck into cabins, before we picked up the passengers in Panama. I can take you down the main hatchway and show you. And the galley, where we serve meals, that's already as good a room as any to meet in."

This may turn out easier than I'd hoped. "What about storage? Is there room enough to stable our horses and store our wagon?"

He points to a hatchway at the center of the ship, currently covered by a tarp. "For certain. We transported some cattle in the hold, at least until it was time to eat them."

Even better. "What about putting a door in the side of the ship, so we can take the horses in and out just like a stable?"

Melancthon goes pale and takes a step backward. "You want to put a . . . *hole* in the side of the *Charlotte?*"

"Two holes," I clarify. "One that would lead to the cargo hold, where we could stable the horses and store the wagon, but move them in and out easily. And then another one right here at the front of the ship, so we can walk in and out without climbing up the gangplank."

"But . . . my ship . . ."

"Is never going to sail again. I'll pay you to do the work, daily wages, whatever a carpenter makes in San Francisco right now. So if you can't find a ship to hire you, by the time you're done working for us, you can buy passage on one. This is your way out of California. In the meantime, you can stay aboard for as long as we're on the ship. Rent free."

The light comes back into his eyes. "So you're going to settle here in San Francisco?" he asks.

It's a reasonable deduction, but I'm not eager to explain our plans to a stranger. "That remains to be seen. But look, no hard feelings if you don't want to do the work. I'll just hire a different carpenter, and you can find somewhere else to stay."

He shrugs. "I guess I'll get started."

"Stable for the horses is the highest priority," I tell him. I'm nervous about leaving them tied up outside, especially Peony, who's been stolen once already.

"That's smart, ma'am," Melancthon says. "Every horse thief in San Francisco will take notice of that pretty palomino of yours."

"It's settled, then. Can you show us to the cabins below? And the meeting room?"

"Cabins and galley. Yes, ma'am. If you'll all follow me this way."

As we crowd together toward a ladder, Becky leans over and whispers, "You handled that *very* well."

"I did?"

"Once you started giving orders, he never once looked to any of the men for confirmation." She squeezes my arm.

Jefferson comes up on the other side. "Don't let it go to your head."

"Huh?"

He nods at my right hand. "You're the only one holding a gun, which kinda demands attention. And you tend to jab with it emphatically whenever you're making a point."

"I do not jab."

"You jab."

He points again. My arm is tensed and I'm thrusting the barrel of the gun at his feet while I talk.

"Huh. I never noticed that before."

Melancthon has been a good caretaker, and the area below decks is spick-and-span. Our steps have a hollow sound that will take some getting used to. Thin wooden walls divide the lower deck into eight smaller cabins, most outfitted with cots or beds. It's not the same as private rooms, but they're semiprivate. Tom and Henry take one together. Becky takes a larger one for herself and the children. She invites me to join them, but there's plenty of room, and Jasper, Jefferson, the Major, and I each take cabins for ourselves. Four empty cots make mine feel a little lonely, especially after we've all been piled on top of each other for days.

Henry sticks his head in the door. "This was a really good idea," he says. "A perfect base of operations for going after Hardwick."

I grin. "We are going to destroy him. Get everyone together in the galley—I'll be there in a minute."

I pick one of the cots and shove the saddlebags underneath it. The blanket from another cot becomes a wrap for Daddy's rifle. I slide it underneath, beside the saddlebags. It's not much in terms of worldly possessions.

But I have friends. And a purpose. And now a ship.

I find all the adults gathered in the galley, seated around a large wooden table that's nailed to the floor. An oil lamp hangs from the ceiling, casting a warm glow. The seat at the head of the table is empty, so that's the one I take.

Becky rocks the sleeping baby in her arms. "Where are Olive and Andrew?" I ask.

"They're amusing themselves in the cabin for now. They're glad to have a larger space."

I waste no time. "It should be clear to everyone now that James Henry Hardwick is coming after us. He provided the money for my uncle's scheme last fall." I nod to Tom and Jefferson, who experienced worse in that ordeal than I did. "Since then, Hardwick has failed to live up to the terms of the contract we signed with him at Christmas."

"But we can take that to court and make him enforce it," Jasper says.

"Is that true, Tom?"

Tom shakes his head. "Right now, California barely has courts worthy of the name. Influence counts for more than the law. The courts do what Hardwick tells them, not the other way around."

"And there's the matter of Becky's house," I say.

Becky stops stroking the baby's cheek and looks up.

"And the fact that Frank Dilley and those roughnecks held you and Henry at gunpoint in the Custom House," I add.

The Major frowns at Becky. "I'm sorry I wasn't there for that."

Becky absently puts a hand on his arm, even as she bounces the baby on one knee. "It turned out fine," she says. The Major stares down at the hand covering his arm, color rising in his cheeks.

"And then we come to the matter of Hampton," I say.

I'm met with nods and murmurs of agreement from around the table.

"There's one more thing," Tom says, his face grave.

"Oh?"

"I can't be the only one who has noticed," he says, glancing around the table. "But Hardwick seems to have taken a peculiar interest in Lee."

"It's true," Becky says.

"Lee, I don't like the way he looks at you," Jefferson adds.

I don't like it much either. He gives my belly the same wormy feeling I always got around my uncle Hiram.

"What makes you all say that?" Jasper says.

"Well, he keeps showing up everywhere we go," Jefferson says.

"He's going to ask for more money for Glory's charter, remember?" Henry says.

"He called Lee 'intriguing,'" Becky says. "Which gave me a shiver, I don't mind saying.

"He knows we've all got more gold than we ought, although . . ." She lowers her voice to a whisper. "I don't think he knows about your particular . . . blessing."

"In any case, his fascination with Lee is . . . unnatural," Tom says.

They're all looking at each other, more than they're looking at me. Finally, Jefferson clears his throat. "The thing is, Lee, there's always going to be men like that in the world."

"And your point is?"

"We can't make that problem go away forever."

"When you're hungry, and you eat, do you expect your hunger to go away forever? When you're sick, and you go to a doctor"—I point to Jasper—"do you expect to stay well forever? Of course not. Hardwick is the problem in front of us right now. We can't solve the problem forever, but we can solve *him*. That's what we're going to do."

"You aren't planning to shoot Hardwick, are you?" Tom asks. "With your daddy's rifle?"

"No!"

"Because that would be wrong—"

"Because that would be ineffective."

"And also wrong," says Jefferson.

"Yes, but it wouldn't get the job done," I clarify. "Jeff, you remember our teacher back in Dahlonega? Mr. Anders?"

Jefferson is leaning forward, fingers steepled. "Yeah."

"What was that monster he told us about? The one where you cut off its head and it grows two more?"

"The hydra?" he answers, as all three of the college men blurt out, "The hydra!"

"That's the one," I say. "Hardwick is the head of the monster, but the body that feeds him is the money and the businesses that are making him rich right now. If he died tomorrow, a bunch of other men would just divvy up his businesses and his money, and they'd all go on doing the same thing. It's not enough to cut the head off the monster. We have to destroy the body too. We're not just going to bring down James Henry Hardwick, we're going to ruin his empire and take every penny he owns. Who's in?"

Silence. Faintly, a burst of distant laughter filters through the hull; probably from one of the nearby saloons.

Jasper spreads his large, capable hands on the table. "I hear what you're saying, and I admire your intent. But I came to San Francisco to learn. And there's so much to learn. Malnourishment, diseases, every kind of wound and injury. But my time is limited. A year from now, when this is a more settled place, those problems won't be here, not in the same degree. I can get a lifetime of experience in the next year if I want it, and that's what I want."

"You're already the best doctor I've ever known," I tell him.

He grins. "And I'm going to get even better."

"That makes perfect sense," I say, even though I'm disappointed. "I wish you well. You're welcome to stay aboard the ship, even if you're not part of our plan."

Jasper stands. "I'd like to maintain a cabin here, if you don't mind, Lee."

"Of course I don't mind!"

"It's just the doctor I'm working with has invited me to board with him on weekdays, because there's no telling what hour of the day an emergency will come knocking. He calls it 'a residency.' My home will always be here, with you." He glances toward Henry and Tom, his face a little apologetic. "But I think I'll take him up on that. Spend most of my nights there, come back to the *Charlotte* on weekends."

Henry and Tom exchange a glance, part resignation, part relief, and suddenly I understand. Henry and Tom have always been especially attached to each other, and Jasper is leaving them be, giving them space of their own.

I swallow hard and force myself to say, "That doctor is lucky to have you."

"Now, this doesn't mean I won't help. Hampton is my friend, and we've been through a lot together, and I'll do just about anything to get him back. So, if you think of something I can do, you let me know, understand?"

"Count on it."

He rises from the table. Becky says, "You'll come around often, won't you, Jasper?"

"Of course!"

The Major shakes Jasper's hand. Jefferson puts a hand on his shoulder and squeezes.

Henry crosses his arms and says emphatically, "See you *soon*."

"See you soon," Jasper echoes.

"See you soon," Tom whispers.

With a final nod, Jasper leaves the room. I stare around the rest of the table. "Anybody else want to go? Now's the time to do it."

Nobody moves. The Major reaches down to rub the stump of his leg. "Just promise me there's a chance to take down Frank Dilley too."

"That's definitely part of the plan," I promise him.

"Then I'm in."

Tom pushes his chair back from the table and rises. Before speaking, he straightens his collar and cuffs. "I think I need to go see a man about a job," he says in a tight voice. "I'll catch up with all of you later."

I nod to him, not trusting my words enough to say anything.

"Tom . . . ," Henry says.

Tom smiles the tiniest bit. "I'll be back."

When he's gone, I lean forward. "All right then. Let's get to work."

Just below us, deep inside the ship, a hammer pounds on thick wood. A moment later comes the rasp of a saw.

Chapter Nine

The first thing we decide to do is find out how much money Hardwick has and where he keeps it.

The day we ran into Hardwick, his entourage included the fellow whom Henry has taken to calling "Mr. Keys," real name unknown. All we do know about Mr. Keys is that he's a small man with a narrow face and no chin, and—most importantly—he sticks close to Hardwick, carrying a large ring of keys and a heavy leather bag full of gold.

It's a sure bet some of Hardwick's money is at that bank. But it's a surer bet that not all of it is. And if anyone is in charge of Hardwick's money, it's Mr. Keys.

Jefferson took off before dawn to make inquiries about Hardwick's main business office and hopefully put an eye on the little fellow.

In the meantime, before the bank opens, Becky and I camp out in the parlor of a hotel kitty-corner to the Custom House building. We find two large armchairs and drag them from the fireplace to one of the windows. The window is dirty but large, and it gives us an unobstructed view of the bank. This is one of the establishments where miners, flush with gold, stay up all night to gamble, and are then late abed, so we have the downstairs mostly to ourselves.

Their gold sings to me, though. Several coin purses' worth, mostly upstairs, but a larger stash hides away in the downstairs office.

The air is especially chilly. Nothing close to a frost, but still the kind of cold that seeps into your bones and makes you ache for a warm kitchen and bread right out the oven; even a chunk of half-burned, half-doughy bread from Becky's restaurant would be just the thing. A light rain falls, so the plaza feels sleepier than usual. The men who come to open the bank have hunched shoulders and dripping hats. They pause beneath the veranda to kick mud off their boots before unlocking the doors.

For the next hour or so, a handful of brave but unfamiliar souls, similarly inured to the cold and wet, are the only ones to enter and leave.

"Excuse me, ladies?"

I'd been so intent on watching the bank that I hadn't noticed anyone approach. The proprietor of the hotel, wearing a green velvet vest and an air of self-importance, looks down his blunt nose at us.

I'm not sure what to say, but Becky doesn't hesitate.

"My dear sir," she says smoothly. The baby kept her up half the night, and it's a wonder she's not dozing in her chair. "How may we be of service?"

"That's just it," he says, hooking his thumbs into his vest pockets. "You can't."

"I'm afraid we don't understand your implication," Becky says.

"That is, what I'm trying to say is, this is not the sort of establishment where we welcome women who provide services."

My head whips back around. *"What?"*

Becky reaches out and taps her fingers on his hand. "Oh, sir, that's such a relief to hear. You've put my heart at ease."

"I have?" he says, thrown off-balance.

I'm torn. I need to watch the bank, but I'm equally captivated by Becky—I have no idea what she plans to say next. It never occurred to me that we'd be a problem sitting in a public parlor on a cold day.

"You have," she says. "You see . . ." She whispers the last phrase conspiratorially, leaning forward. The proprietor bends down to listen closely.

"My dear, beloved husband," she says, "brought our gold into San Francisco to invest it, but I'm very much afraid he's been spending it instead. It's one thing if he gambles a bit of it. Why, that's natural, and any man might do the same, whether for entertainment or in hopes of increasing his stake. But if he's been spending it elsewise . . ."

She lets the last sentence trail off like an unspoken threat. Taking notice of my attention, she jerks her head to the window, and I oblige by turning my head around again to watch the bank, trusting her to take care of the proprietor.

"And you're certain he's a resident of our establishment?" he says.

"Not at all," Becky says. "But he didn't come home last night, and one of his usual companions said he was last seen in your gambling parlor, around midnight. So I've come to check. You say there are no women here who might keep the gentlemen company?"

"Ah," the proprietor says.

In his silence, I hear a different story: that any such women here are discreet enough to avoid being seen in the front parlor in the morning.

"Perhaps he had a bit too much to drink and decided to sleep it off before coming home," Becky suggests.

"That's entirely possible," admits the proprietor. "If you would like to give me a name, I could check our guest ledger."

"Absolutely not!" Becky says. "If my suspicions are unfounded, I would certainly not wish to sully the reputation of our good name."

A short man carrying something heavy walks toward the bank. I rub a circle clean on the window with my sleeve, then realize that Becky and the proprietor are both staring. I suppose that using my sleeve to clean a window is probably ill-mannered. "I apologize," I say, hiding my sleeve under my arm. "I thought I saw . . . him." *Him* being Mr. Keys, not Becky's imaginary husband. "But I was mistaken."

"Have all of your guests come downstairs yet this morning?" Becky asks the proprietor.

"No, ma'am," he says. "No, they haven't."

"Then we'll just wait here until they do. Thank you for allowing us to do that. Your thoughtfulness means everything."

I take another glimpse, just to see his jaw working, trying to figure out how he ended up giving us permission. Finally he snaps it shut and takes a moment to gather himself. "I guess that will be satisfactory," he says thoughtfully, perhaps considering how he can sneak upstairs and warn his customers that someone's angry wife is lying in ambush in the parlor. He turns to go, saying, "If there will be nothing else, then?"

"Oh, thank you kindly for offering," Becky says. "It's so dreadfully cold out. A cup of tea would be perfect. Do you want a cup of tea, dear?"

I realize she's talking to me. "Coffee, please."

"And sugar," Becky says. "Lots of sugar."

We pass the morning supplied with a side table, and restored at regular intervals with fresh tea and coffee. Becky pretends to watch the lobby, deflecting conversations with the proprietor and anyone else who comes along. I keep an eye on the bank.

Gold from last night's winnings pokes at my mind from the rooms above our head. After the proprietor leaves to make his rounds, I feel some of it moving out of the rooms and away, disappearing without coming down the front staircase.

By early afternoon, the rain has let up. We enjoy fresh sandwiches from the kitchen, while Becky pretends to enjoy the company of the hotel's cook. Across the street, the bank's clerks leave in small groups for lunch, and then return. It takes hours, but eventually even Becky's mighty composure crumbles into fidgeting as she becomes bored and restless, ready to call it quits.

But my daddy taught me how to hunt with that Hawken rifle Jim returned to me. He showed me how to hole up in a blind and wait for my quarry to come along, even if it meant staying for hours in the cold and snow. Days, if we were desperate enough.

Sitting in the parlor of a hotel, even a low establishment like this one, is so much easier than sitting in a deer blind. Nobody ever brought me fresh coffee or sandwiches in a blind.

Becky is deflecting a fresh round of questions from the afternoon manager when I finally see our target. "There he is," I announce, rising.

Becky nearly spills her cup of tea.

"You've spotted the lady's husband?" the manager asks.

"Sometimes if you can't catch them going, you get them coming," Becky tells him, and we rush out the door. At the corner, we pause to catch our breath.

"You're sure it's him?" Becky asks.

"Absolutely." I drop my voice to a whisper. "I sense his bag of gold. Also, he has two armed guards." I point to the two men leaning against the wall beneath the veranda. One is pushing a wad of chewing tobacco into his mouth, while the other blows on his hands to warm them. "They were with Frank Dilley the other day. Which means they might recognize us. Are you ready to do this?"

"As long as my constitution holds," Becky says. "I should

have taken the opportunity to relieve myself when I had the chance."

"If I'm right, we won't be in there long."

"We weren't counting on guards. How do we get past them?"

"We've as much right to go to the bank as anyone. We'll just lower our heads and—"

A cry of "Tag! You're it!" rings out at the far end of the building, and Sonia's group of urchins tears around the corner, bumping into everyone below the veranda before scattering in all directions. The guards give chase, patting down their pockets even as they tear after the children.

Sonia's group must be well practiced at pickpocketing to bump and grab so quickly and easily. It couldn't have happened at a better time. While the guards are distracted, Becky and I dash across the street and into the bank.

The moment we pass through the door, a clerk rises to assist us. I pause to catch my breath, because the gold in this room is overwhelming. Here, it's less like a choir singing and more like a giant crowd shouting at the top of its lungs.

"How may I help you ladies?" the clerk inquires.

I blink rapidly, trying to focus. As planned, I pull a handful of large gold nuggets from the plain leather purse I carry, then screw up my face like it's hard for me to think, which is not entirely an act. "Found this. Prospecting."

He's seen larger amounts of gold, but his eyes widen appreciatively.

Becky steps in and covers the gold with one hand, placing her other on my shoulder. "My friend's a hard worker, but a little . . . unsophisticated," she says. "I've tried to tell her not to carry nuggets like these around—that's just asking for trouble. I've told her that she should have it converted to coinage. And she ought to keep it in a bank, where it can be safe."

I take stock of the bank while she's talking, trying to ignore all the gold weighing down my senses. A long counter divides the space. Behind the counter are a few desks, and behind the desks is an iron cage bolted to both floor and ceiling. The cage contains both a small strongbox and a larger safe.

Mr. Keys sits at one of the desks. Across from him is a gray-haired man with heavy jowls, who appears to frown even when he smiles. Likely Mr. Owen, the owner of the bank.

"I don't see many prospectors of the female persuasion," the clerk notes. "It's too hard a life for the weaker sex."

Becky bristles. "I'll hear no more from you about the weaker sex until you've birthed three babes."

"I . . . of course. Apologies." He wisely changes the subject. "Is that all the gold that your friend has?"

"Oh, no, sir, I got lots more," I say, and I flip my purse, like I'm going to dump it on the floor. I can tell the clerk is trying to gauge its weight with his eyes. Becky grabs my hands and stops me again.

"You have to forgive her," Becky says. "She works day and night. I think the mercury has affected her some. She uses so much of it, refining the gold she finds."

"Some people have a knack," the clerk says with a shrug.

He doesn't know the half of it.

"Let's retire to the privacy of my desk," he offers, signaling to the far end of the room.

"I like that desk over there," I whine. "It's by the pretty window." Which is just about the daftest thing to say, but I can't think up another excuse.

Becky shrugs, as if to say, "What can you do?" The clerk accommodates my request by taking us to the desk beside the window. Becky proceeds to ask him a number of pertinent questions about turning gold into coinage and the protection of this bank compared to others.

From here, I have a perfect view of everything behind the counter, everything inside the cage. Which is where the bank's owner is leading Mr. Keys.

Mr. Owen inserts the key into the cage's lock. The iron door creaks open, and everyone stops work for a moment. You'd think the bank would oil the hinges.

"We have one of the strongest cages in the city," the clerk is saying. Then he recites a flurry of details about its manufacture, installation, and maintenance.

The owner steps aside, and Mr. Keys pulls out his namesake ring and sorts through a dozen options, looking for the correct key. I reckon he knows them all by sight, because he slides one into the small safe, and it opens correctly the first time.

Mr. Owen removes himself from the cage and looks discreetly in the other direction. I have no such compunctions and gawk like a child at a carnival.

Before we came, I warned Becky that I wouldn't be at my

level best, not surrounded by so much gold, and we decided I would act a bit touched to cover any lapses. Good thing we did, because there there's enough gold in that safe to ransom a kingdom. Stacks of coins and ingots. Hundreds of pounds. More than I have ever seen—or sensed—in one place at one time.

Mr. Keys removes even more gold coins from his little bag and stacks them carefully inside. When finished, he makes a notation on a ledger inside the safe; then he pulls a small notebook from his bag and writes what is certainly a matching entry. He locks up the safe and exits the cage. Mr. Owen latches the cage behind him. They shake hands, and Mr. Keys passes us on his way out. Becky has her back to him. I lean against my hand to hide my face. If he recognizes either one of us, he gives no indication.

"So you're saying you can turn these nuggets into gold coins for a small percentage of the weight?" Becky says, pulling me back into the conversation.

"A nominal fee. The Pacific Company is known to charge up to twenty percent, and many other banks in town will require a similar amount. Our fee is only ten percent."

"What about impurities?"

He smiles. "Yes, our assayer determines the level of impurities in the gold, and that amount is also charged against the weight."

I imagine that it amounts to at least another ten percent.

"But everyone does the same," he assures us. "Did you know that forty million dollars in gold was collected by miners last year?"

It boggles the mind. "How many gold coins is that?" I ask.

"Let's use the fifty-dollar eagle as the standard. In that case, the total number of coins would be . . ." He pauses to think.

"Eight hundred thousand gold coins," Becky says.

"No, it's . . ." The clerk counts his fingers. "Oh, yes, it's about eight hundred thousand gold coins. You guessed right." He smiles at her like she's a performing dog.

"That seems impossible. Where would people keep it?" she says.

"We estimate that half of it went out of the country, back to Mexico, or Peru, or Australia, maybe Sweden or China—wherever the miners came from. They struck it rich, packed up their money, and took it home. Once California is a state, we'll pass more laws to keep foreigners out in the first place. We want as much of that gold as possible to stay right here in the United States where it belongs."

"We're all foreigners here," I point out, forgetting for a moment that I'm supposed to be a bit addled by mercury.

Becky shoots me a warning look. "If my friend wants to keep her money safe until she needs it, she can store some of it here?"

"Absolutely." He twists in his seat and indicates the cage. "Our strongbox is the most secure in the whole city."

The strongbox is little more than a traveling trunk, with breakable hinges and a flimsy padlock. It doesn't contain a quarter of the amount in the safe that sits beside it. There's so much gold in the safe that I feel slightly sick, like I would after eating a whole pie, when all I needed was a single piece.

"But the safe," I say. "The safe looks safe. I want my money safe. In a safe."

"My friend likes the safe," Becky says. "The big black one. Is it available to customers?"

"That's a Wilder Salamander safe, one of only a few in the entire state of California," the clerk says. "It's got double walls, insulated, to protect the items inside in case of fire. State of the art. But that's the personal safe of one of our most elite customers."

"But I just saw somebody put something in there?" I say.

The clerk smiles at me. "As I said."

Becky says, "He must be a very good customer."

"He's very nearly a bank unto himself," the clerk exclaims, and then, glancing at the gray-haired owner, decides that circumspection is called for. "But let me assure you that your friend's money will be triply protected here. First by the strongbox itself, which only the manager has keys to. Then by the cage, which is similarly locked. And finally by the guard who patrols our building at night."

"That's a lot of protection," Becky says.

"It's not safe if it's not in the safe," I say, failing to sound angry.

Becky puts a hand on my arm. "Why don't you go outside and get some air? I'll join you shortly."

"Yes, ma'am." She knows I want to lay eyes on Mr. Keys if I can. I give her a grateful look and exit the bank without another word. Beneath the veranda, I scan the square for Mr. Keys and his guards, but they are already gone.

Becky joins me outside a few minutes later. "You've upset the poor gentleman. He's very concerned that if you take your business to another bank, they'll take advantage of you. On the positive side, young Mr. Owen—he's the son of that other fellow—is impressed by my mathematical abilities, considering that I'm a woman, and he asked me to tea, which I reluctantly declined."

I grin, in spite of the churning in my belly. "I'm getting sick from being near so much gold," I whisper. "Let's walk."

We stroll into the plaza, and I feel a little steadier with each step. Halfway across the square, Jefferson slides in beside us.

"Hello, Lee, Becky. How'd you like the distraction? I ran into Sonia's little gang and paid them to make a ruckus so you could slip past Mr. Key's guards."

"That was clever," Becky says.

"We saw where Hardwick keeps his gold," I say, and I describe everything we observed in the bank. "It's more gold than I ever imagined. More than one man could ever spend or need."

"Then I have some bad news for you," Jefferson says.

"Worse news than 'He has more money than we could ever steal'?"

"Yes, worse than that." We cross the street and head downhill toward the *Charlotte*. The scent of saltwater marsh rises to greet us. "I found Hardwick's main business office, which is at his house. His mansion, I mean. Takes up half a block. And I started following our pal, Mr. Keys, first thing this morning.

This bank wasn't his first stop. It wasn't even his second."

"Where was he going?" I ask.

"To other banks," he says. "He took a large bag from Hardwick's office, went to a couple of banks, made deposits, and then went back to Hardwick's house to collect another bag."

"I counted forty-seven gold coins in his deposit," Becky says. When I look at her in astonishment, she says simply, "Well, something like that. It was hard to count and talk at the same time, so I might be off a coin or two. Assuming they were all fifty-dollar coins, which seems to be the most common denomination, that's a deposit of two thousand three hundred fifty dollars. Three of those comes to more than seven thousand dollars! Just this morning."

"More than three banks," Jefferson says.

"Exactly how many banks?" I ask, my voice rising to a near-panic register.

"Eleven," Jefferson says.

Becky and I stop in the middle of the street to stare at him.

"This was his eleventh bank visit of the day," he assures us. "In and out within a few minutes at each stop. Like it's something he does every day. But that's not possible, right? There's not that much gold in all the world."

"Maybe there is," Becky says. "According to Mr. Owens Junior—who seems a reliable compendium of details, even if he's a bit slow at multiplication—California is home to at least twenty million dollars in gold."

"No wonder I was so distracted when our boots first

touched this territory," I say. "It was like a constant ringing in my ears."

Jefferson nods. "And Hardwick is trying to get it *all*."

Becky resumes her journey toward the *Charlotte* and gestures for us to keep pace. "This job just got a lot more complicated," she says.

"Yep," I say. "We need to think bigger."

"And smarter," Jefferson adds.

Chapter Ten

When we paid Hardwick four thousand dollars to settle my uncle's debt, we thought it was a lot of money. But it was nothing.

Four thousand to settle a debt.

A few thousand to auction off the pieces of someone's house.

A few thousand more for a man's freedom.

These little bits and pieces add up. No doubt this is how Hardwick's fortune started. But it's clear that the big money in San Francisco is now being made in property, through land sales and rents. If Hardwick is filling safes in eleven banks, then this is how he's doing it.

Jim Boisclair has been in San Francisco for months, and I figure if anyone can help me suss it all out, it's him. So I arrange to meet Jim early the following morning at Portsmouth Square.

I spring out of bed and scarf down a quick breakfast, eager to see my friend. Even though it's not raining, the air is so damp with fog, it might as well be. I don a wool coat over a flannel shirt and sturdy trousers, and I'm still cold.

Jim is already waiting for me, leaning against a lamppost. He tips his hat and grins.

After we exchange greetings, I say, "Are you *sure* we can't ride? Peony could use the exercise." She's taken well to being stabled in the hull of a ship; it's the not smallest or worst place I've had to keep her. But I know she likes to stretch her legs.

"You don't see as much when you're riding," Jim says, pausing to blow on his fingers and rub them together for warmth. "You rush by, in too much of a hurry. Might as well hire a carriage with curtains on the window—that way you don't have to see the truth or talk to anyone at all."

I sigh, but I don't disagree.

"But I'm real glad to hear that pretty mare of yours is all right," he adds. "I remember the day she was foaled."

"I couldn't have made it here without her," I say. "Which way are we going?"

"Up," he says. "We're going to tour some of the city's most profitable areas, where Hardwick makes most of his money." He leads the way west, up the city's hills. The steep climb warms me quickly. "Pay attention as we go, and tell me what you see."

"And what are you going to do?" I ask.

"I'm going to point out the things you're not seeing." It's exactly the kind of thing my daddy would say, and it puts a lightness in my heart.

Everywhere we go, people are already up and working.

Clearing land and roads. Loading wagons full of dirt, unloading wagons full of supplies.

"I see a lot of people working hard," I tell Jim.

He smiles. "That's a good start."

Jim has always been one of the most sociable people I've ever known, and traveling across a whole continent has not changed him one bit. He stops and talks to everyone who will speak to us, and he isn't shy with his questions. Do they own the land or rent it? Some rent it. More say they own it, but when Jim asks about prices, it sure seems like they're paying installment plans at rates that sound a lot like rent. Why are they working so hard to improve it? So they can sell it for a profit once they've paid off the loan. A handful of the laborers are Negro, and they take plenty of time to answer Jim's questions and give specific answers. We spend almost half an hour talking with an enthusiastic fellow named Isaac who hails from Cincinnati.

Before we take our leave of Isaac, Jim says, "You hear the news about Hampton Freeman?"

"Sure did," Isaac says. "We're praying for him."

"We'll be taking up a collection."

"I've already told the fellows down at the foundry."

"That's good, that's good."

When we near the peak, Jim turns north. Outside a two-room shanty is a family of five—husband, wife, and three young children—just sitting there with a pile of belongings. Must be moving day.

But as we walk past, two white men carry a bed frame

through the doorway and drop it carelessly to the ground.

The family is not moving by choice. They're being evicted.

I glance up at Jim, who nods. "If we'd been on horses, you might've missed that," he says.

After crossing a muddy street, we find ourselves in a whole new neighborhood. It's similar to the first one we passed through—rows of shanties interspersed with the occasional house, lots of men and only a few families—but the faces here are mostly Chinese. They regard Jim and me with suspicion. No one wants to answer our questions.

We head farther north toward Goat Hill, where the semaphore tower raises flags to signal ships coming into harbor. Hammers sound in the quarry, breaking rock to use as ship ballast. Neighborhoods are forming here as well—mostly shacks and tents, though they're laid out along regular streets. We stop and talk to a few people, and nearly all the accents are Irish.

We head downhill toward the bay. Jim pauses at the corner of Sansome and Vallejo. It's a whole block of open land, without a single house or structure.

"It's a cemetery," I say. Crosses and gravestones stretch before us.

"They call it the Sailor's Cemetery," he says. "It's where all the sailors used to be buried. Now it's where all the outsiders are buried. People like me. Foreigners. Are you hungry?"

It's past lunchtime. "Starved. And you're not a foreigner." But as soon as the words leave my lips, I know they're not true. We're all foreigners, everyone but the Indians, that is, who have made themselves scarce in this city, or more likely been forced to leave. Very few Indians remain in San Francisco, and almost all who stayed are at Mission Dolores.

"Anyway, I know a place," Jim says. "Just found it a couple days ago."

Thinking about how we treat the Indians is chasing away my appetite, but I say, "All right, sure."

He leads me past the cemetery and down toward the choppy gray bay.

"Have I seen what you want me to see?" I say as we walk.

He shrugs. "Maybe." Jim wants me to put the pieces together myself, but so far I can't solve the puzzle. I see a lot of people working hard, improving the land, making something for themselves.

We duck into a building without any signs or special markings on it. Conversation trickles off the instant we come through the door.

The room is low ceilinged with exposed rafters, and it's filled with the darkest-skinned men I've ever seen, all clustered around a series of small tables. Most wear something between a robe and a blanket, thrown over one shoulder, all in bright colors. The air bursts with the scents of coffee and spices.

I'm sure it's a mistake to be here, but Jim takes a seat at an empty table and motions for me to join him. When I do, Jim looks to the proprietor and holds up two fingers.

After a moment's hesitation, the proprietor nods. The men stop staring and resume their conversations. The room buzzes with unfamiliar words.

I glance around nervously. "Why'd you want to meet here?" I'm whispering.

"Makes you feel a bit uncomfortable being around faces that don't look anything like yours," Jim says. It's not a question.

"No," I say. A bit too quick and sharp, which gives life to the lie. "Maybe."

"That's right," Jim says. "And it makes Hardwick and all the fellows who work for him uncomfortable, too. Hardwick has spies, maybe even spies close to you. Remember? He *knew* you were going to the bank that day to get that southern lady's house back."

"You're thinking it was Tom," I say darkly. "Tom wouldn't do that."

"If you say so." He waves his hand around the room. "In any case, these fellows came all the way from Ethiopia to dig gold. They're just waiting for spring to get sprung. I figure this is the one place in town we can talk privately, because a spy would stick out like a snowball in summer."

The shop's owner brings us two bowls of food, which is a stew with flatbread. The spices are unfamiliar, and I'm a little afraid to eat it. But I don't want Jim to know that.

I wave at the proprietor. "Some silverware, please?"

Jim shakes his head. "Like this," he says. "You break off bread to scoop up the stew. No, use your right hand only. You don't want to be rude."

I follow his example. The bread is spongy, like a pancake, but it has a sour tang.

Jim laughs at my expression. "You get used to it." He scoops more stew and pushes the bread into his mouth. After he swallows, he says, "Tell me what you saw this morning."

So I tell him what I've been thinking: the people of San Francisco work hard, improve property, build better lives for themselves.

"What I saw," Jim says, "are a whole bunch of folks not protected by the law."

I open my mouth to argue. Close it. Take another bite of food.

"You saw how Hampton's not protected by the law, right? Well, neither am I, nor any other Negro man or woman," he says. "Same goes for the Chinese, the Indians, and all the other immigrants. The Mexicans did all right at first, but that's changing, and it will change even more when California's statehood becomes official."

"I see your point," I say, thinking of the family being forced out of their home by Hardwick's men.

"So Hardwick owns land in every neighborhood we walked through today. He doesn't sell it outright. People jump at the opportunity to *rent* from him when they first arrive, expecting to pick up gold on every corner. They make outrageous payments, figuring the next month, the month after, they'll be rich beyond their wildest dreams. Instead, they go broke, and Hardwick rents the land to some other newcomer with a nest egg."

"And that's how Hardwick made his fortune?"

Jim shakes his head. "We're just getting started. Sometimes he sells property on an installment plan. A fellow with a lot of optimism buys a house lot for twelve thousand dollars. Only he doesn't have twelve thousand dollars, so Hardwick promises to sell it to him for just a thousand dollars a month, plus interest and some handling fees. The man signs the contract, but the interest and fees bring the payment closer to fifteen hundred a month, and meanwhile he's not getting rich like he planned. After a few months of hard work, during which he's been improving the property, he's broke. He can't make payments. So Hardwick's men kick him out."

"That family sitting in the street . . . they'd been evicted."

He nods approval. "Hardwick's men reclaim the property—now worth more—and he resells it for a higher rate as improved land."

"And not everyone lives long enough to go broke," I say, thinking of that huge cemetery. "California is a dangerous place."

"Exactly. Most people left their loved ones behind. They come alone, and they die alone. There's no effort made to contact a family back in France or Australia or China."

"Or even back east."

"Or even back east. The property goes into probate, which means it goes to the court. Hardwick owns the court, so the property reverts to the previous owner, which is him, and he starts the process all over again."

I take a bite, chew thoughtfully. This sour bread isn't so bad. "So Hardwick is selling the same land over and over again."

"Exactly."

"You know, a while back I met a pickpocket. Sonia. She

told me San Francisco was full of thieves. Real thieves. The kind who take everything from you, even the clothes off your back."

Jim nods. "A lot of folks are on the streets these days because Hardwick put them there. It's gotten worse in the past month or so, since that Frank Dilley showed up. When I found you and Jefferson at the law offices that day, it sounded like you all knew each other."

"Wish we didn't. He was master of our wagon train on the way out, once the Major got hurt. Left us to die in the desert, seemed disappointed when we didn't. Ended up working for my uncle Hiram."

Jim pauses midchew. "So Hiram did make it out to California," he says around a mouthful of food.

"Yes, and I need to talk to you about Uncle Hiram when we're done here. But Jim—be careful of Dilley. He's . . . an unsavory fellow."

"The world's got plenty of those," Jim says.

"Yeah, but Frank Dilley's a special sort. He *likes* to hurt people, especially anyone different from him."

"The world's got plenty of those, too. There was an overseer who . . ." Something awful flits across his face, but it's gone before I can put a name to it. "Well, I was lucky to buy my way out when I did."

The proprietor brings two cups of the strongest coffee I've ever smelled. I look up to thank him, but he won't make eye contact with me.

Jim continues, "Anyway, most of the land we saw today has

been sold, and resold, four or five or six times, just in the past year."

I give a low whistle. "Why do people keep doing business with Hardwick?"

Jim shrugs. "What other choice do they have? A couple years ago this was a town with a few hundred people. Now there are thirty thousand. Most of them spent everything they had to get here. They can't exactly turn around and leave."

The Hoffman family gave up and went back home after arriving in California. But they had a golden candlestick and a witchy friend to help them pay for return passage. If not for that, they would have been stuck here like everyone else.

"And the whole city almost burned to the ground just two months ago," Jim continues. "Hardwick profited from that too—folks lost everything and couldn't afford to rebuild, so he bought their land out from under them and then rented it back at twice the price."

I've lost most of my appetite, but I force myself to sip the coffee. It's sharp and bitter enough to penetrate the constant buzz of gold, which I appreciate. I take another sip and say, "If he's investing all this money, how come he has so much of it locked up in banks?"

"You remember my general store, back home in Dahlonega?"

"I'll never forget it."

"When I wanted to buy supplies, I had to buy them with cash up front. Nobody would extend credit to a Negro. That's not the deal Hardwick has."

"Huh?" I clutch the coffee mug close; maybe I'm seeking comfort.

"Hardwick owns everything on paper, but that doesn't mean he paid for it all. The banks extend him credit. So he takes the title on the property, and collects rents, and he gives everyone else their cut. He pays his gang more than they could make doing carpentry work or prospecting. He pays the sheriff to look the other way, and I guess the politicians and judges, too. Maybe even the bank. In the end, he has a nice chunk of money left over. And he never had to buy anything up front in order to get it."

I think back, trying to remember if I saw Mr. Keys count out a portion of coins to the bank manager, but I wasn't paying close enough attention.

"Don't like the food?"

I glance down at my bowl. Most of it is uneaten. I'm pushing the remaining stew around with a piece of bread. "It's just . . . you've given me a lot to think about."

Chairs scrape as a handful of customers rises to leave. When they exit, light pours in through the door, and I have a brief but perfect view of the street. Two tall fellows stand there, peering inside and not even trying to be subtle about it. I recognize them as the polite gunmen in nice wool suits we met at the Custom House: Large and Larger.

"We were followed," I tell Jim.

He nods. "As long as they don't come inside. Just keep your voice low."

I'm not sure Large and Larger can see me from where they

stand, but just in case, I take a defiant sip of coffee and stare over the edge of the mug at them as if I'm not afraid at all.

"Anyway, I came to San Francisco planning to set up a new general store," Jim says. "It's like Dahlonega all over again. In two or three years, once the rush settles and regular business gets established, that'll be the way to make a living. But every piece of property I look at costs too much. And your best business is regular customers, folks that come in month after month, year after year. There can be no regulars if your neighborhood changes every time the moon wanes. All because of the problems I've been describing to you."

"So what are you going to do?"

"I'm not going back to Georgia, that's for damn sure. I hear parts of Canada are pretty nice." He pushes back from the table.

I put a hand on his arm. "Wait."

He sits back down, eyeing me warily. Gray hair grows at his temples now, which is new since I last saw him. The trip west was hard on us all. "That's right. You wanted to ask me something about your uncle."

If Jim thinks it's safe to talk freely here, then I have to get my questions out now. "Well, him and Mama, actually. After I got to California, Uncle Hiram found me. He . . . kidnapped me."

"Oh, Miss Leah, I'm so sorry." He leans toward me, forearms on the table. "But you got away? You said Hiram wasn't a problem anymore."

"He held me captive. Dressed me up in clothes my mama

used to wear. He had this mine going, worked by local Indians. It was awful. They were sick and starving and there was an uprising and . . ." My heart beats too fast, my breath comes in gasps, as memories pour in. I'm not over what happened yet. Not by a long shot.

"Take your time," Jim says.

It's a long moment before I trust my voice to obey. "Before I got away, he told me something. I thought maybe you'd know if it was true or not."

"Oh?"

"He said I was his very own daughter. Not Reuben's girl, but his. That he and Mama . . ."

"Ah," Jim says. "I see." He regards me with frank honesty. "I always suspected."

"You did?"

"Your mama, Elizabeth, was all set to marry Hiram. They were sweethearts. But then one day she suddenly got herself hitched to his brother, Reuben, instead. No one was more surprised than Hiram. He carried a grudge ever since."

I'm frowning. "But that was years before I came along."

Jim nods. "Hiram carried a torch for Elizabeth for a long time. It was plain as day to anyone with eyes. But a man like that can't truly love another person. He can only love selfishly, his heart full of his own needs. I think . . . I think maybe he . . ."

"You think he raped her."

His lips press together into a firm line.

My next words are a whisper. "Did Daddy know?"

"I reckon so." Jim's gaze turns fierce. "Your daddy loved you more than life itself, don't think he didn't. You were his very own daughter in every way that mattered."

"I know."

"But you might have noticed that Hiram left Dahlonega. He wasn't much welcome after that."

"I hardly saw him or heard tell of him, growing up."

"And when your parents were murdered, and you came to my store all forlorn but with the fire of determination in your eyes, I had a pretty good idea who had done it. I knew you had to get out of town as quick as possible."

I reach for his hand and give it a squeeze. "I wouldn't have made it without you."

Another group stands and clears out. The proprietor is giving us the side-eye. Maybe we've overstayed our welcome. Maybe he's a spy for Hardwick after all, no matter what Jim thinks.

But there's one more thing.

"Jim, I have to ask." My voice is a deadly whisper now. I trust Jim, I do, but I can't risk being overheard. "Did Daddy ever tell you anything about me? I mean . . . anything special that . . . I can do?"

His eyes sparkle. "You mean the way you can recite the presidents backward and forward?" he whispers back.

"Um, no. I mean—"

"Oh, I know. It's the way you can hammer together a sluice in under twenty minutes."

"Well, that too, but—"

"I've got it! Reuben once told me you could blow a spit wad through a piece of straw and hit something at four paces."

"Six paces!" I glare at him, realizing he's funning me. "So you do know."

"Yep. Since before you could walk. It's an amazing thing, Leah. An amazing thing."

"It's one reason Hiram chased me all the way across the continent."

"I figured. He was the only person besides me who knew. If your mama had had her way, even *I* wouldn't have known."

"But the thing is . . ." I glance around. Lots of customers remain, and no doubt plenty of them understand English just fine. "Jim, do you have any idea where it came from? I mean, I know Mama left Boston in a hurry. She hated it whenever I said the word 'witch' or even just mentioned what I could do. She had a mighty fear. And I was wondering . . . did she have a gift too? Something special *she* could do?"

He doesn't hesitate. "She did."

"What?"

The proprietor turns, startled. My face flushes.

"What was it?" I repeat, back to a whisper.

"She could find lost things."

I shake my head in disbelief. "I don't remember anything like that. Not one single instance of . . ."

"She only used it once that I know of," he says. "It was a few weeks after the Cherokee were forced out of Dahlonega by President Jackson. Old Man McCauley came bursting into the store, saying he couldn't find his five-year-old boy."

"You mean Jefferson!"

He nods. "Your daddy was with me that day. McCauley told us Jefferson had been missing for hours. He was afraid the boy had gone after his mama, who was halfway to Oklahoma Territory by then."

I know this story. Well, part of it. Jefferson told me my daddy found him in a ditch by the road, several hours out of town.

"Daddy found him," I said. "But you're saying it was really Mama?"

Jim nods. "We looked for half a day. Finally Reuben went home to your mother, carrying Jefferson's favorite blanket, and begged her to use her gift, *just this once.* And forgive me, Leah, I don't know the details of how it all worked; your mama and daddy didn't like to talk about that sort of thing, even with me. All I know is that blanket helped her somehow, and she sent Reuben off with specific directions on how to find the boy."

"Well, I'll be." I knew. Somehow I had always known there was more to my mother than met the eye. Her final words make a lot more sense now. *Trust someone. Not good to be alone as we've been. Your daddy and I were wrong. . . .*

She wasn't just talking about my gift; she was talking about hers, too. About feeling so alone with a certain bright, screaming knowledge you think you might die of it. About being so full of fear that you never dared trust anyone with that knowledge, not even your own daughter.

But I've dared. I've dared a lot. Even in my darkest days,

hemmed in on all sides by awful people like Hiram and Hardwick, I'm surrounded by people I can trust.

That was Mama's final wish for me.

I put my hand to her locket, dangling at my throat. *I did it, Mama. Just like you hoped.*

The proprietor clears his throat. It's definitely time to go. I pull out some coins to pay for our meal, and Jim tells me when I've counted out enough. "Let's go," he says, rising from the table.

I squint at the light when we step from the building. The sky has cleared, and the air has warmed. Large and Larger are still keeping watch from across the street.

"It appears your caution in choosing our establishment for lunch was well founded," I say.

"Friends of yours?" he asks.

"Friends of Hardwick. Or maybe just employees. I don't think Hardwick has friends."

"That's as sure as heaven. Most of his friends would turn on him in a second if he couldn't pay them. Let's head to the waterfront."

Eyes bore into my back as we amble along the shore. I know this part of the city better than any other. Ships on one side. Warehouses on the other. Streets turning into docks as they stretch out into the bay. We stroll down Battery as far as California Street, Large and Larger continuing to trail casually behind.

"Sorry to bring my troubles your way," I say.

"What? Oh, you mean them. Negros are followed all the

time, everywhere we go. White folks just assume we're up to no good."

How have I never noticed that before?

"You all right, Miss Leah?" he says. "That was an awful lot to take in back there."

"I . . ." I reckon it *was* an awful lot. "I'm fine. Better than fine." And it's true. It almost feels like a weight has lifted from my shoulders. I make sure Large and Larger remain a safe distance behind us before adding, "I'm eager to get back to the business of figuring out Hardwick."

He shrugs. "In that case, what are we standing on?"

I glance at my feet. "I don't know. Land that used to be water?"

"Exactly. We're standing on the most valuable property in all of San Francisco. This is where all the business happens. It's flat and easy to build on. If I could open a store anywhere, I'd do it here." A sweep of his arm indicates the water. "And all of that?"

"Future land."

"Yep. And here's the thing—Hardwick doesn't have to wait for it to be land in order to sell it. The whole thing is marked out in a grid several blocks into the bay. There's an auction every month—"

"Let me guess. Next Tuesday."

"That's right. A sheriff's auction."

We had made inquiries about the auctions when we were thinking about buying Becky's house. "Cash only, paid in full up front."

"In the morning, right before the auction starts, one of Hardwick's men passes out maps showing available lots. Prices vary widely month to month, depending on how much cash he thinks people have."

"How do you know all this?"

"I thought future land might be cheaper than real property, so I went to a couple auctions thinking maybe I'd buy a lot to build my general store. I had my eye on a particular corner at Market Street and Drumm." He points to a spot on the water, which is, I'm guessing, the future intersection of Market and Drumm.

A man is rowing a small boat out in the bay. Jim waves at him, and the man waves back. Jim beckons him in our direction.

"That's going to be the heart of the business district some-day," Jim says. "Now, if you were Hardwick, and you didn't plan to stick around long, what might you do?"

It takes a few seconds for my mind to put the pieces together and find the answer. "Sell the same piece of future property to a bunch of different buyers."

"Last two months, I watched the corner of Market Street and Drumm get auctioned off twice."

"Cash in full, up front, both times."

"You got it."

I rub my forehead. "So Hardwick is planning to leave. He's not going to wait around for the courts to settle this."

"That's my guess. You want to go visit Hampton?"

The man in the rowboat has pulled up to the edge of the

dock. "Whoa. We can do that?" I say.

Jim grins, saying, "Sometimes it's better to ask forgiveness than permission." He helps me into the boat, which wobbles precariously as I settle onto the bench. The sailor pulls away from the shore, and I wave merrily to Large and Larger, who stand on the dock with their hands on their hips, watching us go.

Wind whips my hair, and salt spray stings my face and chills my fingers. Fortunately, it's only a short paddle across choppy water to the sheriff's floating jail. I assume we'll climb up and go inside, but the sailor rows us around to the far side of the brig, out of sight of shore. The water is rougher out here, and our little rowboat rocks unsteadily as Jim raps hard on the side of the jail ship. A small round porthole opens just above, and a dirty white face peers down.

Jim calls out, "We're looking for a fellow by the name of Hampton!" A moment later, Hampton's face appears in the porthole, and I think, *Surely this is the strangest visitor calling I've ever done.*

I cup my hands to my mouth. "How're you doing?"

His forced smile doesn't fool me even a little bit. "The quarters are small and the meals are smaller, but at least nobody's working me to death."

"Hang in there," Jim says. "We're working on your situation."

"Does my friend Tom know about this?" Hampton asks. "He could set it to rights."

I hesitate, and the waves bump our rowboat against the side of the brig. I start to grab the edge of the boat, but think better of it. If we hit the side of the ship again, I could lose those fingers.

Finally I shout, "Tom had to a take a job in one of the law offices."

"I trust Tom," Hampton says. "He'll help, regardless of where he's working."

"You need anything?" Jim calls up.

There's shouting inside, and Hampton glances away from the porthole. "Gotta run," he says. The porthole slams shut.

"Well, that visit didn't last long," I say.

"I'm not sure the prisoners are technically allowed to receive," Jim says.

The sailor says nothing, just picks up the oars and rows us back to shore, taking us close to the _Charlotte_.

"Thank you, Jim," I say as we reach our familiar dock. "For today. For everything."

"Anything for Reuben's girl," he says. Then something in my face makes his eyes narrow. "What are you thinking, Leah?"

"I'm thinking I have one big advantage over Hardwick, but only if he never, ever learns what it is."

Chapter Eleven

My uncle Hiram wanted to be rich because he thought it would make him important. He thought money would make people show him the respect he wanted. He had a picture in his head: politicians and businessmen asking for his opinion. A big chunk of land. A wife, servants, maybe even a daughter like me.

And everything he did, from speculating down in Georgia, to murdering my mama and daddy, to following me out to California and making me dress up and parade around his gold mine—it was all about building that picture in his head.

We all have something like that. I've got one, too. The picture in my head includes me and Jefferson together, neither of us hungry, in a nice cabin with a woodstove and a big bed with a pretty quilt like my parents had. It makes me blush a little to think about that bed.

Hardwick has something he wants, too. Some picture in his head that requires all this money. Something he does with the gold coins besides pile them up in banks.

So that's why, come nightfall, Henry and I are waiting in a hired carriage outside Hardwick's San Francisco mansion. I'm wearing a nice dress Becky picked out for me—she spent part of the day searching the best shops for wedding dresses—and the bodice makes me itch. Henry is wearing yet another new suit. I had to pay for it, but he insisted it was necessary.

Hardwick is the last fellow I care to get to know or spend any time with, but for our plan to succeed, I have to learn more about him. I have to figure out what picture he sees in his head.

I pull aside the curtain in the carriage window and take another look: adobe walls, tile roof, several sprawling wings and outbuildings, nested in a garden property, all surrounded by a wall. The only entrance is a wide iron gate. Guards shadow the gate, the orange glows of their cigars and cigarillos like stars against the night. This was once the villa of some Mexican official, and it survived the recent fire without any damage.

"I wonder how much a place like this costs to buy," I say, not really expecting an answer.

But Henry says, "He didn't buy it. He rents it from one of the local dons, a man who prefers to live on his ranchero than in the city."

I can't imagine renting a place so huge. "So he's not putting down roots." Just like Jim suggested.

"Maybe," Henry says. "He's been here less than a year. He was living in Sacramento, but when the weather turned cold last year, or maybe when they had the convention for statehood, he sold off a chunk of his interests in Sacramento and elsewhere. Shifted his operations to San Francisco."

"How do you know so much?"

"I always come home from a night of cards poorer in cash," he says solemnly, "but richer in knowledge."

"I'm glad that's . . . paying off for us. For some reason, I thought Hardwick had been here a while."

"His interests are spread out all across the territory," Henry says. "But his activities here have increased noticeably. Seems like he's old friends with the new sheriff, and they figured out some deal with the auctions."

"I keep hearing about this sheriff," I say.

"He and his deputies used to be part of a notorious gang of steamboat robbers."

"Really?"

"Really."

I peek out the curtain again. Hardwick will leave his compound eventually, and we aim to follow him. Surely the guards have noticed our carriage by now, skulking here in the dark. "Do you know how Hardwick came to be here in the first place?" I ask, to pass the time and keep my mind off what might happen if the guards grow suspicious.

"He probably landed in San Francisco with the navy in 1846. He was a war profiteer, buying supplies on the cheap and selling them at marked-up prices to the army. His nickname was John Mealy Hardtack."

"Hardtack? Like the biscuits?" We ate an awful lot of it on

the trail to California. If I never do battle with those molar breakers again, it will be too soon.

Henry nods. "He bought old hardtack biscuits, usually filled with mealworms, and sold them to the army, who didn't have a lot of other options."

"And the sheriff—wait, something's happening." Beyond the wall, lanterns bob across the property. A team of horses noses toward the gate, ready to leave.

"Seems like the army is how Hardwick met Sheriff Purcell," Henry says, dropping his voice, though I'm sure no one can hear us from all the way across the street.

"How much do you know about Purcell?"

"Not much. After the war with Mexico, he and his gang left the army and returned to their old ways, only this time they robbed and terrorized Mexicans and California Indians. Apparently that qualified him to be elected sheriff. That's why you don't see too many Indians here in the city, outside of the mission anyway, and the ones you do see are most likely to be Sioux or Cherokee, come west like the rest of us."

"You found out all of this by gambling?"

"Of course," he says. "There's no more popular topic of conversation in all of San Francisco right now than Hardwick. Every man of money either wants to work with him, copy what he does, or avoid him like the measles. But he has an advantage, something no one can quite put their finger on."

"What do you mean by that?"

Henry lifts the curtain and points. "I think it's her. Most

folks think he's courting her, but no one is sure. I'd bet my first edition of the *Coquette* there's more to it than that."

Guards pull open the iron gate to let out the carriage. Hardwick, dressed in a suit and top hat, offers his newest associate, Miss Helena Russell, a hand as she climbs inside and takes a seat.

"Henry, what's an associate?" I whisper.

He looks puzzled. "Someone who associates?"

"No, I mean, is it a polite way of saying something else? Does it mean something like . . ."

"Business partner?" he suggests helpfully.

"Prostitute? Mistress?"

"Not as far as I know. Why?"

"When Hardwick introduced Helena Russell to me, he described her as his newest associate. I've been struggling ever since to figure out what that means."

"You're not the only one."

Hardwick's carriage pulls out of the gate and clatters down the street. Henry sticks his head out the door and tells our driver to follow, not too closely, and to stop when it does. Our carriage lurches forward. The road is not as smooth as I'd like, and I find myself grateful for the seat cushions.

"From what I can gather," Henry says, "Hardwick has never been married, and never been publicly involved with any woman. It's a common problem here, seeing as men have outnumbered women ever since the war. So a month or two ago, when Miss Russell showed up, everyone assumed that Hardwick had finally found himself a lady."

I think of her strong arms and calloused hands. "I don't think she's a lady."

"Lee! Are you being catty?"

"No! I didn't mean it like that. I mean she's not . . . refined. She's . . . like me, I guess."

"Nothing wrong with that," he says sternly.

"I wasn't fishing for reassurances."

"Well, Miss Russell is an odd one, that's for sure. She doesn't accept lunch invitations from the wives of the other rich men and politicians. She's not engaged in charitable work for the improvement of the city. She hasn't hosted any parties."

"What does she do?"

"She accompanies Hardwick to all his business meetings. She's met every one of his partners and major clients and political allies. Some find her unnerving."

It *is* unnerving, the way she always whispers in his ear.

The carriage rattles to a stop. Henry peers out the window. "Ah, the Eldorado. Miss Helena Russell is accompanying him to a gaming house."

"Is that unusual?"

"Not lately. But before she arrived, Hardwick never gambled. Now he plays high stakes every night. Apparently he's as lucky in cards as he is in business."

The door opens, and Henry tips the driver as we step down.

The world shifts beneath my feet, and I grab Henry's arm for balance. "Henry, there's an awful lot of gold in there," I whisper.

He gives me a sympathetic look. "You're sure you want to do this?"

I take a deep breath, letting the gold sense surround me, pass through me. Things have been a whole lot easier since I learned not to fight it. "I'm sure," I say, already steadier on my feet.

A huge crowd is gathered outside, and we start to push past elbows and cigars to reach the entrance. But the dress I'm wearing is like magic; men part for me and tip their hats like I'm a one-woman Fourth of July parade. And maybe I am. All the gold here is setting off fireworks right behind my eyes.

Inside is a high-ceilinged, smoky parlor. Eight gambling tables take up most of the space, and an excited mob surrounds each one. Lots of Mexicans here, in dusty serapes and more elaborate boots than I'm used to. White men in shirtsleeves and suspenders shout in a variety of accents, announcing their origins from the Yankee north, the cotton south, the Irish isle, and faraway Australia.

A long bar runs the length of the parlor. On the wall behind it are shelves with row after row of bottles. Lots of men and a very few women crowd against the bar, drinking and laughing. In a little balcony above, a pretty Negro woman plays the fiddle.

The room smells of sweat and booze and cheap tobacco, which I'd normally find distasteful, but this time I inhale deep, letting the scents ground me. Because otherwise I'd be overwhelmed by gold, not just by the amount of coins in play, but by their constant movement. It's like a whirlpool of stars.

For a brief, fool-headed moment, I imagine calling all of that gold toward me. Part of me _wants_ to do it. But this time, it wouldn't be a cloud of soft dust, coating me, turning me into the Golden Goddess of miners' tall tales. It would be a deadly hail of coins. Enough to bury me.

Or I could push it all away. It would be a relief.

I close my eyes. Sweat rolls down my forehead. My hands shake.

Maybe, with one burst of power, I could send every gold coin, every lucky nugget and pin and button in this room flying.

"Lee," Henry whispers. "Lee? Are you all right?"

"I'm . . . not sure."

"People are staring. Let's keep moving."

The size of the crowd makes it hard to see the players at each table, so we circle the room once, and then twice, looking for Hardwick and Russell. Henry pauses to talk to a number of people he recognizes, and then gets distracted by one of the games. A cherub-faced miner is on a winning streak, and the crowd cheers as he keeps doubling his bet and winning.

"He started the night with a fifty-dollar coin," explains a redheaded man standing beside us. "And now he has more than three thousand dollars."

"Maybe he should quit while he's ahead," I say.

"He should keep going while he's lucky!" Henry says, exchanging a grin with the redheaded man.

Two hands later, the miner has doubled his money again. On the third hand, the cards fall against him, and he loses everything. A collective groan of disappointment sweeps around the table on his behalf. Several bystanders offer to buy him drinks.

But he looks crushed. He's a boy barely old enough grow a beard, not even Jefferson's age. Tears roll down his sunburned cheeks.

Under the nearest table, trapped beneath the shoe of a man who's doubling down on a losing streak, I sense a small coin, dropped and lost. I bend down to pretend to adjust my boot, focus my energy very carefully, and call the coin.

The coin skitters across the floor and into my hand. But my control isn't as focused as I would like; on the table, the loser's stack of gold coins topples over.

I rise and turn to the young boy being consoled by his friends. I press the coin into his hand and say, "So you won't leave broke tonight. Here's a second chance."

His jaw hangs open. I expect, sooner or later, a thank you will emerge.

Instead he spins around and shoulders his way back to the table. "I'm in the game," he says. "I'm back in the game!"

"That was very kind of you," says Henry.

The boy sits down and scrubs away the tears with the sleeve of his shirt. "I'm not so sure," I say. "Where's Hardwick? I don't see him anywhere."

"Oh, he's almost certainly in the private rooms in the back."

"Why didn't you say so?"

"Because we won't be able to get in, at least not until much later in the night, when they start to relax the rules. In the meantime, we should just enjoy the entertainment, and if Hardwick leaves, we'll follow him to the next place."

"Why can't we get into the private rooms?" I ask.

"It's high stakes. You need at least a thousand dollars just to walk through the door."

When we came into San Francisco, with my saddlebags full of gold, I had thought I was the richest woman in the world. Now my resources are rapidly dwindling before we've even put a dent in Hardwick's enterprises.

But I came here to see him in action. I need to know who he associates with, how he spends his leisure time, figure out what he cares about.

"What if I happened to have twenty gold pieces with me? The fifty-dollar gold pieces."

He grabs my arm, then promptly lets it go again. "Are you teasing me?"

"Henry, am I a person who teases?"

"But you have a thousand dollars in gold on you?"

Slightly more than a thousand. The weight of it tugs at me, both physically and mentally, from the small purse hung over my shoulder and tucked inside my sweater. "I always carry gold with me now. Jefferson keeps some of my stake. A fair bit is with Peony. Even Mary has some, back in Glory. Never keep all your money in one place, right?"

"True enough."

"So, where do we go?"

He stares at me, as if torn. I don't get to ask him what he's torn between, because he grabs my hand and leads me through the parlor and down a long hallway.

Two men in wool suits stand outside a door: my old friends, Large and Larger.

"There's a thousand-dollar minimum," Large says.

"Do I need to count out the coins for you, or will you take my word for it?" I ask.

The two behemoths glance at each other. Finally Large shrugs.

"We can take your word for it," Larger says.

"Mr. Hardwick thought you might be coming tonight," Large explains. "Told us to look for you."

Unease fills me. We didn't go to huge pains to keep our presence a secret, but even if he had noticed the carriage, how could he have known it was us inside? Maybe someone had spotted me peeking from the window.

Henry and I move to enter, and Larger places one of his huge, meaty hands on Henry's chest. "But _your_ thousand dollars, we'll need to see."

"Mr. Hardwick didn't say anything about _you_ visiting tonight," says Large.

Henry's eyes plead with me for a moment. I'm not carrying enough for both of us, and I doubt Henry has more than one or two coins left. "He doesn't intend to gamble," I say. "He's my _associate_."

Larger rolls his eyes. "Nice try."

My heart sinks. It's one thing to be brave when you're with a friend; it's another thing entirely to do something brave all by yourself. "I'm sorry, Henry."

He squeezes my hand. "I'll wait for you in the main parlor."

My gold sense flutters my stomach as I enter the room. This parlor is much smaller. In one corner is a short bar manned by a single bartender. Even so, there's a lot more gold in this room. Four tables play host to a number of distinguished-looking gentlemen who are sipping from glass tumblers, smoking fragrant cigars, laughing. Each one has a stack of gold coins at hand.

I feel like a fish in a tree, and everything in me wants to escape. But then I spot Hardwick, sitting at the farthest table from the door. He's as impeccably dressed as ever, with a gold watch chain swooping across his left breast. His stark-white sideburns are combed flat over gaunt cheeks, and a cigar dangles from thin lips. Helena Russell stands beside him.

She notices me first and whispers in his ear. My heart rocks in my chest as Hardwick says something to everyone at the table. In response, the other gamblers gather their coins and stand. Staring quietly at me, they disperse to other tables.

One fellow pauses to smile. "A pleasure to see you again," he says. "Still golden, I hope."

It's the governor of California, and the pleasure is all his. I met him once before, at the Christmas ball in Sacramento, when all the tall tales about the Golden Goddess were spinning around. If they're still spinning, I'm in a heap of trouble.

But the governor tips his hat and moves on without another word. I breathe relief.

Hardwick beckons, and I stride over and sit like it's the most natural, normal thing in the world. I open my purse and set my coins on the table while the dealer shuffles the cards.

Miss Russell seats herself on his left, slightly behind him, with one gloved hand slipped through his arm. Perfect for leaning forward to whisper in his ear.

Hardwick watches me the way a cat watches a bird's nest in an apple tree. "How would you like to come work for me, Miss Westfall?"

My heart hammers in my throat, and the air suddenly seems a bit thin because all I can think is *He knows. He knows what I can do.*

After too long a pause, I manage to say, "Doing what?"

He takes a sip of whiskey, then wipes his mustache with a handkerchief. "I'm not sure. I admit, I don't quite have you figured out."

Well, that's a mercy.

"But you keep showing up in the most interesting places," he continues, "and it's clear that you have some ability for accumulating resources."

So maybe he doesn't know after all. I try to keep the relief from my face. "In other words, you've determined that I have some gold, and you'd like to take a portion of it."

His sudden laugh is surprising for how genuine it seems. "No one acquires gold by accident," he says, eyes twinkling. "I have gold, you have gold. There's a chance that both of us could acquire a lot more gold by working together. How do you want to bet?"

The dealer has turned up a pair of cards. "I'm sorry, but I don't know how to play. You'll have to teach me."

Hardwick makes a small circular motion with his finger, and the dealer reshuffles the cards. "This game is called Spanish monte," Hardwick says. "The rules are simple, and it's almost impossible to cheat."

I only half listen to Hardwick's instructions, because Miss Russell is peering at me in the most peculiar way, like she's seeing through me, or beyond me, and—most disconcerting of all—her irises are saturated with a deep shade of violet.

I could have sworn her eyes were blue.

The dealer lays down two cards, a two of hearts to his right and a jack of diamonds to his left. He places the remaining stack of cards between them.

"And now we bet," Hardwick says, tossing a fifty-dollar coin onto the jack.

I toss a coin onto the deuce, determined to ignore Miss Russell's violet gaze.

Hardwick makes the go-ahead motion again. The dealer turns over a seven of hearts. "The young lady wins," he says.

"The odds change as he works his way through the deck," Hardwick says. "Someone who pays close attention can increase their chances of winning after a few hands."

The dealer deals, and again I choose the card that Hardwick doesn't. This time I lose, but so does Hardwick, and both our coins get taken. "I should have quit while I was ahead."

"That's the trick, isn't it?" Hardwick says. "To exit the game when you're at your peak? But you're young. You're just learning how the game's played, and you've barely started."

I'm not sure we're still talking about gambling. "What about all the people who never get ahead enough to quit?"

"That's their problem, isn't it?" he says. From behind him, Helena Russell reaches for his whiskey, takes a sip, sets the glass back on the table. Hardwick doesn't seem to notice or care. "But that doesn't apply to you or me. Your friend Tom is a very good lawyer."

If he's trying to throw me by changing the subject abruptly, it might be working, because I lose on the next hand, and Hardwick wins. "I'm not sure I would recommend him," I say. "He only negotiated the one contract for me, and I thought it was airtight, but it turns out there's no way to enforce it."

"Sometimes that's a temporary problem, with the system, not with the contract. I was just talking with the governor and with California's new senator. They seem to think that when statehood becomes official—in a few more months, maybe a year at most—we'll have the rule of law here, as strict as any state in the nation, with honest judges, and checks and balances, and all the other trappings of civilization."

I can't tell if he finds the prospect appealing or not. "I didn't realize you had so much respect for the law."

This draws another belly laugh. "I respect the laws so much I want to make them," he says. "Your bet."

Hearts come up again, and it's been several deals since I saw them, so I toss two coins down, and this time I win. One hundred dollars, just like that.

Helena's eyes widen. They've returned to their normal blue, which doesn't make me feel the least bit better. She hasn't said a word since I sat down, not to Hardwick or to me, but my skin prickles under her gaze.

Maybe it's nothing. A trick of the light. But maybe it's quite a bit of something. I know one other person whose eyes change color—me. And only when I'm sensing gold.

In the next round, I lose everything I'd won. I say, "One thing I can't figure out is why you started gambling. Everything you do is so careful and planned, but this is a game of chance. You can't help losing."

He finishes his glass of whiskey and smiles. "Who owns this parlor?"

I think about Large and Larger watching the door. "You do."

"So when I win, I win. And when I lose, I still win. Excuse me, I need to refill my glass. Would you like something to drink?"

"No, thank you."

He rises and heads toward the bar in the corner. As the dealer gathers up all the cards and starts shuffling, Helena scoots her chair closer to mine.

Something tingles at the back of my neck, and I freeze, like a ladybug caught in a spider's web. Helena leans forward, avidly, hungrily, and places a hand on my knee. I open my mouth to ask her what in tarnation she's doing, but a small bolt of lightning shoots through me. Her eyes are so dark now, the color of ripe plums.

"You have to tell me," she says breathlessly. "Quick, before he comes back. How do you do it? How do you do that thing with the gold?"

My heart starts racing.

Her gaze is awful. Like she's looking right through my skin and into my heart. Her nose is a tad too long, her skin a bit too world-weary, her lips pressed thin. But there's a compelling wild energy about her that makes me shiver just as much as that violet glare.

"I don't know what you're talking about," I manage.

Her eyes narrow. "You're up to something, and I'm going to figure you out. You're not going to get his money."

I shoot to my feet and start gathering my coins.

Hardwick returns. "Quitting so soon?" he asks. "Sweet girl, the first rule of the game is you can't quit before you're ahead even once."

I sway dizzily. There's too much gold in this room for me to risk making abrupt moves, but I can't help scrambling backward, away from the table and Helena's horrible eyes. The backs of my knees knock the chair as I push it back. "Sometimes it's better to know when to cut your losses," I say, and I rush out the door before he can respond.

Chapter Twelve

I find Henry sharing drinks at the bar with the cherub-faced gambler. Henry babbles and sways, noticeably in his cups.

"We have to go, Henry. Now."

Drunk or not, Henry doesn't hesitate. He tosses a coin at the bartender and follows me out the front door.

Once inside the relative safety of the carriage, he asks, "You talked to Hardwick, yes? Did something go wrong?"

My heart still feels like a drumbeat in my throat. "I'm not sure what happened. I . . . I'm not quite ready to talk about it."

He doesn't press, but he says, "I got some good information tonight. Let me know when you're ready to hear it."

"All right. Thanks." I'm grateful to be left with my own thoughts as we ride back to the *Charlotte*.

We pull up, and the sight of the ship ought to give me great comfort, because Melancthon's handiwork is beautiful. A new door greets us, framed by a small porch and two lanterns that cast warm, buttery light onto the stoop. But all the hominess just reminds me that I'm _not_ home, that my real home was taken from me, and all our efforts to establish a new one depend on making sure Hardwick is no longer a threat.

Melancthon and a man I've never seen before are sitting on their heels, huddled in front of the door. As we exit the carriage, Melancthon rises and greets us with a wave.

"Just putting the final touches on this great big hole. How many keys do you want?"

The fellow with him stands, wiping his hands on something that looks a lot like Wilhelm's blacksmith's apron, but with a lot more pockets. "Name's Adams," he says. "Locksmith." He's tall and angular with a long, narrow nose and a meticulous black mustache.

"Nice to meet you Mr. Adams," I reply. "How many keys can you make?"

"As many as you need, ma'am."

"In that case . . ." I count companions in my head. "I need eight keys."

His eyes widen slightly, but he says, "No trouble at all."

Adams pulls a flat tray the size of a writing slate from a bag. From his pocket, he withdraws a large iron key. He presses the key into the tray; I peer closer and see it's filled with milky wax.

When he lifts the key out, a perfect impression remains in the wax. Adams wipes the key on his apron and hands it to me. "This will have to do for now. I'll deliver seven copies tomorrow."

I look back and forth between the key in my hand and the wax tray in his.

Melancthon hands a few coins to the locksmith, who takes his leave. I stand back, admiring my new porch.

"Nice work, Jones," Henry says, admiration in his voice.

"It's beautiful," I agree. "Thank you."

Melancthon beams.

We step through the doorway, and voices echo up from the galley. Henry goes off to join them, but I'm not ready to be around anyone yet. I've learned too much today—about Mama, about Hardwick's *associate*—and I need time for things to settle. So I head up to the deck and climb the stairs to the stern—the poop deck, as Olive and Andy inform me every single time.

My intention is to sit and gaze at the stars over the hilltops and pretend I'm someplace far away. But someone else has gotten there first, and I recognize his lanky, perfect shape even in the dark.

Suddenly, having company doesn't seem so bad. I sit beside him, my back against the railing. The sky is covered with clouds, not a star to be seen.

After a while I reach over and squeeze his hand. He squeezes back. We sit in darkness holding hands, not saying a word. I find I don't miss the stars at all; the hills of the city are covered with lights.

"I'm scared I'm doing the wrong thing," I say finally.

"We could leave. Go anywhere."

"Is that what you want?"

"No." I'm relieved to hear him say it. He adds, "But as long as I'm with you, I'll be right as rain, no matter where we go."

"We can't leave. You promised Becky you'd wear a plum-colored suit for our wedding in Glory," I say.

Both of his warm hands fold around mine, and he pleads. "Please, please, let's get out of here and run away before we have to do a big wedding. I already feel sick every time I look at a plum."

I flash back to Helena Russell's plum-colored eyes.

"Lee?"

I blink to clear the memory. "Becky will be so disappointed in us."

"Becky lives to be disappointed in people. If we get out of her way, she'll expand her horizons. She'll find all sorts of new people to be disappointed in."

I chuckle while Jefferson leans back against the railing. "You know, I think that baby girl is going to be full-grown before she gets a name," I say.

"The Major's been calling her Rosy, 'cause of her rosy cheeks. Becky caught him doing it the other day, and I thought she was going to rip off his other leg before she was done."

"Jeff!" I say, but I'm laughing.

"I'm serious. She wants to control everything, so nothing can go wrong. She won't even give that baby a name because she's afraid it'll be the wrong name." He takes a deep breath, like he's carefully considering his next words. "You can't get so scared of doing the wrong thing that you don't do anything at all."

I let that sink in for a moment. Jefferson's voice has changed.

It's deeper than it used to be. Warmer. A voice a girl can trust. "That's not why I'm scared," I tell him.

"Then what are you worried about?"

"Something happened tonight. When Henry and I followed Hardwick."

"Tell me."

And just like that, my heart starts pounding all over again.

"Lee?" His fingertip traces my left eyebrow.

I wanted to keep this to myself a little, hold tight to it, let it stew. It feels so monumental. So personal. But this is Jefferson. I can tell him anything. "It's about Helena Russell, Hardwick's associate. I think she knows what I can do."

Jefferson sits straight up, his fingers leaving my face. "You mean, your witchy powers?"

"I don't know. Maybe." I explain what happened at the gambling parlor.

He rubs his chin with a hand, pondering my words, and it turns out it's a *relief* to tell someone I trust, to share the burden of thinking with him. At last he says, "That thing about the eyes. More than a little bothersome."

"Yeah." I scoot closer so our thighs touch. He's like my own personal woodstove, a shield against the cold night.

"You think she can find gold? The way you do?"

"No. Not exactly. I mean, she asked me how I did 'that thing with the gold.' If she could do it herself, she wouldn't ask, right?"

"That makes sense."

"But I do think she has . . . magic. Something miraculous

and amazing that she can do. And Jeff, I have to tell you. I talked to Jim today." It pours out of me, everything about Hiram and Mama and her ability to find lost things and how, one time, the lost thing she found was Jefferson.

Jeff is silent a long time. "So this kind of thing is passed down, generation to generation."

"Maybe."

"And Helena Russell can recognize it in someone else."

"It's possible." A bit of wonder tinges my voice.

"Does that mean Hardwick knows about you?"

I force myself to consider this sensibly, without panicking. "He noticed my particular affinity for gathering wealth, for sure and certain," I say. "But he always seems baffled by it. Maybe Helena knows but hasn't told him for some reason."

His arm drapes my shoulders again, and I lean into him. "So that's why you're so scared," he says.

"We need to tell everyone. If Helena knows . . . things . . . it will be very hard to make a good plan."

He's silent a long time. "But maybe, also, it's a little bit wonderful? It must be hard to hold those two things in your heart at the same time. Fear. Delight. All about the same darn thing."

I can't help it; I turn my face and kiss him hard on the lips. Because he understands without me having to say. I'm not the only girl with witchy powers. I'm not alone.

Chapter Thirteen

The next morning I wander to the galley, drawn by the smell of coffee and the sizzle of bacon. That alone would leave me more than satisfied, but the big table also contains platters of scrambled eggs and fried potatoes. My mouth waters. Before I take the first bite, I know that Becky didn't cook this meal. I pour some coffee, cup it in my hands, and hold it to my face, just breathing in the aroma.

The lanterns are lit, and a candle brightens the table. If we're here for any length of time, maybe I should commission some windows. And it's as though I summoned him with a thought, because Melancthon enters with a huge platter of flapjacks and thumps it down on the table.

"I hired you to be a carpenter, not a cook," I tell him. "You're under no obligation to feed us."

"Who's feeding you? All of this is *my* breakfast." We both grin. "No, seriously, I just wanted to show my appreciation."

"It's no problem for you to stay here. There's more space than we need."

"It's not just the room and board, and giving me honest work for honest pay, although I appreciate that. It's my thanks for saving the *Charlotte*. This was my home for three years, and I've worked on every part of her—I know every beam and strake, every inch of timber. Thought I'd see her torn apart and used for lumber. But you saved her."

"So you've forgiven me for wanting holes in her."

"Let's not get carried away."

I sip the coffee. "Have you given any more thought to your long-term plans?"

He sits beside me and pours a cup of coffee for himself. "It's been on my mind. This meal is a bit of a thank-you, yes, but it's also a bid-thee-well. Word has it the *Argos* is setting sail for New York next week."

The thought of losing Melancthon saddens me. I barely know him, but he's already proved himself a decent fellow, and pleasant company besides. "Do you have enough to purchase passage?" We've paid him fairly for his work, but I have no idea how much it costs to sail from San Francisco to New York by way of the Panama Isthmus.

"That's just it; I wouldn't have to buy passage. The captain and I sailed together before, on a whaling ship out of Newport. He says the ship is privately chartered. Won't say for who, but he did say that the customer is paying very well for his privacy. He wants to hire me as a carpenter—his last one caught gold fever."

I am now fully awake and alert, and it has nothing to do with coffee. Well, maybe not everything to do with the coffee. "That's . . . interesting."

Melancthon stares into his cup. "He also says they have valuable cargo that might create some problems, and they'll need a steady hand moving all of it once they get to Panama."

This definitely sounds like Hardwick. "When exactly are they sailing?" I'm willing to bet the rest of my savings it's not before Tuesday's auctions.

"End of the week," Melancthon says. "After the auctions."

Time enough to collect all the money first. *Sometimes you have to quit when you're well and truly ahead,* he told me.

"Do me a favor, Mr. Jones," I say. My mind is churning, churning, churning. Hardwick leaving so soon could present an obstacle. Or maybe . . . an opportunity. "Wait a day or two before you accept that offer."

He opens his mouth to ask why, but Jefferson wanders into the galley, whistling like a yellow warbler with a mouthful of spring. He pulls up a chair and sits beside me.

"You're in a good mood this morning," I say glumly. "Like every morning." This is what I have to look forward to for the rest of my life: Jefferson's morning cheer assaulting me like a bag of bricks.

"Yep." He grabs a plate and helps himself to a large serving of everything.

Becky enters carrying the baby, who is most certainly not named Rosy. The Major follows behind, guiding Andy and Olive toward the table. He and the children eye the flapjacks with distrust. I reckon they're not used to seeing such a fine, evenly cooked repast. Henry stumbles in a moment later.

"I'll make myself scarce," Melancthon says, gathering up his plate and coffee.

"You can stay," I tell him, but I don't enthuse too hard.

"I expect you all have things to talk about," he says. "And I like to sit on deck in the morning."

He leaves, and everyone starts eating. Once we all have a bit of food and coffee in us, I spring the bad news. "We have to move up our timetable."

"We had a timetable?" the Major says around a mouth of flapjacks. He's chewing them uncertainly, like a cat with a feather stuck in its mouth, and I get the strangest notion that he might prefer Becky's.

"But we've barely started gathering information," Becky says.

Jefferson nods. "I'm still trying to find an angle on Mr. Keys. I've never seen him alone, without at least two guards. And he doesn't gamble or have any bad habits, as far as I can tell."

"It doesn't matter. It's not *our* timetable; it's Hardwick's." I tell them everything I've learned over the past few days. Hardwick selling off his other properties in the state, wringing every dollar out of his San Francisco interests, bragging to me about getting out while he was ahead. "And then there's this news: according to Melancthon, someone's chartered a ship called the *Argos* to take valuable cargo out of San Francisco to New York. It has to be Hardwick, leaving town with all his gold."

"Why would he do that?" Jefferson asks.

"People sometimes make rash choices when they're in love," Becky says. "He's got that new lady friend, right? We met her at the law offices. What's her name?"

"Helena Russell," I say. My voice squeaks a little.

"So maybe he's ready to get married and settle down. Maybe they want to start a family."

I shake my head. "They have a closeness, an . . . intimacy, I suppose," I say, thinking of the way she hung on his arm, drank from his whiskey glass. "But I don't think they have marriage in mind."

"Why not?" Becky asks.

"He calls her his associate, and she goes with him to all his business meetings."

"Like a secretary?" Becky says.

"Not exactly like," I say. "She watches everything. She . . ." I hesitate. I should tell them about her eyes, about my suspicions, but the words lodge in my throat.

"Last night I learned that she used to be a fortune-teller," Henry offers. "A few months ago she was running a scam, mostly on miners, pretending to tell their futures, if they'd find gold, that sort of thing."

I give him a sharp look. "Who told you that?"

"That girl Sonia."

"The pickpocket?"

"She and Billy and their mob of runaways were hanging around the Eldorado last night. Looking for easy takes, I suspect. She didn't have any information about Mr. Keys. But she and Helena Russell targeted some of the same people."

"Marks," Becky says.

"Yes, they targeted some of the same marks. So she knew all about Russell's scam."

The air around me is suddenly hot and tight. I'm not sure I'd discount Russell's fortune-telling as a scam.

"I asked about Hardwick," Henry continues, "but Sonia said they avoid him—his guards kill anyone who crosses them. Or *worse*. When I told her he was back in the private room she and her crew made themselves scarce."

"That explains what Helena wants with Hardwick," the Major says. "She's trying to run some kind of scam on him and take his money. But what does he want with her?"

Silence around the table. Beneath it, Jefferson grabs my hand and squeezes, as if to say, "Go ahead. Tell them."

Before I can change my mind, I blurt the previous evening's events, leaving nothing out.

Another silence follows.

"The second sight," the Major says at last.

"Huh?" I ask.

He wipes his mouth with a napkin; before keeping company with Becky, he would have wiped it with his sleeve. "I mean, what if Hardwick keeps her around because her fortune-telling powers are real?"

That's exactly what I was thinking.

"I knew some women like that, not on the Craven side of my family, but the O'Malleys. Something passed down from the old country. We called it the second sight. They could find lost items, tell a person's future just by looking at him, dream about things far away. I've seen it with my own eyes."

I lean forward. "Seen *what?*"

He takes a sip of coffee and considers his next words. "When we were small, my little brother fell out of a tree and broke his right arm. The same day it happened, my mother got a letter from Aunt Lizzy, her sister, warning that she had had a dream about my brother breaking his arm, and telling my mother to be careful. It'd been written days before."

"That's not exactly proof," I say.

He shrugs. "No, but there were other things, too. Even now, for example, there's this girl . . ." He gives me a knowing look. "Who can sniff out gold better than a bloodhound on the trail. When she does, her brown eyes turn the most mesmerizing shade of gold."

"Really?" Becky says. "I never noticed that!"

Everyone is suddenly staring at me, as if expecting my eyes to shoot daggers. Like I'm *dangerous.*

Something inside me breaks just a tiny bit. Sniffing out gold is the most valuable, wondrous thing I can do. But even the people closest to me, the people I love with all my heart, sometimes view my power with suspicion. And maybe they're right to do so.

Mama was the same way. She loved me, for sure and certain, but she never wanted to talk about what I could do, even when it was just me and her and Daddy all alone by the box stove. *Magic makes mischief,* she always said, and left it at that. If she'd had her way, I never would have used my powers, even if it meant holes in the roof and a bare cellar.

She changed her mind at the very end, but it was too late. She was murdered for my gift. So I don't blame my friends one bit for being a little bit scared sometimes.

"It's one of the prettiest things I ever saw," Jefferson says, breaking the silence.

"A marvel, truly," the Major agrees.

"Well, I've never noticed Lee's eyes," Becky says, "but her particular abilities have been an incredible blessing, and I'm grateful to be among the lucky few who benefit."

Henry raises his coffee mug. "To Lee and her . . . second sight."

Everyone grins, raising their own mugs, and I look around at them all, tears filling my eyes as it slowly dawns on me: I misread their stares. They're not afraid of what I can do. They're not like Mama at all.

"In any case," the Major says, "I'm concerned about Miss Russell, but I'm even more concerned with how Hardwick is using her. Her fortune-telling is giving him an edge in all his dealings."

Becky shakes her head. "I bet she can't do anything at all. Not like our Lee. It's a confidence game." She's feeding bits of scrambled egg to the baby, who tries to grab them from the spoon with her chubby hands. "She's fishing for information," she explains. "'That thing with the gold?' That's just her way of getting you to reveal how you attained so much. I mean, you were in a gambling parlor owned by Hardwick, and she said that you aren't going to get any of his money." She waves the spoon in the air. "*I* could make that prediction."

The Major says, "But the things my aunt Lizzy knew . . . of course, with her, it was only family members. Or people she was well acquainted with. I don't think her sight ever worked on strangers."

Becky reaches over and pats the Major's hand. "Now, Wally, I'm sorry. I didn't mean to impugn the memory of your beloved aunt Lizzy. I just think there are good reasons to be skeptical."

He covers her hand and smiles at her, and she smiles back. Maybe Jefferson and I aren't the only ones who think they invented falling in love.

I grab the napkin and wipe my mouth to cover my smile.

Henry taps the table like he's forming a message in Morse code. "I think we're missing the point here. What is Hardwick's goal?"

This is exactly my question. What's the picture in his head? The perfect life he envisions for himself?

Henry's eyes light up like a city on fire. "What if . . . ?" And then his mouth stops, to make room for his spinning brain.

"What if *what*?" I ask.

"What if he's going back to New York to get into politics?"

"Then good riddance to him," I say. "But why would he have to go to New York to get into politics? He already controls every politician in California."

"No, think about it," Henry says. "California isn't even a state yet, not officially. And it's way out on the far edge of the country. It takes weeks or months for news to reach us.

Being governor here is like being a bullfrog in a washtub. It makes a big noise, but it's still just a washtub. But New York is different! Just think about who ran for president in the last election."

We all shake our heads until the Major says, "Well, Zachary Taylor ran—that's how he ended up being our president."

"But why did the Whigs put Millard Fillmore on the ballot with him? Because he's from New York. Why did the Free Soil Party pick up ten percent of the vote with Martin Van Buren on their ticket? Because he's from New York."

This is the most passionate I've ever seen Henry on a topic. But I'm pretty sure everyone else is staring at him just as blankly as I am, because I don't know what he's getting at.

Seeing our confused expressions, he opens his hands, like he's begging for understanding. "New York has thirty-six votes in the electoral college—no other state is even close. Didn't any of you vote in the election of 1848?"

Becky folds her hands on the table and sits up primly. "Henry, dear, I'm not allowed to own my own property, much less vote."

"I'm not old enough, but if I was, I've got the same problem," I say.

"Well, of course," Henry says, looking from us to Jefferson. "But . . ."

"Don't look at me," Jefferson says. "My mother was Cherokee. Government says I can't be trusted to vote."

Henry's mouth drops open. Then he turns toward the Major. "What about you, Wally?"

The Major shrugs. "I never worried too much about politics—as long as the system works for me I'm happy. The system always seems to work for me."

Henry throws up his hands in disgust.

"You're awful worked up about this," I observe.

"Think about it," Henry says. "A self-made millionaire returns from California to New York—a man who is now rich beyond imagination. People will love that story. He decides to get into politics on his claims of being a successful businessman—because it was the frontier, it's like being a war hero, only more glamorous. Meanwhile, nobody in New York knows his character, what he's really like. Someone like that could get nominated to run for president. It doesn't even matter which party."

Jefferson leans forward. "You think that's Hardwick's plan? He's going to take the millions of dollars he's made and go back to New York to get elected president?"

"I'm not sure," Henry says. "The timing is good. It's three years to the next election. He goes back now, invests his money in a bunch of legitimate businesses, spends the rest to establish himself. He'd be in prime position."

"I don't know," Becky says. "It seems far-fetched."

"He mentioned something last night," I say. All the faces turn toward me. "I accused him of not respecting the law. He told me he respected laws so much, he wanted to make them."

Henry leans back in his chair and folds his arms, as if putting a period on his argument.

"This is a good thing, right?" the Major says. "He'll be out of California and out of our hair. We can go back to living our normal life."

"How can you think that?" I snap.

The Major looks at me, genuinely confused.

"He paid to exterminate Indians—whole tribes of them, all of their families, destroyed. Muskrat is probably dead, and it's because of *him*. He ignores the rights of free men, and profits off buying and selling people's lives. He takes advantage of the poor and people without legal protection, and gets rich by using the law to rob people of their hard-earned wages." I point across the table at Becky and the kids. "He steals from widows and children. It's bad enough that he does it out here, but what if he's in charge of the whole country? Think about everyone he'll hurt."

By the end, I'm shouting. My face is hot with anger. The longest silence yet follows, broken only by the uncomfortable shifting of Becky's children in their chairs.

"Ma, may I be excused?" Andy whispers.

"Olive, take your brother, and the two of you go play in our room for now," Becky says.

Olive quickly gathers up her brother and flees.

"You're right, Lee," the Major says softly. "It was a thoughtless thing for me to say."

I overreacted, and I'm fixing to apologize, but Jefferson says, "Once Hardwick leaves California, we can't touch him. The minute he sets sail on the *Argos*, our chance to stop him is gone."

"The auction is Tuesday," the Major says. "How can we stop him before then?"

"I wish I knew." I stand abruptly, gather my dirty dishes, and carry them to the washtub, where I stack them loudly.

Jefferson brings his dishes over. "Do you want to talk about it?" he whispers.

Guilt twinges in my chest. I'm being rude. "No, I want to think. But thank you." I should scrape and wash my own dishes, but I leave them and flee down to the hold to see Peony.

It's neat and tidy, with four separate stalls and space to store the wagon. The stalls have fresh straw, and somebody has mucked them out recently, so it smells familiar—like the clean barn my family always kept. The last time I set foot in that barn, I was hiding from Hiram, waiting for my chance to escape.

And once again, it only serves to remind me that this is *not* home. Not really. Not yet. No place can be home until we're safe from Hardwick and people like him.

Peony snorts when she sees me, shuffling eagerly. I imagine she's tired of being cooped up in here. I find a brush and groom her.

"Sorry I'm not taking you out for fresh air," I say. "You deserve better. We all deserve better." She nuzzles my hand for the treat I didn't bring, so I spend extra time cleaning her coat, especially the little swirl of hair on her withers she likes brushed just so.

Thumps on the ramp signal someone stepping down into

the hold, and I have the urge to hide, but within a split second I realize that hiding will not stop Hardwick or solve any of my problems.

Melancthon approaches with that peculiar rolling gait of his, like he's compensating for waves that aren't there anymore. He pauses when he sees me.

"You did a good job down here," I tell him. "The horses seem as comfortable as can be expected."

He nods. "Thank you. It's been a long time since I was around any kind of creature that couldn't swim."

"Peony swims just fine. Most horses do."

"Huh. Haven't worked with horses since my canal-digging days. Would rather be on the water, though."

"Weren't you ever afraid?" I ask.

"Of horses?"

"No, of sinking, when you were sailing the ocean." I touch the smooth, curved hull with my fingertips, thinking of the ship Hardwick will sail to New York. Maybe we'll get lucky and he won't make it that far. Which I recognize for a bit of meanness, considering all the other people aboard. "This doesn't look like much to keep between you and the bottom of the sea."

He grins, pounding the hull with his fist. "Those are three-inch planks, and the hull is double planked, so that's six inches of solid oak between us and the water. We needed it, the one time we took her around Cape Horn."

"So it's hard to break the hull of a ship like this."

He rubs the back of his neck thoughtfully. "Not if you drive it onto rocks, or get rammed by another ship, I suppose. But that takes a particular kind of bad luck. Although I once had the misfortune to be aboard a ship that capsized, so I figure I've used up my bad luck for a spell."

"Capsized?"

"Another whaling ship, the _Salem_—got caught in swells in the North Atlantic. It shouldn't have been a problem, but we only had half a hold full of cargo, and a new cargo master who didn't know better, and the barrels broke loose in the waves. Shifted from one side to the other, before we could stop them, making the ship roll more with every wave until it rolled right over."

I stare at him in horror. "I hope all your crewmates survived."

"We got safely into the ship's boats, not a soul lost. But the ship and all the cargo sank to the bottom of the ocean. Lost everything except the clothes on our backs."

I rub Peony's nose, and she nuzzles my face. I lost everything once, everything except this horse and Mama's locket. "That sounds awful. I'm so glad you—"

"Lee?" A familiar female voice shouts down into the hold. Peony's ears flick with recognition. "Lee?"

I drop the brush and run to answer. "Mary?"

Chapter Fourteen

My friend stands at the stable door, and even though she's supposed to be back in Glory, taking care of the Worst Tavern, I'm so glad to see her. She's wearing a printed wool challis dress, with beautiful patterns in swirling red and purple. I throw my arms around her and hug tight, before remembering she doesn't much like to be hugged.

I step away sheepishly. "Sorry. I'm just really glad to see you."

"I forgive you."

"What are you doing here?"

"About a week after you left Glory, I missed you and decided to come to San Francisco to find you."

I study her face. "That sounds like a bunch of hogwash."

She frowns.

"Mary? What happened?"

She becomes fascinated by the bridle hanging beside Peony's stall. "Nothing. I mean, I left before something could happen."

"Mary! Tell me!"

Her frown deepens. "It wasn't safe for me, all right? Once my friends left, everyone expected me to . . . be like I was before. Some of the men were . . . demanding. They just assumed that because I'm a girl from China, I'm in a certain line of work. So I left."

"Oh. I see." And I do. Mary was a prostitute before she joined up with us in Glory. At barely seventeen years old.

"This town is even bigger than when I was here last," she says, but I won't let her change the subject just yet.

"What about the Worst Tavern? Becky left you in charge." She glares, and I hold up my hands in protest. "Not judging. Just asking."

She sighs. "Old Tug and some of his Buckeyes are working the place in shifts—when they're not working claims. They're terrible cooks, but no worse than Becky."

"And how is Tug? Wait . . . is he one of the fellows who—"

"No! He's the best man in Glory, if you ask me. Kept an eye on me as best he could, but he couldn't be there every waking moment. Even Wilhelm could only loom so much. But you and Becky and the Major—you're the leaders in our town. And once you left . . . one of the Buckeyes' claims was jumped. And a group came down from Rough and Ready trying to make trouble. Almost had our very own gunfight, but Tug talked them down. It's just not the same without you all there."

"So you set off for San Francisco. All on your own. Mary, that was dangerous! You could have—"

"Hey! I stowed away on a ship and traveled across an ocean

all by myself. And if I recall correctly, you covered half a continent with nothing but your mare and a saddlebag. So don't be lecturing me about it now!" Her eyes are bright and fierce, made more so by the meager lantern light.

"You're right. I'm sorry. And I'm sorry we left you there all alone." It doesn't set well, that Glory could turn out as lawless and frightening as any other frontier town. As if Glory's residents are a parcel of naughty children who play dangerously when their mama and daddy are away. That could be Glory's future, instead of the "sanctuary" Jefferson imagines.

"Wasn't your fault," Mary says. "I was the addle head who said she wanted to stay." The fight melts out of her, and she leans against the stall, looking a little defeated. "If I go back there, it has to be with friends. And when I do, I think maybe I should find someone who will marry me. A single girl from China . . . it's just not safe. You know, California isn't a very good place, if you're not white."

She'll get no argument from me.

"But now I've found you—which, by the way, was easy as pie. Everyone knew you from your description. Not many white women in San Francisco."

This does not sit well at all.

She says, "I can stay here, right? You don't mind?"

"Of course. Actually, we might be able to use your help with something."

I fill her in on everything that has happened with Hardwick. By the time I'm finished, she's grinning like a kid at Christmas. "This will be *fun*," she says.

◆ ◆ ◆

After Mary leaves to claim a cabin of her own, I go to my room and grab my saddlebag. It's easier to heft than I'd like. I spent so much money buying the _Charlotte_. Doing something about Hardwick is proving more complicated and expensive than I expected.

I sit on the floor at the end of my cot, saddlebag between my feet. Inside is a small pile of gold. A few eagle coins remain, along with a handful of gold nuggets I could get assayed if I need more money—though plenty of folks here take raw gold in payment. Still, there's more saddlebag than gold by weight.

Back in Glory, I practiced working with gold every day, and although I've had a few opportunities here in San Francisco to use my witchy powers, I need to be more disciplined about it. No one becomes a dab at something by laying about, Daddy always said.

I close my eyes and reach out with my gold sense. The shape of it eludes me at first; there are so many individual pieces. The coins ring loudest at first, at 90 percent gold. Nuggets are sometimes purer than that, but not these. One is so muddled up with quartz ore it's barely fifty percent. For my idea to work, I need this pile of gold to hum a single, familiar song, but this seems more like church ladies at a picnic all vying for attention.

I concentrate harder, trying to imagine all the little bits of gold as a single entity. It doesn't work. There are too many tiny pieces to keep track of, and they insist on singing their own tunes.

So instead of focusing on the whole mess as one, I wrap my thoughts around as many individual pieces as I can, holding their shapes in my mind. A twenty-dollar piece, a half eagle, the largest nugget.

I stretch out my hand, and I close my fist as if grasping that sound-shape in my mind. Then I open my palm and fling it across the room.

The saddlebag slithers along the floor and thumps into the far wall. I gasp, my eyes popping open.

I did it.

I've called gold to me before, and pushed it away, but it's another thing entirely to move something else with it. My shoulders ache, like I've been lifting hay bales. A throb is forming at the base of my neck.

I clench my fist and summon the gold back to me, but the saddlebag doesn't move, just gives a little hiccup on the floor and stays stubbornly still. I stretch out again with my gold sense. What did I do wrong? I used the same . . . aha. All the bits of gold settled into new places when it slid across the floor. I have to wrap my focus around the mess all over again if I'm to move it.

I take my time about it, going slow and careful. It's several heartbeats before I've latched on well enough to give it another try. My patience is rewarded; the saddlebag slides—faster this time—back across the floor, and I stretch out my boots to stop it. The impact shivers through my knees.

Eyes closed, thoughts swaddled tight around the gold, I open my fist and fling it away again. The saddlebag rips across the floor and slams into the wall. My fist closes tight, and it returns; this time I open my hand and stop it just before it hits me.

Over and over again, I practice: slide _thump_, slide stop, slide _thump_, slide stop.

The muscles in my neck and shoulders burn, and my head feels like there's a tiny miner inside, jabbing with a tiny pickax. But in a way it's also calming. It takes so much concentration, leaving no room to think about anything else.

Slide _thump_, slide stop.

A soft tap at the door interrupts me.

"Come in," I say.

The door creaks open, and Jefferson pokes in his head tentatively. "I cleaned up your dishes," he says, as though it was a monumental feat of heroism.

"Thanks."

His gaze goes from me, to the saddlebag against the wall, and back to me, sitting cross-legged on the wood plank floor. "Practicing again?"

"Yep."

He frowns. "Lee, are you feeling all right?"

"Why? Don't tell me I'm covered in gold again."

"Your face is flushed," he says, plunking down beside me at the end of the cot. He stretches his legs out. "Like you've gotten too much sun. And your eyes are as bright gold as I've ever seen."

"Huh. Well, I've been trying something new."

"How's it going?"

"It's going."

"Show me."

"All right." I'm suddenly nervous, like I'm performing for the most important person in the world, but I concentrate a moment, and sure enough, the saddlebag goes scooting across the floor.

"Isn't that something!" Jefferson says. His gaze turns thoughtful. "We can use this. Somehow . . ."

"I'm trying to figure out how to direct it better. Stop and start, change direction, that sort of thing. But it's hard. It . . . makes my head hurt a little."

He's staring at my face now, in a peculiar way that sets my heart to thumping. "Your eyes. They're almost glowing."

"Oh?"

Jefferson's fingers reach up to gently touch my cheek. "They're beautiful."

"Oh."

His gaze drops to my chest, and his eyes narrow.

"What?"

"That locket," he says, indicating the charm with his chin. "Have you tried working with it?"

Of its own accord, my hand goes to the golden heart shape hanging from my neck. Inside is a lock of hair, taken from my baby brother, who only lived a few days. "No, not really. Why?"

"You wear it every day. Remember how you found little Andy with it? When he was lost on the prairie?"

I nod, seeing what he's getting at. When I told Mary about

my gold sense, I was able to make it float in the air a little.

"You once told me that you feel the shape of things. You know the shape of that locket like your own hand."

I reach behind my neck and undo the clasp. I lift the tiny chain so the locket slips off into my palm. Though I see it clear with my eyes, feel it cool and firm against my skin, my magic perceives it as a sparkling ember, ready to do my bidding.

Just like with the gold inside the saddlebag, I wrap my mind around its shape, then I push the locket away. It flies forward until, with a thought, I command it to stop. It hovers in mid-air for the space of a breath before dropping to the floor.

"Well, I'll be," Jefferson breathes. "You saw that, right? It . . . floated."

"Yep." I blink to clear vision that's gone a little fuzzy. "I've done that before. It's easy compared to moving a mess of gold in my bag."

Jefferson's eyes dance. "This is going to be useful."

His excitement is catching. "I don't know how yet, but we'll think of something. Maybe you could help me practice?"

"Sure," he says. "What do you need me to do?"

"I'd like to test my range. Can you take the saddlebag to one of the other decks and leave it in an open space?"

"Which deck?" He stands, tossing the bag over his shoulder.

"Don't tell me. That's the whole point. I want to see if I can figure out where it is."

"If I took the locket, you'd find it, no trouble at all."

"Well, yes, but I want to get better at this."

"Then let's give it a try," he says. He bends down, kisses me quick on the lips, then closes the door on his way out. My cabin is suddenly empty and quiet without him.

His footsteps fade down the hall, toward the hatch that leads to the lower deck with the horses. Listening to his footsteps feels like cheating, so I close my eyes and focus on the gold instead of Jefferson's boots. It's like a torch in my mind, descending to the lower deck, growing gradually fainter, then brighter again as it passes directly beneath me and up the other stairs. Clever Jefferson.

The saddlebag finally comes to rest on the poop deck, where Jefferson and I watched the stars last night.

It's at the end of the ship farthest from me now, but the torch in my mind is still bright. I reach out my hand, close my fist, and try to pull the gold.

It slips through my fingers like water.

I squeeze my fist and try again.

My arm shakes. Fingernails dig into my palm hard enough to hurt. My head pounds like a steam engine about to explode. I yank my fist toward my stomach.

The gold moves.

It slides across the deck, thumps down the wooden steps to the quarterdeck, and slams against a railing.

I fall backward, panting, dizzy, partly because the use of power is heady and strange. But partly because I think I've figured out what we're going to do with it.

Jefferson's boots pound down the steps and through the hallway. "Lee! Lee!"

The baby starts crying, and Becky shouts, "Jefferson Kingfisher, I just got this child to sleep!"

"Sorry, ma'am! Won't happen again."

I stand up and fling open the door. Jefferson is wide-eyed and grinning as he comes down the hall, saddlebag over his shoulder. He fights hard to keep his voice a whisper: "Did you do that?"

I grin back at him. "You know I did. I need to rest, then I need to practice again. I might have an idea."

He plants a quick kiss on my lips. "You are a wonder," he says, with that almost smile I love so much.

I want more than a little kiss. "All this practice. My shoulders hurt—do you want to come rub them for a bit?" As soon as the words leave my mouth, I know I'm the daftest girl who ever tried to flirt. My cheeks flame.

But Jefferson grins. He slips the saddlebag off his shoulder and quietly shuts the door. "That's a good idea."

He lifts my hair and kisses the back of my neck, sending tingles up and down my spine. "Jeff," I say. Like it's a warning. Or maybe an invitation.

"Just a little kissing, right?" he says.

"Right."

His strong fingers sink into my muscles, hurting and relieving hurt at the same time. The throbbing in my head starts to subside. I let myself sink down into the cot like it's the most comfortable featherbed that ever existed. Doing something about Hardwick can wait for a while.

Chapter Fifteen

$\mathcal{I}$ allow myself one more day of thinking and practicing with my gold and plotting with my friends. It takes all of us together to figure out how to take Hardwick down. And it will take all of us together to do it, even Jim Boisclair and Melancthon, though the sailor will never know the particulars. By evening, after several meetings and a few errands, we have the skeleton of a plan. Tonight, we begin putting it into place.

To blend into the night, I'm wearing dark trousers and an old black sweater that Henry found at a general store. A miner's hat made of dark brown leather will hide my hair. For the first time in months, I've bound my breasts with a shawl.

The goal is to go unnoticed. But if I am noticed, it's best I be seen as a boy, which makes me a dime a dozen in this city, not unusual at all.

"You sure you're ready?" Jefferson says, as we walk together toward the galley. Like me, he's dressed in dark trousers and a dark woolen shirt. "You're about to take an awful risk."

He's right. We could use several more days of planning. Weeks, even. "The auction is in two more days, and after that, Hardwick's going to take his money and run. We have to do this now."

"We have to steal his money, his reputation, and his allies—that's what you keep saying."

"I like how it sounds when you say it. We have to steal justice."

He grins. "Let's start with his money. I asked Mary to—"

"Stop right there," I say. "I can't know the details of your part of the plan."

"Why not?"

"Because of Helena Russell!"

"You don't believe in her _second sight_, do you?"

"If someone told you about a poor orphan girl from Georgia who knew how to witch up gold, what would you say?"

He rubs his chin. "That's different."

"Only because you know me." I grab his hand to steal some of his strength. "Did you know that I'm Irish, too? On my mother's side? What if Miss Russell can tell the future? Or read my mind? Maybe the fact that I have powers of my own makes it easier for her to scry my footsteps. Or even my thoughts. So, I can't know too many details, or maybe Hardwick will know them. And you have to stay away from her. We all do."

He squeezes my hand in reassurance. "I'm not sure about seeing futures or thoughts or whatever, but better safe than sorry, right?"

"Right."

We've reached the galley. A cast-iron stove now rests on a tile platform in the corner, with a stovepipe running up and out the side of the ship. Poor Melancthon—another hole. A small fire inside has made the room toasty warm.

Melancthon and the Major are at work on their own part of our plan—though Melancthon has no idea what he's laboring on; he's simply following the Major's orders. They're cleaning a hose that looks like it's been salvaged from one of the ship's pumps. An empty rain barrel stands nearby, and their tools are spread out over most of the table. I turn my gaze away. I don't want a picture of it in my mind, lest Helena Russell susses it out.

At the table's corner, Olive sits beside Henry. She clutches her new rag doll while he reads to her quietly from Washington Irving's *Sketch Book*, pointing to the words and sounding them out. Andy plays on the floor with his menagerie. Becky sits in a rocking chair with the sleeping baby. The chair rocks back and forth. Becky's lids are half closed.

"Where did you get a rocking chair?" I ask.

"Wally and Melancthon put it together for me," she says, smiling. "They're exceedingly clever."

The Major looks up from his current work just long enough to wave off the compliment, but I can tell he's proud of his work.

"Becky," I say, "Now that Mary's here . . ."

Becky pauses midrock, and then continues, rockers creaking on the floor. She pulls the baby's blanket tighter, as though she'd been fussing. "I saw her this morning at breakfast. She left to run errands in town."

I bet she did. Where Becky is concerned, Mary prefers to make herself scarce. "I understand if you need to pack up and head back to Glory right away."

She sits up straighter. "Not until we're done here and I've gotten my cottage back. No low-down, mean-spirited, pusillanimous, thieving scoundrel is going to keep me from collecting what's mine." There's so much vehemence in her voice that the baby startles and fusses for real. "Now see what you did?"

"Sorry," I say in a lower voice. "So you're not mad? About Mary?"

Becky lifts her nose into the air. "I let her know she's welcome here, and she always has a place to stay with us." As if she's a queen bestowing favors on the unworthy.

"Well, I, for one, am awful glad to see her," I say.

"Are you and Jefferson going out soon?"

"We are," I say.

"Please be careful. If something happened to you . . . well, the children would miss you a lot."

I glance over at Jefferson, who hides a small smile.

"Will do, ma'am," I tell her.

Jefferson and I exit the *Charlotte* and step out into the street. It's a quick walk to Portsmouth Square, which is busier at night than most places are during the day.

One side of the square is formed by the long building that contains the Custom House, the law offices, and the bank.

The other three sides are filled with hotels and gambling dens. The square is crowded with people, drunk, joyful, weeping, fighting people, alone and in groups, stumbling from one hotel to the next, abandoning one gambling parlor for another, climbing in and out of carriages as they arrive from private parties or prepare to return home. Light fills the square, thanks to lanterns hanging beside almost every stoop, even a few torches. It's no wonder this place burned almost to the ground.

It's a perfect environment for Jefferson and me to blend in while we watch the Custom House building. Arm in arm, like two chums out for a stroll, we pretend we aren't in the least bit nervous as we go from one hotel to the next, fall in or out of one group or another, and skirt the square as we watch the bank. A guard paces the veranda, or sits on a cane chair outside the door and smokes. From time to time, some of his friends come by to chat, but nobody draws him away.

"That seems like hard duty," I say to Jefferson as we stroll past.

"I bet it gets harder a few hours after midnight, when the gambling dens close their doors and everyone goes home or finds a bed. That's when we'll have our chance."

"I've never broken the law before," I say, speaking in a low whisper.

"Me neither," he says. "And I'm man enough to admit I'm a bit anxious."

A large, cold drop of water lands on the tip of my nose. When I look up, a few more patter on my face. Rain might make tonight's task especially difficult and dangerous.

The rain does us one favor, which is bring an earlier end to the evening's festivities. By the time the ships' bells in the harbor are ringing midnight, the streets are already clearing, and some of the parlors close their doors. Jefferson and I find a bench and sit. It's chilly, and I'd love to burrow into his chest, let his warm arm wrap me tight. Instead, we sit shoulder to shoulder, barely touching.

We're in the dark, in the shade of an awning, unmoving, so I don't *think* the guard can see us. But we can see him just fine in the light of his lantern. He sits alone for a long time, smoking, rolling one cigarette after another. I start to doze off.

"There he goes," whispers Jefferson.

I snap to and sit up straight. The rain is still falling, a dismal curtain of cold droplets. The guard is standing, shaking out his empty tobacco pouch. He peers into the dark for a long minute. He paces to one end of the veranda and looks around, then heads back to the other. Having assured himself that no one is about, he runs across the street for the parlor of the hotel where Becky and I stood lookout a few days earlier.

"What time is it?" I ask Jefferson.

"The ships just rang five bells," he says. "So, two thirty in the morning,"

I stand from the bench. "Then I had better get moving. I might not have much time."

"He'll probably want something hot to eat, something hard to drink, and take time to relieve himself. But if he comes back early, I'll distract him."

"All right. Here I go—"

A sharp whistle cuts through the night, slicing from one end of the square to another. A dark shadow slips around the far corner of the veranda, carrying a pry bar. The shadow sprints down the length of it, staying close to the wall, pausing only long enough to blow out the lantern.

The rain muffles the sound, but there's a soft, woody snap. The pry bar forcing the door open.

"Whoa," I whisper, my heart sinking. "I think the bank is getting robbed."

"Seems like we're not the only ones up to no good tonight," Jefferson says.

"This is bad for us," I say. "We can't do this if they get there first."

"They won't be successful," he says. "Not going through the front door like that. We'll just come back tomorrow night."

"Hardwick will double his security. We won't be able to touch his gold."

"Do you want to go across the street and tell the guard?"

I stand up and start moving toward the Custom House building. Jefferson follows me. Then I pause. "Won't matter," I say. "Whether the robbery is successful or not, Hardwick will double the guard. Let's see how far they get." I'm not sure it's the right decision, but it's my best guess.

A metallic clang rings through the rain. The cage lock is broken.

The clomp of hooves and the creak of wheels freeze me against the wall. A mule plods into view from a side street.

Jefferson leans over, like he's a drunkard and I'm helping him keep his feet, but both of us watch the mule cart.

The driver glances our way, but he chooses to ignore us. He pulls the cart up to the front of the bank.

Jefferson and I ease closer, all the way to the corner of the veranda.

The first man pushes Hardwick's safe through the bank door.

"They put it on wheels," Jefferson whispers.

"That's one way to do it," I whisper back. But now I'm worried the robbers will get away with their theft, which could make our task impossible. Hardwick needs to feel confident. Overconfident, even.

The driver stretches a plank from the back of the cart to the hard porch. The safe is heavy, but together the two of them muscle it up the ramp into the cart. The wheels sink several inches into the mud, and the mule snorts and fights against his traces.

No movement from the hotel. The guard shows no sign of returning.

They're going to do it. The robbers are going to get away with Hardwick's money.

"What do we do?" Jefferson whispers.

The thieves toss the plank on the back of the wagon and leap onto the seat. The driver lashes the mule, which lurches forward, straining against its harness. The traces rattle, and the shafts snap tight. The wagon doesn't move, and for a second I think we might be saved by the mud.

The driver lashes the mule again, harder, and the other

man jumps down to push from behind. With a huge sucking sound, the wheels break free of the mud, and the wagon begins to slowly roll forward.

"That poor mule," I say.

Jefferson says, "I'll follow them, see where they go."

"Wait a second," I say, grabbing his wrist.

I can sense the gold in the safe, and for once, we've had a bit of luck. Because inside that safe are several gold bars, which have as large and regular a shape as a military marching song. All I have to do is beckon it.

I concentrate hard, reaching with my mind.

The driver whips the mule again, and the wagon starts to surge forward. The thief jumps onto the bench seat.

I pull the gold harder than I've ever pulled.

The safe slides backward off the cart and lands in the mud. It's so heavy it sinks half a foot deep, maybe more.

I drop to my knees, light-headed, gasping for air, like I just sprinted up a hill.

"Lee," Jefferson says, kneeling beside me. "Lee, are you all right? Did you just—"

"I just," I say.

The thief leaps down from the wagon bench and tries to shove the safe, but it won't budge. The door of the hotel slams open. The guard runs out, followed by several others. The driver whips the mule, and the cart clatters into the night. The other thief starts to chase after, shouting "Wait!" The mud trips him up. The guard and his friends fall on him, punching and kicking.

Jefferson pulls me to my feet, but my knees are wobbly. "We have to get out of here, Lee, before someone sees us," he whispers.

"I can't," I tell him. If I try, I might lose my supper. Hearing the wet *thunk* of feet and fists against flesh isn't helping. I should have let the poor man get away.

"I'll carry you," Jeff says.

Which he does. He puts an arm around me and lifts me like I'm passed-out drunk. We make our way back to the hotel awning. Carefully he lowers me to the bench to rest.

"Lee! I can't believe you moved that whole safe."

"Good thing I've been practicing," I say. My head won't stop spinning. I topple sideways, falling slowly, like the drizzle.

Chapter Sixteen

$\mathcal{I}$ wake up in my cabin in the *Charlotte*. Jefferson sits across from me, a worried look on his face. Dark hollows circle his eyes. Olive, bless her heart, sits on the floor beside my cot, holding my hand.

"Ma," she cries, with all the piercing volume of a child with important news. "Lee's awake!"

"What time is it?" I ask.

"Around noon," Jefferson says.

I start to rise, but Becky bursts through the door, sees me, and pushes me firmly back into the blankets. "Don't even think about getting up, young lady."

"But—"

"I'll have absolutely no buts from you."

"No butts," says Andy, following her into the room. "No butts on the poop deck!"

"Andrew Junior," Olive says, with all the imperiousness of her mother. "Lee's sick. Be quiet."

"La poop, la poop, la poop," he says, dissolving into giggles.

"We have to *be quiet*," Olive says, in the loudest whisper I've ever heard. "Lee, are you ready to drink some water? Jasper says sick people need to drink a lot of water. I brought a pitcher, just in case you woke up." She indicates an old spouted bucket on the floor beside my cot.

Before I can answer, Becky puts her hands on her hips, looks down her nose at me, and says, "What exactly did you think you were doing?"

"I was trying to—"

"That was a rhetorical question, Miss Westfall." She wags her finger at me, and that's when I know I'm in real trouble. "I once saw a man try to lift a fallen tree. It was after a June thunderstorm, and it was blocking the way of several carriages, including ours. Some of the men were hitching up a team of horses to drag it out of the way, but this fellow couldn't wait and he wouldn't ask for help. He strained and groaned and then, with a prodigious heave, much like Samson, he flung it aside. And do you know what happened then?"

"Is that another rhetorical question?" I ask. Meekly, I hope.

She glares. "It's a story, and it's a story I think you should attend to."

"What happened?"

"The tree dropped on one side of the road, and he dropped on the other." She imitates by flopping her hands to either side. "The strain was so great that his heart burst, and he died right there on the spot."

I swallow. My throat feels drier than the Humboldt Sink

we crossed last summer, and my head pounds fiercely. "Could I get that drink of water, Olive?"

Olive leaps for the "pitcher," but Becky doesn't slow down. "So what do you think would happen if a little slip of a girl like you tried to move a safe full of hundreds of pounds of gold all by yourself?"

I am most certainly not a little slip of anything, but she's on a roll, and I can tell she's genuinely worried about me. Olive hands me a cup of water. I drink greedily.

"I had to do something," I say. "I didn't know what would happen."

"Well, now you do," she scolds. "And I don't want you doing anything foolish like that again."

"I'm pretty sure she'll find something else foolish to do," Jefferson mumbles under his breath.

Jefferson and I exchange a knowing look. I have way bigger plans for my gold sense than simply moving one little safe.

But Becky doesn't know that part, and it's best we keep it that way. Because if everything goes as intended, Becky will be close in Helena Russell's company at least once before our work is done here.

We are saved by a slight tap at the door. Melancthon stands there with a tray containing a tureen of chicken soup, along with a bowl, spoon, and napkin. The soup smells like sunshine to me, and if my mouth wasn't so dry, I'm sure it'd water.

"There's lunch in the galley for them that want it," he says. "I brought this for Lee, so she wouldn't have to get up."

"I can make it to the galley," I protest.

"You most certainly will do nothing of the sort," Becky says. "Come, children, it's time for lunch."

Olive takes Andy by the hand and leads him away. She pauses at the door to look sternly over her shoulder. "I'll be back to check on you soon, Lee."

"Thank you," I say.

Becky follows her children from the room, and Melancthon sets the tray down on an empty cot. Beside the soup are bread and butter and a variety of cold meats. "For Mr. Kingfisher," he says. "If he's hungry, too. Holler if either of you need something more. Can I do anything else for you?"

I glance over at the wall. "Well, there is one thing."

"Just name it," he says.

"Is there any chance I could have a window in my room?"

His mouth drops open and he pauses. Then he tosses up his hands. "What's another hole? You're the captain of this vessel now, more or less. Windows for everyone, I suppose."

"I think the fresh air would be good, and I'd love to have some daylight in here."

He stops at the doorway on his way out. "I don't know precisely the nature of your . . . accident. But I'm glad to see you up and well."

"Thank you. And Melancthon?"

"Yes?"

"Have you made up your mind yet about the *Argos*?"

"I haven't."

"Is the captain a close friend of yours?"

"He's not the kind of man you can be close friends with. If

you help him with something he needs, he'll help you with yours. A matter of expediency."

"I see."

When he shuts the door behind him, Jefferson slides closer. He brushes the hair from my face and looks me right in the eyes. "You scared me half to death," he says.

"How bad was it?"

"Bad enough that you scared me half to death." He grabs a hunk of bread and gnaws off a huge bite. I ladle some soup into the bowl and spoon a sample into my mouth.

"I meant specifically," I say, between sips.

"You keeled over on the bench, and I didn't know anything was wrong for a moment, except that you were weak, because your eyes were still open and you were saying words. But the words didn't make any sense. Then you just collapsed, and nothing I could do would rouse you. So I picked you up and carried you back here, and then I woke Henry and made him run and fetch Jasper."

"You didn't need to do that!"

"Oh, yes, I did. You were really pale, and your eyes were half open—and uncanny bright, like tigereye gemstones—but you wouldn't respond to anything. Jasper came and tested your reflexes and listened to your heart and your breathing, and said he thought you'd be fine with some rest."

"Jasper was here and I missed him?"

"He was here until after sunrise, when he said he needed to get back to his office and take care of his other patients. He plans to come by and check on you again this evening."

My bowl of soup is already empty, so I ladle out some more. "So what did he say was wrong?"

"He was worried that maybe you'd had a stroke."

"A stroke?"

"Like an apoplexy. But he said your reflexes were equally responsive on both sides of your body, and you were talking in your sleep. Your words were clear, so he decided that was a good sign, too."

I pause with the spoon halfway to my mouth. "What was I saying?"

"Stuff about gold. Becky kept Melancthon away, in case you started babbling about your power. You were just shining and smiling like you'd done something amazing."

"To be fair, it *was* pretty amazing."

He grins, which lights up his whole face. "Yes, it was."

"I moved a whole safe full of gold."

"From almost a hundred feet away!"

"It's like, the bigger the gold is, the more it magnifies what I can do." I shake my head, half in disbelief. "Do we know what happened to the gold and to the robber?"

All the light in his face is extinguished.

"Tell me."

"Way I heard it, the guard spun a tale. Said he noticed the robbers hanging around earlier in the night, and he set a trap to catch them in the act. Had to let them get the safe out the door, so there was no question of their guilt."

"And Hardwick believed that?"

"The boys from the hotel backed it up, said he came to them

for help. Hardwick rewarded them all. But the safe was well sunk into the mud by the morning. They couldn't budge it, so Hardwick hired some Chinese laborers to do the work."

None of that explains his dour expression. "What aren't you telling me?"

He takes another huge bite of bread, and follows it with a cut of sausage, and I can tell he's playing for time to think about his answer. There's still soup in my bowl, but I've lost my appetite, so I put it down.

"Jeff?"

"The guy in the wagon got away. They didn't catch him, and he's probably halfway to Mexico by now. His friend refused to tell them who he was."

"And the one they caught?"

"The guard called the sheriff, and the sheriff came and arrested him."

Trying to get the story out of him is like trying to weed dandelions from the garden. I might get a handful of truth, but every yank leaves just as much behind in the ground as I clear away.

"Did they take him to the jail with Hampton?" I ask.

"No," he says, staring off at the floor. Then he turns to look at me. "They hanged him. Right there in the square."

"Without a trial?"

"Sheriff said he was caught in the act, so he didn't need a trial. There's no tolerance for theft around here. They put up a gallows and hanged him just after sunrise."

I cover my face with my hands, and then grab my pillow and

pull it over my head. "It's my fault," I mumble through the pillow. "I got that poor man killed."

"You did nothing of the sort," Jefferson said. "That's on the men doing the killing."

"But I made sure he got caught!"

"You didn't know what was going to happen. His friend got away, and he might have gotten away, too, if he hadn't run back for—"

"Don't! I don't want to hear any excuses."

My eyes are closed and my face is covered, but all I can see is that day back in the Hiram's mine when I tried to give one of the Indians a drink of water, and Frank Dilley shot him dead. I tried to do a good thing, for selfish reasons, and it got a man killed. Now it's happened again.

Jefferson's hand rests on my shoulder, and I flinch away.

"Lee," he says.

I fling the pillow at him, which he catches neatly. "You know, that could be you! Our plan to rob Hardwick could get you killed."

He sets the pillow aside and comes over to sit beside me.

"Maybe," he says. "But it's still the right thing."

"Not if you get hanged."

"That won't happen. My father's name is McCauley, right? Maybe I have a second sight of my own."

He wraps an arm around me, and I've never been the clinging type, but I can't help clutching fistfuls of his shirt and holding him tight against me, absorbing his warmth, taking him in. He smells of wood shavings and clean hay. "That's not funny."

"We're going to be fine. Besides, this is proof that you've been right all along."

I lift my head. "Huh?"

"Hardwick has no respect for laws and the process of justice," Jefferson says. "If he's not stopped, more people are going to get hurt. More people are going to die."

"At least it won't be you."

"But it'll be someone," he says. "I've been thinking a lot about what Henry said. It's all the people who don't have a say in the government who get hurt by it. Indians, Negros, Chinese, women, children. Poor folk. We don't mean anything to Hardwick and men like him. We can't stop all of them, but we can stop him."

"This robbery put a hiccup in our scheme."

Jefferson reaches around me for another bite of bread. "Tomorrow is the auction. We'll stick to that part of the plan and steal his reputation. We'll figure out the rest too."

"I guess." I pick up the spoon and force myself to eat another bite. "Nobody ever got hanged for stealing a reputation, did they?"

Chapter Seventeen

*T*uesday morning comes, cold and plodding. Five of us attend the auction under a grim gray sky—me, Jefferson, Becky, Henry, and Mary. An auctioneer's platform has been set up in Portsmouth Square, near the Custom House. A body hangs from a hastily constructed gallows, swaying in the wind. A group of dirty children makes a game of throwing pebbles at it.

It casts a pall over me, a long shadow that seems to follow me no matter where I stand or the angle of the shrouded sun. There's no way to look at the auctioneer's platform and not notice the limp body out of the corner of my eye. I can't help staring at it, feeling that the dead man is staring right back, accusing.

"It's not your fault," Jefferson says as we wander through the milling multitude. "It's Hardwick's."

"Are you sure you should be up and around?" Becky asks. She's wearing a beautiful dress of soft green calico, which she gleefully chose in spite of it being an inappropriate color for this time of year. Her own minor mutiny, I suppose. "Jasper says you should rest and take it easy for a couple days."

"I'm fine," I say. It's true. I do feel fine. Maybe I feel better than fine, the way you do after you run a mile to the neighbor's house, chop an extra cord of wood, carry two full buckets from the spring instead of one. At first, the day after, you're tired and sore. But then you get busy again, feeling stronger than ever.

Henry slipped away for a moment, but now he returns, handing out sheets of paper to all of us. "These are the preliminary auction items," he says. "The map shows plots of land for sale, along with their estimated values. The other list is marked with opening bids."

Mary skims the list and glances over the map. "Why did you say preliminary?"

Henry and I exchange a glance. The preliminary lists circulate first, and that is part of our plan. But I shut the thought down as soon as it forms. I don't see Helena Russell anywhere, but she's sure to be near.

"At these auctions, they often circulate one list early to see what people's reactions are, then print another, final list, with prices higher or lower, based on what they think they can get," Henry says.

"They'll hand out the final list right before the auction starts," Jefferson adds.

"Well, that's clever," Mary says.

"There's my house!" Becky says. "They have no right to sell my house." She turns toward the crowd and shouts it again.

"They have no right to auction off my house!"

"Right doesn't come into it," I say.

"It's whatever they think they can get away with," Jefferson says. "Speaking of getting away with things . . ."

He tenses, like his hackles are going up, and I follow his gaze.

Two workmen in muddy coats stomp up the platform steps, hauling an auctioneer's podium. They're followed by a thin man in a blue-striped shirt and a pair of round spectacles. He wields a gavel, like a judge.

Following the auctioneer is Frank Dilley. The burned half of Dilley's face shimmers with glycerin, making his sneer gleam like the edge of a knife. His jacket is pulled back to reveal the guns in his holster, one on each hip.

Dilley is the last fellow I care to see, but I'm a little relieved at the same time. If he's here as Hardwick's representative, then maybe Hardwick won't be coming at all. Which means we might be clear of Helena's second sight for a spell.

The workmen deposit the podium in the center of the stage. Frank Dilley drops a lockbox beside it; it thumps hollowly. It won't be hollow by the end of the auction. And from here, it's just a short walk to the bank, where he'll add it to the rest of Hardwick's money.

Watching it all makes me wish our practice run had gone a whole heap better. There's still so much we don't know, and tonight will be for real.

Dilley twirls the key to the lockbox on his finger, bored as he surveys the crowd. He gaze lands on me. He snaps his fist closed on the key and shoves it into his pocket.

"We've been spotted," I say, remembering that we have as much right to be here as anyone, that of course Hardwick and his people knew we'd come. I shuffle my feet and fight the urge to run.

"At least Miss Russell isn't here," Jefferson says, softly, soothingly. His calmness is an anchor as my emotions roil like a storm. "After our failed practice run, we deserve a spot of luck."

I glance around for Helena one last time, but as far as I can tell, Becky, Mary, and I are the only women here. Still, I discipline my mind, just in case. I will think only of my tiny role today. Concentrate on my outrage. Nothing else.

"Final prices! Final prices!"

A towheaded little boy, not much bigger than Andy, scampers into the crowd from the direction of the printer's office. He lugs a huge stack of papers and hands them out to everyone he sees. The crowd murmurs at the updated sheets.

Henry grabs a handful. "Well, this is it, then," he says, distributing them to us. "We should probably split up for better effect."

Jefferson grins and heads off to the far edge of the crowd, in the opposite direction of Henry.

"This should be interesting," Mary says, then weaves nearer to the podium.

Becky reaches out to squeeze my hand. "Good luck," I tell her.

"We don't need luck."

The little boy hands the remaining copies to the auctioneer. I watch for his reaction. He stares at the price list, then takes his glasses off, wipes them clean, and stares at the sheets again.

A voice whispers at my side. "Are you ready?"

I look up and find Jim Boisclair. "Ready, willing, and able. You?"

"Always," he says. "Might even pick up a lot for my general store."

"Better be careful—I hear they'll sell the same lot right out from under you."

"You don't say?"

The auctioneer places the list on the podium before him. He stares at it one last time. Then he picks up the gavel and bangs. "We'll begin with the sale of future lots!"

Jim steps forward, lifting his sheet high. "Hold on! They're auctioning off a lot I already bought and paid for!"

I give it a few seconds to sink in, listening to the growing unease around me. Then I wave my sheet in the air like a battle flag. "They're trying to rob us! Selling the same property twice!"

From across the crowd, I hear Becky's voice. "They're selling my house! Which I own free and clear!"

From another direction, Mary, with a strong Spanish accent: "They're robbing us! *Ladrones!*"

The voices of women in peril have gotten everyone's attention. People in the crowd bow over their lists, studying them with a critical eye.

Henry yells, "Is that my trunk you're selling?"

Jefferson: "You can't sell my land without my say-so!"

The auctioneer bangs his gavel, but the crowd is provoked now. The murmur swells to a roar of angry voices. Frank Dilley's right hand moves to his gun belt.

"I already own this lot on Front Street! I paid for it last week!"

"Lot twenty-two on Fremont belongs to me!"

"What's going on here?"

"Crooks!"

Jim leads a surge toward the podium, and I follow in his wake. "I demand an explanation," he says. "What's going on here!"

"We have a right to know," I shout. "Why is Hardwick trying to rob us?"

Someone, a stranger, hollers, "Hardwick's trying to rob all of us!"

The crowd is riled up, turning into a mob. The auctioneer bangs his gavel and shouts, but nobody listens. Frank Dilley hollers, "Pipe down! Pipe down! Hardwick ain't robbing nobody! Shut up or clear out of the square! We've got an auction to run!"

Jim and I push all the way to the front of the crowd. "Hardwick is selling the same property three and four times!" I shout.

Frank Dilley sees us. Smiles.

"I demand an explanation," Jim shouts.

"I got your explanation right here," Frank Dilley says. And he draws his gun and aims.

I don't know if Dilley is aiming at me or at Jim. All I know is Dilley is capable of killing in cold blood as easily as you can say boo.

I yank on Jim's sleeve. "Jim, get d—"

The crack of gunfire. A puff of smoke. The sharp scent of gunpowder.

Jim drops to the ground like a sack of flour.

The crowd goes dead silent.

Everyone steps back, and I'm kneeling in a semicircle of aloneness while a scarlet flower blooms on Jim's side. We lock gazes, and God help me, but I'll remember this look on his face for the rest of my life. "Damn fool, he shot me," he mumbles. "This . . . not part of our plan. . . ."

Frank Dilley holsters his Colt, yelling, "We've got an auction to run here! If you don't want to buy anything, then clear out. If you got a problem with the items for sale, then go talk to the sheriff!"

Everyone stares, cowed. After a moment, the crowd begins to thin as several slip away, quiet but fast.

The auctioneer picks up his gavel and bangs it again. "Our first lot up for sale is . . ."

Why is no one helping us? A man lies bleeding on the ground and no one cares. It dawns on me: because he's a Negro.

Jefferson and Mary appear at my side. Jefferson says, "Jim, are you . . . is he . . . ?"

"Alive," Jim murmurs. Flecks of blood land on his lips. "Stings a fair bit."

"We have to get him to Jasper," I say. "Now."

"I could fetch the wagon," Jefferson says.

"No time," Mary says.

"He didn't shoot my legs," Jim says. "Help me up."

I'm terrified that letting Jim walk is an awful idea, but I'm not sure what else to do. Jefferson squats to put Jim's arm around his shoulder. "Jasper's office is in Happy Valley," he says, lugging Jim to his feet. "Nearly ten blocks away."

"Then we better get going," Jim says, and he starts toward Kearney Street.

"Walking will just make him lose blood faster," Mary says.

Becky and Henry rush over. "We're coming with you," Becky says.

"Here, let me help," Henry offers, reaching for Jim's other arm, but Jim shrugs him off.

"Someone needs to stay," Jim says. "If we can't shout the truth, we can still whisper it where people will hear. Stay here and finish what we started."

"We can do that," Becky says.

"You're a born performer," I tell Henry. "You stay with Becky and help her."

He nods solemnly. Behind us, the first tentative bidders are shouting offers for a scrap of land that's still ten feet underwater.

We move fast for the first four or five blocks, with me and Jefferson helping Jim along while Mary presses a handkerchief to his side. Maybe that bullet just grazed Jim, I tell myself, but there's a hole in the front of his shirt and nothing in back. More worrisome is the way he's coughing up blood.

By block six, Jim is flagging. Mary bolsters his armpit and grabs his belt in her fist. "Run and get Jasper," she says to me. "As fast as you can."

I sprint down the final blocks as fast as I've ever run in my life, through the courtyard and into the parlor of the house, where a variety of sick people are waiting to be seen. A clerk or secretary of some kind sees me. "The doctors are busy, but if you'll have a seat—"

"Jasper!" I shout, running from room to room. In the second room, an older doctor with remarkable whiskers looks up from his examination of a red-faced businessman. I find Jasper in the third room, wrapping plaster around the arm of a little Mexican boy. He's standing there in shirtsleeves, with his cuffs rolled to his elbows. "Jasper!"

"Lee?"

The clerk appears behind me. "I told her to wait!" he says.

"It's Jim. Frank Dilley shot him," I pant out.

Jasper beckons the clerk over and orders him to finish wrapping the boy's arm. Jasper wipes his hands on a towel while he says, "Where is he?"

"In the street outside, a block or two away." The words come out in tiny desperate gasps. "We couldn't get him all the way here."

He grabs his stethoscope and puts a hand on my shoulder, as calm as I am terrified. "Show me."

As we dash through the parlor, Jasper calls out in broken Spanish to a couple of men, who grab a stretcher and follow. Together, we sprint up the block.

Jim has collapsed to the ground. A small group of neighbors has gathered around Jefferson, who is kneeling with Jim's head propped up on his lap. Mary is still doggedly pressing her handkerchief to his wound, but it is now soaked with crimson.

Jasper bends down to check Jim's pulse and listen through the stethoscope.

"You did a good job getting him this far," he said. "He has a chance."

Jasper beckons the workmen over with a wave of his hand, and they put the stretcher down and gently lift Jim onto it. "We'll take him through the side door and directly to the operating room in the back of the house," Jasper says. "Mary, keep pressure on that wound as we go. Lee, walk with me and fill me in on the details."

Blood covers Mary's hands. There's even a bit of it matting her black hair, just above her ear.

The workmen rush Jim back to the office, the rest of us following behind. I babble the whole way, telling Jasper everything. I end with, "I think Dilley wanted him dead because he figured out Hardwick's scam to rob people."

The older doctor with remarkable whiskers meets us at the side door. He's taken off his suit coat and is now wearing a clean white apron.

"I suppose this is another one of your charity cases, Clapp," he says, not unkindly.

"No, sir," I tell him. "We'll pay whatever it costs." Even if it's the last of my gold.

Jasper blocks the door. "You can't come in. You'll have to wait in the parlor."

"I . . ." I hate feeling so helpless. "You'll do everything you can for him, right?"

"I always do everything I can for my patients," he says, turning away.

The door closes. We stare at it a moment.

At last Mary says, "I know you're worried about Mr. Boisclair, but this may have presented us with an opportunity."

"What do you mean?" I say, still staring at that door. My oldest friend in the world besides Jefferson is behind that door, his life hanging in the balance.

"I mean, it depends on how things turn out, but—"

"What do you mean, Mary?" Jefferson repeats, more sternly.

Quickly she sketches out the beginnings of a plan. A plan within a plan. Another thing we can't dwell too hard on, lest Helena Russell pluck it from our thoughts.

"So, what do you think?" she says.

"It's a good idea," Jefferson says.

"Better than what we had already come up with," I concede. "It solves one of our remaining problems."

Mary wipes her hands on her skirt, leaving bloody smears. "I guess I'll go find the others. Let them know what we're about."

She turns to go, but I grab her arm. "Thank you, Mary," I say.

"Of course." She yanks her arm away and heads off at a jog, as if our recent exertions have not winded her even a little.

Jefferson takes my hand and leads me back to the parlor, where we find seats. The red-faced businessman is leaving. The clerk escorts the little boy with the broken arm to his mother, and a short while later, he brings Jefferson and me some tea.

Jim is in surgery forever. People come and go while we wait. Gold changes hands, small amounts, unlike in the hotels and gambling dens. It's a relief of sorts, not to have so much of it around.

The sun is low, shining through the parlor window, when the older doctor with remarkable whiskers appears at the end of the hall, wiping his bloody hands on a white towel. He glares at us and glances away, saying nothing.

"If Jim dies," I whisper to Jefferson, "is it my fault?"

"Don't be daft."

I give him a sharp look.

"You're scared," he says. "You're sad and you're angry. Dilley shooting Jim is a reason to stay to the course, not doubt it."

I feel numb, maybe too numb to take in what he's saying, but a distant part of me knows he's speaking the truth.

Jasper appears at the end of the hallway, blood on his shirt and pants, beads of sweat on his upper lip.

I jump up, and Jefferson follows. "Can we see him now? Is he going to be all right?"

Jasper's expression conveys a world of bad news. "Come this way," he says, gesturing. "We have some things to talk about."

Chapter Eighteen

We spend a long time with Jasper, talking things through, making all the proper arrangements.

Before returning to the *Charlotte*, we hire a boat to row us out to the prison barge. The water is rough today, and the little boat can't seem to keep its course, no matter how valiantly the boatman rows. But eventually we reach the sheriff's floating jail. I bang on the hull, just like on my previous visit with Jim, and call out for Hampton.

When his face appears in the porthole, a lump lodges in my throat.

"How are you doing?" I manage to shout.

"If it weren't for the rats and the lousy food, it'd be just like the county fair," he says. The false cheerfulness in his voice doesn't hide the strain. "Come to think of it, the county fair also has rats and lousy food."

"Need anything?" Jefferson calls up, and I give him a sharp look, because that's not like Jefferson at all. It's one of those things that feels good to say, I guess, but I don't know how we'd get Hampton anything he needed.

"I need out! Won't be much longer. Yesterday Jim said they raised enough money to get me free. They just need to take it to the sheriff and sign the papers."

"That's why we came to talk to you," I say. "It's about Jim. I'm afraid we have bad news."

Hampton's face in the porthole is an unreadable mask, like a man so accustomed to bad news it doesn't even land.

"Frank Dilley shot him. It turned out bad."

Anger flashes across his face. Then he pulls away from the porthole. He returns a moment later, wearing the same mask as before. "Shouldn't make a difference. Jim said one of the preachers is handling the money. He has standing in the community, even with the sheriff."

Jefferson and I exchange a look. "That's . . . good news," I say.

"Have you talked to Tom?" Hampton asks.

After too long a pause, Jefferson says, "We haven't seen much of Tom lately."

"He's been working," I add. "We see him at supper and sometimes breakfast."

"You ask him about my Adelaide."

"We'll do that," Jefferson says.

The waves are growing more violent, knocking our boat against the side of the ship. I grip the bench to keep from losing my seat.

"We gotta go," Jefferson says.

Hampton nods once, and his face disappears from the porthole.

We reach shore, pay the oarsman, and trudge home toward the *Charlotte*. The daylight fades early this time of year, especially with the sky so overcast. It's almost dusk by the time we make it home. The wagon is parked outside the ship. Inside the wagon is a huge barrel.

Everyone is gathered in the galley, including Mary. The table is cleared of the Major's and Melancthon's latest project, and fixings for dinner are spread. The Major bounces the baby on his knee, the end of his wooden leg tapping on the floor.

Becky's eyes go straight to the bloodstains on Jefferson's clothes and mine. "How is Mr. Boisclair?"

"He's . . ." I glance at Mary, who nods quietly. Yes, she arranged everything after she left the doctor's office, just as she promised. Even though Helena Russell is nowhere near, I'm afraid to say or even think too much.

"There's going to be a funeral for him tomorrow," Mary says finally. "In the Sailor's Cemetery at the corner of Sansome and Vallejo."

"Oh, Lee, I'm so sorry," Becky says. "I know he was a long-time family friend."

I just nod, unable to form words.

"The view from that spot is positively poetic," Henry says. "I think your friend Jim will approve."

"But . . . Sailor's Cemetery?" Becky says. "He was never a sailor, was he? I thought he was from Dahlonega, like Jefferson and Lee."

"A lot of folks buried there," Mary says. "Indians and Negros. Chinese. The funeral is going to be a small affair. Henry and I made all the arrangements today."

"Mary is a marvel," Henry says. "Did you know she speaks English, Chinese, *and* Spanish?"

Mary glares at Henry, as if complimenting her is the worst thing ever.

But Becky says, "Of course." As if it's nothing. "She interprets for me all the time at the tavern."

"In any case," I say, "I'd sure appreciate it if everyone could be there tomorrow. Jim is . . . *was* one of my oldest friends."

"Which reminds me," Jefferson adds, looking to the Major. "We'll need to take that barrel off the wagon to make room for a casket. I told Jasper we'd come pick it up tonight. He promised to have it ready."

The Major and Melancthon exchange a glance and a nod. "We can do that right after supper."

"I'd be grateful," I say.

Jefferson and I grab plates. I serve myself a helping of everything on the table—smashed potatoes, green beans with bits of bacon, and a slice of salted ham—but I don't have much of an appetite. I sit beside Mary. She puts her arm around me and gives me a quick squeeze—a rare gesture from her.

"How'd the auction go?" Jefferson asks around a mouthful of food. Nothing affects his appetite.

"Nothing we said, in shouts or whispers, did anything to slow it down," Henry says.

"The starting prices were too good to pass up," Becky

explains. "I think even people who thought Hardwick had robbed them in the past wanted to get a piece of things."

"But did you get your house?" I ask.

Becky brightens. "I think so! I have to pick it up in the next few days. We'll see if the auction . . . holds."

"I'm so relieved to hear it," I say. We needed something to go right for us. "I can't wait to set it up in Glory."

"So Dilley collected all the money and took the strongbox to the bank?" Jefferson asks.

"They were done before noon," Becky says.

"Sold off everything and closed up shop," Henry adds. "I was able to spend the whole afternoon helping Mary arrange things."

I stop playing with my food and put down my knife and fork. "Which means that tonight, a huge portion of his fortune is going to be at Owen and Son, Bankers, right on Portsmouth Square."

"We may have some news about that," Mary says, with a nod toward Henry. "When we were out making funeral arrangements, we had a little trouble finding the help we needed."

Henry adds, "The first two people we asked had already been hired out by Hardwick. To fetch all his safes from various banks around the city."

"Whoa," says Jefferson.

"When?" the Major asks. Melanchthon is looking back and forth between us all, obviously curious about why these details are important, but not butting in. He knows we're up to something, but he hasn't once pestered us with questions. I hope he's trustworthy. The Major assures me that he is.

"Tomorrow," says Mary. "They'll start first thing in the morning, and deliver all of them to Hardwick's house before a big party tomorrow night."

"A party, huh?" I say, and Jefferson draws in a small breath. A party would be perfect. Exactly what we need for the last part of our plan. We'll have to work fast, though, to put everything into place.

Maybe all those safes will . . . I shut my thoughts down as quick as I can. I need to practice *not* thinking about the plan. Then again, it's not like Helena is standing outside the door, hoping to eavesdrop on our thoughts.

"Can you do me a favor?" I ask Mary.

"Of course."

"Any chance you can find the folks Hardwick hired and give them a message?"

"Probably."

"They'll be watched by Hardwick's men every step of the way. They should be warned that the safe at Owen and Son will be the heaviest safe and the hardest to move."

Mary tugs her earlobe. "That is a very good thing for them to know. Thank you."

Jefferson eyes me, but he doesn't say a word. Melanchthon looks at Mary, then me, then back again.

Mary rises. "I need to go. I got myself a job serving drinks in a gambling den tonight."

"Serving drinks?" Becky asks with a raised brow.

Mary has the grace to smile. "Just serving drinks."

"I suppose it's good not to be idle while you're here," Becky says, which I think is a callous and uppity thing to say, as Mary has never been idle a day in her life. But my thoughts toward Becky soften when she adds, "Will you be coming back with me to Glory? After we've finished here? I . . . I've gotten used to having you around the tavern."

Mary looks at her a long moment. "Maybe. I'm not sure."

Becky opens her mouth, but nothing comes out.

To me, Mary says, "Be careful."

"You too. Mary . . . I know you volunteered for these assignments, but I'm not sure it's safe."

Mary shrugs. "I'm the only one who speaks Chinese and Spanish. It has to be me."

Melancthon stands. "I'd be happy to accompany you, ma'am, and see to your safety."

Mary's smile lights up the galley. "I'd like that, sir."

After they leave, the Major hands the baby to Becky, along with her fistful of smashed potatoes. "I should hitch up the wagon and get over to Jasper's before it's too late."

Olive and Andy clear their plates and run off to play hide-and-seek. The sounds of counting and running echo hollowly through the ship. Henry, Becky, Jefferson, and I all linger at the table, unwilling to let the day go.

"What exactly do we know about this party tomorrow night?" I ask.

"Not much," Henry says. "Hardwick has been sending out invitations to all the local politicians and bigwigs, but they take turns hosting parties for each other all the time.

It didn't sound like anything special."

"We'll make it special," Jefferson murmurs.

I think about the city and get the map of it clear in my head. "Hardwick's house is in Pleasant Valley, right? Melancthon says the *Argos* is sailing for New York. It's currently anchored in Mission Bay, which is right next to Pleasant Valley. If all of Hardwick's safes are being delivered to his house, that's the first step to loading them onto the ship."

"If we hadn't hired Melancthon ourselves," Jefferson says, "he'd be on the *Argos* already, overseeing the hold retrofit. The carpenters will be finished soon, and Hardwick could be gone with the tide on Thursday."

"So this is our only chance."

Henry nods.

Becky tries to spoon some green beans into the baby's mouth, but the tiny thing can't be fooled. She tightens up her lips and shakes her head. Becky widens her eyes and grins hugely and says to the baby, "Say 'Hardwick is a baaaaad man!'"

"Bah!" says the baby, and Becky slips a spoonful into her mouth.

Jefferson folds his arms. "It's comeuppance time," he says.

"It is," I agree. "Then home to Glory." With its sunrise hills and golden grass and wide-open space. So different from this busy, rickety city.

"Which reminds me." Becky hands the baby to Henry, who uses his table napkin to wipe at the smeared potatoes on her round cheeks. "You two wait right here. I had time to go shopping after the auction today, and I found something for you."

She disappears and returns with several bundles wrapped in brown paper. She puts the first in front of me and unfolds it to reveal a gold-and-yellow damask linen.

"What's this?" I ask.

"Material for your wedding dress! I realized I was never going to coax you into a dress shop. And then I thought about it—why must you have a boughten dress, anyway? We could get one tailored just for you."

It looks like a tub of butter exploded in a vat of cream. "It's . . . nice."

Becky beams and starts tearing open another package. "And I found the perfect lace to go with it!"

I admire the lace and try not to think about how, when I get married, I'm going to look like a giant pastry covered in spun sugar. "You're so thoughtful, Becky."

"This one is for you," she says to Jefferson, opening the final package to reveal wool and satin in varying shades of plum— unripe plum and juicy plum and nearly prune. I'm going to look like butter and sugar, but Jefferson is going to look like a giant walking bruise. I glance over at Henry, but he's no help at all, because he stares at the nearly prune satin like it's manna from heaven.

"You shouldn't have," Jefferson tells Becky flatly, and I have to stifle a giggle.

"Don't be ridiculous. Glory's first wedding is going to be a special event. Historic. It's the least I could do for the two of you."

"I . . . thank you," Jefferson says, looking at me with panic in his eyes.

"The tailor will be here Friday to take your measurements," Becky says. "I would have scheduled it sooner, but they're very busy right now, finishing up new clothes for Mr. Hardwick's party. I declare, any person with an aptitude in San Francisco right now is bound to make a fortune."

Movement catches my eye, and I look up and see Olive and Andy peering around the corner. I beckon to them, and Olive runs over and climbs onto my lap.

"Do you love it?" Olive asks.

"I love it," I say. "Your ma is a very good friend."

"This is the color I would have picked," Andy announces, grabbing at the fabric for Jefferson's suit. Becky slaps his hands away.

"No touching. You haven't washed your hands," she says.

Andy sticks his fingers in his mouth and licks them vigorously, then wipes his hand on his trousers. "Now can I?" he asks.

I am eager to see the result of this inquiry, but we're interrupted by banging at the door.

"I'll see who it is," Jefferson says, and he heads down the hallway to the entrance.

Before he gets halfway, he starts backing up. Following him is Frank Dilley, his hand on one of his guns.

I slide Olive from my lap and push her behind me.

My Hawken rifle is in my room, beneath my cot. I'll have to get past Dilley.

"I let myself in," he says. "Well, ain't this a proper reunion with you wagon-train bootlickers, the Johnny-come-latelies. I don't suppose Wally Craven is around here somewhere?"

"Your former wagon master and *superior* is momentarily engaged," Becky says. "If you have a message for him, you may leave it and go."

"No, I have a message for you," he replies. "Well, you, specifically," he adds, indicating me. "But I'll extend it to all of you, even the brats."

He reaches into his left vest pocket; Jefferson starts forward.

"Slow down, tiger," Dilley says, and draws his gun just far enough to make Jefferson freeze.

He removes a gilt-edged envelope, which he tosses onto the galley table.

"Mr. Hardwick requests the pleasure of your company, and that of your guests, at a little soiree he is hosting at his home tomorrow night. It's a farewell party for all his business associates before he leaves for New York. He's done business with you, as a representative of the town of Glory, and would like to show his appreciation. The details are in the invitation. Be sure to bring it with you. I'll tell them at the gate to expect you—the children too." He glances at Henry. "Your good pal Tom doesn't need an invitation. He'll be there working for Mr. Hardwick. And I understand the doc deserted you, like he should have a long time ago. But he's still invited."

"Why'd Hardwick send *you*?" I ask. Hardwick knows our history with Dilley.

"Oh, I volunteered. A chance to see some old friends one last time."

He tips his hat and backs out the way he came, keeping his hand on his gun the whole time.

The second he's gone, I run to my room and grab my rifle. I have my powder horn out and I'm shoving a wad of shot and cotton down the muzzle when Jefferson stops me. "You can't shoot him," he says.

"I'm not an idiot. But he was here. In our home. He just walked right in. So I'm keeping this gun loaded."

"Lee, you know better. That gunpowder will get wet. Next time you shoot, it will backfire in your face. There's nothing to be done that we aren't already doing."

I glare at him, hating that he's right. It's exactly what my daddy would have said. "We have to do _something_, damn it."

"You're entirely correct," Becky says softly. "He shouldn't get away with just walking into our home. But the children are listening, and I would still ask you to mind your language."

All the fire goes out of me, doused by the ice-cold water of Becky's words. "I'm sorry."

"Damn it!" Andy says, in perfect mimicry of my voice.

Becky spins on him. "Andrew Joyner Junior! If you ever say that word again, even as a grown man, I will scrub your mouth with soap until it's clean enough for serving Sunday dinner, is that clear?"

"Yes, Ma," he says contritely.

"Besides, you don't want to shoot him, you want to thank him," Henry says.

I spin on him. "What . . . ? Oh. You're right."

He holds up the invitation, which he has unsealed and read. "Now we have a way into Hardwick's house. The final part of our plan, the only part we hadn't figured out yet. Delivered to us on a silver platter. My friends, we are going to a party!"

Becky grins ear to ear. "I haven't attended a proper party since Chattanooga. We have to find something appropriate to wear!"

I recap my powder horn and return the rifle to my room, Jefferson trailing behind me. "Helena Russell will be there," he says.

"Yep." I sit on my cot, and Jefferson settles on the one across from me. "But we'll worry about that tomorrow."

He puts his elbows on his knees and rests his chin on his hands. A tiny bit of soft, dark hair is growing along his jawline now, and I resist the urge to trace it with my fingers. I wonder if he'll choose to grow a beard, like his da, or shave it clean, like his mother's people.

"We have a long night ahead," Jefferson says. "Maybe you should get some shut-eye."

I stare at his lips. "Maybe you should get some with me."

He grins. "I like that idea."

My cot is too small for us both, so we shove two cots together and lie down side by side. He cradles me close, twining my fingers with his, and it reminds me a little of being on the trail, sleeping together beneath the wagon. Back then, I thought he was holding my hand in friendship.

I smile to myself. We aren't just friends, and maybe I

can take liberties now. I reach up and touch the hair on his jawline, because I can.

Hours later, Jefferson shakes me awake. I snap to, shivering with cold. This is our last chance. If we can't do what we plan tonight, we'll run out of time.

I don a skirt—the bright yellow calico, given to me by Lucie Robichaud before she took her leave and went to Oregon Territory. I need to be visible. A distraction.

Jefferson wears dark trousers, brown leather gloves, and a miner's hat, all meant to help him blend in with the night. Together, we exit the *Charlotte* and head toward Portsmouth Square. A few blocks short of our destination, we pause. Jefferson plants a quick kiss on my lips. "Good luck," he whispers.

He'll need luck more than I will tonight. "Be careful," I warn. "Take no chances."

He tips his hat to me and dashes away, into the darkness.

I continue on alone. It's the quietest part of the night, when all the gamblers are abed and a body can hear the water of the bay lapping against the docks just a few blocks away. The sooty wet smell of the city has faded with recent rains, only to be replaced by the more pungent smell of an overflowing outhouse. Everyone has been doing their business wherever they please, and when they're drunk, wherever they please turns out to be wherever they are.

The gallows still stand in the corner of the square, like a tall, angular scarecrow. The body has been removed, but a single crow remains, perched atop the crossbeam, its head tucked under a wing for the night. Near the gallows, a lantern hangs in front of the bank, illuminating not one, but two guards.

Apparently Hardwick learns from his mistakes. With two guards, there's one to spell the other, and no reason to leave the door unguarded even for a second. It reminds me not to underestimate him.

The guards sit quietly in their chairs, positioned on either side of the door. I recognize them instantly: my old friends Large and Larger.

Chimes echo from the harbor. The ships, ringing five bells.

I walk boldly across the square toward the veranda. No short cuts, no misdirection, straight and brisk. "Hello, gentlemen."

They straighten in their chairs, faces brightening. They're likely bored out of their minds, and I provide a welcome diversion. Still, I have to be careful what I say. The moment I cause any trouble, they'll chase me off.

I stop at the edge of the veranda and lean against the post.

"Nice night for a stroll?" Large asks.

"I can't sleep," I admit.

"It's hard to sleep when you're walking around," Larger points out.

"It's usually easier to sleep when you have a bed," Large agrees.

"Why aren't you home in bed?" Larger asks.

Tiles rattle on the rooftop.

"Quite a breeze tonight," I say, which is true, but not the reason for the rattling roof tiles. I jerk a thumb toward the gallows. "I didn't see the hanging. Were either of you here for it?"

"See, that's interesting to me," says Large.

"Me too," says Larger. "The way I heard it, someone fitting your description was loitering the night of the attempted robbery."

"Two people," says Large. "Someone about your height, and a taller, skinny boy. The guard who caught the robber thought they might have been lookouts."

My heart races. Right now I'm giving away more information than I'm getting. "You don't say?"

"I just said," says Larger.

"Yeah, I'm pretty sure he did," adds Large.

"So what are you doing here tonight?" asks Larger.

I'm here to distract them from what Jefferson is doing right this very second, but I think hardest about my second reason for being here, which is knowledge.

And maybe that's not such a bad thing to admit. So I take a chance and try honesty on for size. It's the opposite of what Hardwick would do. "I need information about James Henry Hardwick. He took a bunch of money from me, promised to give my town a charter. Only he never delivered. Now he says there are going to be additional expenses."

Large looks at Larger. Shrugs.

"Sounds like Hardwick," Large says.

"There are always additional expenses with him," Larger agrees.

"And now he's invited me to this big soiree at his house

tomorrow night. I'm wondering what I'm in for if I go, and whether I have any chance at all of getting what he promised me, or if I'm just walking into some sort of awful trap."

The roof tiles rattle again, and I press on, thinking about what Becky would say. "You may have noticed there aren't a lot of woman out here in the territories. It's enough to make a girl downright lonesome. I'd dearly love to make some connections, and this party seems like the place to do it." I do my best to look forlorn and frightened. "But attending might be _dangerous_. Anyway, it was keeping me awake, and so I started walking and ended up here."

The two men look me over, like they're sizing up a stray dog to see if it's going to bite. The night is cold and sharp. The salt-laden wind cuts through everything now, even the latrine scent. Which is the bigger threat, me or boredom? They glance at each other and reach an unspoken consensus. Boredom wins out. Large stands up, fishing a key from his pocket. He turns to open the bank door.

"Mr. Owen lets you go inside his bank?" I practically yell it out, loud enough to wake everyone in the hotel across the square.

"He lets Mr. Hardwick have keys to his bank," says Larger.

"Sort of an apology for what happened the other night," says Large. "Hardwick would never let us have access to the safe, though."

"Never that," Larger agrees.

My heart is in my throat as the door creaks open and Large disappears inside. I shuffle my feet, clear my throat, make any natural noise I can think of. When he reemerges a moment later with a chair, I barely keep from gasping with relief. He drops it on the boardwalk and slides it over toward me. Then he relocks the door.

Larger holds out a hand the size of a paddle. "Have a seat."

I've never been so glad to comply with an order. The roof creaks, so I loudly scrape the chair a little closer to the guards.

Large hikes up his trousers as he sits down again. "What do you want to talk about?"

I cross my arms. "I have a list. . . ."

Two hours later, when I'm yawning too much to keep talking, I thank them for their time and wander home again. The wagon with the casket is parked outside the *Charlotte*. Jefferson sits in the wagon, legs dangling over the side, and I'm so relieved I can hardly breathe. I run forward and throw my arms around his waist.

"Glad you're back safe," he says into my hair.

"It worked!" I say. "I can't believe it actually worked."

"It did." I hear the smile in his voice. "You were out there long enough."

"I wasn't sure how much time it would take. I kept them talking as long as I could think up questions."

He pulls away and holds my shoulders at arm's length. "Well, that's the end of that. No more going anywhere alone in this city. For either of us."

He's probably right. "How are the horses?" I ask.

"I think they were happy to stretch their legs. Did you learn anything interesting from the guards?"

"No. I just pretended to. And then I was suitably grateful afterward." I yawn hugely. "The rest can keep until after I get some shut-eye."

"Did you at least learn their names?" he asks.

"Never thought to ask." And I head inside to bed.

Chapter Nineteen

$\mathcal{I}$ sleep for just a few hours before morning sunlight pours through the new window in my room and wakes me. The rest of the crew is eating a solemn breakfast in the galley, but I don't have any appetite. I pour myself a cup of coffee, then head down to the stables to fetch the team of horses.

Peony and Sorry immediately start to complain. I feed them first and muck out their stalls, but it's not enough to placate them. They're even more restless than usual, as if watching the team head out on an adventure just made them hanker for more. During the long walk from Georgia to California, they got used to being out in the open, under big skies with lots of fresh air.

"Sorry, girl," I tell Peony while I brush her. "But we need the carthorses again today. A couple more days and you'll be on the road again."

The brush does some kind of magic, because she seems more cheerful after, but no amount of grooming or coaxing cheers Sorry. The sorrel just stands there dejected, mane and tail hanging limp, which is more or less the creature's usual state.

I'm probably imagining the way Peony and Sorry glare knives into my back as I fetch their neighbors and lead them up the ramp to the wagon and fresh air. They've made this trip a few times now, and they're all business. Makes me miss the pair Daddy and I trained up back in Dahlonega.

The pair I sold to Jim Bosclair, who knew I had no right to sell them, but bought them anyway to help me out.

The rest of our group gathers outside—everyone but Mary, who insists that she shouldn't be seen with us in the light of day in order for our plan to work. She's right, of course, but I find myself wishing she was here anyway.

Jefferson wears his usual shirt and trousers, but everything is clean and pressed. Henry has donned yet another new suit—I think he must have traded the last one for it—this time in melancholy colors. The Major struggles with his tie, but Henry's deft fingers soon fix it for him. Andy and Olive wear somber wool, their collars freshly pressed. Andy's hair is combed, although nothing can keep a big cowlick from sticking up. Becky wears a deep blue that's almost black, and has the baby wrapped in a navy blanket.

I've donned an ordinary gray dress and a warm sweater that's a little too big. But I decide not to change them. This is how Jim always knew me.

Melancthon emerges from the ship with a wooden cross, which he holds up for us to examine. JAMES BOISCLAIR is carved into the crossbeam, along with yesterday's date.

"It's not much of an offering," he says. "But he's not being buried at sea, so the least he deserves is a decent grave marker."

"Thank you," I tell him. "It's perfect."

We form a sad procession through the streets. The residents of San Francisco are used to death and dying, so folks hardly glance at us twice. It saddens me, that a man's life means so little to them, especially a man like Jim, someone given to helping out strangers.

A small group of four has already gathered in the cemetery. I recognize Jim's friend Isaac, who I met the day Jim took me on his tour of the city. Beside him is the minister who has been raising money to help get Hampton out of jail. The cemetery caretakers, also Negros, stand by with shovels. They've dug a hole for us, and I pay them the amount we agreed on. It's not six feet deep, but I reckon it's deep enough for what we need.

"Is this everyone?" the minister asks.

"I guess so," I say. "Jim didn't have any family when he came west. . . ."

My words die away as several people crest the hill and approach—mostly Negroes, a couple Chinese, one white man with an eye patch.

Isaac moves to greet them all and exchange handshakes. It warms my heart to see folks turning out to pay their respects. Jim was only here a few months, but already he was putting down roots, acting as a leader in his community. Just like back home.

"Isaac tells me you knew Boisclair from Georgia," the minister says to me.

"We both did," I say, indicating Jefferson and myself. "He was good friends with my daddy, and always kind to me. Helped me out of trouble when I needed it most."

"Amen," Isaac says. "That's the kind of man he was."

"Amen," the minister says. "Well, let's get started. Who's going to help lower the coffin?"

Jefferson and I both step forward. With help from Henry and Isaac and the two caretakers, we do a creditable job of lifting it off the wagon and lowering it with ropes into the hole.

"Whew!" says one of the attendants. "He was a heavy fellow."

"He was solid gold," I say, wiping sweat from my forehead. "The stone on which you set your foundation. Worked hard every day of his life."

"Amen," Isaac says.

"Amen," echo the others.

The minister lifts a well-worn pocket Bible, its leather cover flaking at the edges, licks his finger, and opens to the right page without any help from a bookmark.

"Today's word is from Matthew, chapter six, verses nineteen to twenty-one. 'Lay not up for yourselves treasures upon earth, where moth and rust doth corrupt, and where thieves break through and steal.'"

I suffer a brief pang of conscience, and I share a glance with Jefferson, who also lowers his face in what I assume is a fleeting twinge of shame.

" 'But lay up for yourselves treasures in heaven, where neither moth nor rust doth corrupt, and where thieves do not break through nor steal. For where your treasure is, there will your heart be also.' "

He delivers a short sermon about people coming to California in search of gold, when what they really need to find is a congregation of souls, a community of like-minded spirits. He says that when the gold fails and the money runs out, as it surely will, God will still be there to help us, and the way he helps us is by surrounding us with the right people.

Brother Jim, he points out, was one of the right people. Even though he'd only been in San Francisco a few months, he'd made it his business to look out for others, like Isaac here, who needed a hand finding a home, or Brother Hampton, who needed the community to lead him out of Babylon and rescue him from unjust imprisonment.

For where your treasure is, there will your heart be also.

I glance around at my own small community—Becky and the children, Henry, the Major, and most of all Jefferson. I have treasure richer than gold, if I have friends like these. And it's true; they have my heart.

The minister would say I'm laying up treasure in heaven, where thieves do not break through nor steal, but he'd be wrong. My treasure is still worldly, still vulnerable, and I've already lost too much of it. Theresa and Martin, my parents, and now Jim—all stolen from me.

Maybe I'm just as greedy as any ne'er-do-well taken by gold fever. It's just that I'm greedy for friends. Greedy for a home.

The minister ends by leading us all in a hymn. It's not one that I've ever heard, but I appreciate the sentiment.

"Steer well! The harbor just ahead
Aglow with glory's ray,
Will on thee golden luster shed,
From out the gates of day,
And waiting there are longing hands
That thrill to clasp thine own,
And lead thee through the heav'nly land
Into the bright unknown."

It's fitting we sing this song as we view California's Golden Gate to the bay, still strewn with morning fog, lit on fire by the sunrise. Jim would have loved it.

The minister bows his head and prays. Then we take turns tossing handfuls of dirt onto the casket. Andy enthusiastically throws fistful after fistful, until Becky guides him clear. The two cemetery attendants finish the job with their shovels; I imagine filling a grave goes a lot faster than digging one. When they're done packing down dirt, a little mound remains. I lift Melancthon's cross from the wagon and jab the long, pointed end into the ground, leaning hard until it's firmly set.

I reach into my pocket for gold coins to hand out, two to the minister, and one each to the attendants and to Isaac.

"You don't need to do this," the minister says, but it seems like more of a formal protest than a genuine one. The other coins disappear quickly into their owners' pockets.

"I do, for Jim's sake," I say. "Thank you for coming out today."

"Thank you, and God bless all of you," the minister says.

"When will you know about the fate of Hampton?"

"As soon as the sheriff has time to see me and sign the papers. Seems he's busy at the moment, with the auction just yesterday."

"And evicting people from their houses all week long," Isaac adds.

"We mean to see Hampton free," I say.

"We're handling it," the minister assures us firmly.

"We look out for our own," Isaac adds.

There's a lot of hand-shaking and farewelling, and after all of Jim's friends have trickled away, our group finds itself standing in the cemetery at the foot of Jim's grave. Jefferson just stares at it, shaking his head, as if he can't believe what's just happened.

"So what's next?" Becky asks me.

"We go into the lion's den," I say.

"Might be tricky," Mary says. "The hardest part yet."

Jefferson kicks a clod of dirt at the foot of the grave. "Let's ruin him."

The Major clasps Jefferson on the shoulder. "Even *I'm* willing to put on some frippery and attend a party, so long as there's a chance to set Frank Dilley to rights. That son of a—"

Becky clears her throat abruptly, and the Major jumps.

"Beeswax. That son of a beeswax."

"Ma, what do bees whack?" Andy whispers.

"Hush, darling," Becky says.

Henry is the only one who seems delighted at the prospect. "This is going to be the biggest, most exclusive party in the history of San Francisco. Maybe in the history of California. You couldn't drag me away with horses. And that's before we get to any of the other business."

I can't help grinning at his enthusiasm. "And you, Becky? This all depends on you. I would never do anything to put your children in harm's way, on purpose or by accident. If you have any doubts or reservations, just say the word and we're done."

Becky bites her lower lip, which is never a good sign. She pulls Olive close and gives her a tight hug, puzzling the girl. Then she reaches out for Andy, to tousle his imperfectly combed hair, but he dodges her and starts darting around everyone's legs.

"Bees whack this," he sings. "Bees whack that, bees whack the bear with the bowler hat!"

Becky gazes at her unruly son, her face full of warmth. Full of love. My mama used to look at me like that.

"Oh, of course I'm in," she says at last. "That man's so low he has to reach up to rub the belly of a snake. He should be stepped on like the vermin he is."

"That's what I hoped you'd say." I grab Andy as he runs by and make as if to toss him into the back of the wagon. He squeals in delight. "Let's get ready."

Chapter Twenty

*H*enry offered to hire a coach for the evening, something to convey us to Hardwick's soiree in style and comfort—at my expense, of course. But it turns out there are a limited number of carriages to be hired in San Francisco, and we were too late to schedule the lowliest driver with a dung cart.

"I could take all of you in the wagon," Melancthon offers when Henry breaks the news to us.

"I would rather walk a hundred miles," Becky says, "than be bumped around in a wagon like some poor country girl on a hay ride."

She had enough wagon riding to last a lifetime.

I add, "Plus, it's better if you aren't seen with us."

Melancthon presses his lips tight, making me wonder how much he has guessed. But then he nods, and that's that.

So we're going to walk.

As the night falls, we gather in the galley of the *Charlotte*, dressed in our best finery. For Becky and the Major, that means the same clothes they wore to Jim's funeral, but brightened with a few decorative flourishes. Becky paces nervously, irritating Baby Girl Joyner. I don't pretend to know much about babies, but from what I've seen, they must be like cats, sensitive to every fleeting emotion of the person who holds them. Before the tiny girl can get too upset, the Major offers to hold her, and both she and Becky calm right down.

Jefferson sidles up to me. "We might have one of those one day," he whispers in my ear.

"We might have a whole mess of them," I say. "I just hope we can bring them into a world a little safer than this one."

"Becky seems to be doing all right with hers," he points out. "And so will we."

And that's a good thing, because the only thing about children I know for certain is that they tend to follow a wedding the way light follows the sun. I reach out and squeeze Jefferson's hand.

Mary rolls her eyes at us from her seat at the table. She is taking Jasper's place tonight, since the invitation doesn't specify names except to say "Leah Westfall and seven companions." She wears a nondescript dress of brown muslin, and a heavy cloak with a cowl that will hide her face from Frank Dilley.

"You ready for this?" I ask.

She grins. "You know I am."

Henry wears a suit of deep navy blue, with a bright yellow double-breasted waistcoat. He struts around, waiting for someone to notice. Mary has no patience for frippery, and Becky and the Major are too preoccupied—with the children and possibly each other—so I take pity.

"No peacock ever looked finer," I tell him.

He straightens, head held high. "I look dashing, don't I?"

"San Francisco agrees with you."

"I just wish it would agree with me in a more financial capacity." He sighs.

Jefferson is trying to fix the narrow tie that he's added to his shirt.

"It looks like you're tying a halter hitch," I tell him. "You aren't pulling a cow out of a ditch. Here, my daddy taught me. Just"—I slap his hands out of the way—"let me take care of that for you."

He waits patiently while I undo the horrible knot. He says, "If my da owned a tie, I never saw him wear it."

"Your da didn't do a lot of things he ought to have done."

He flinches.

"I mean, you're twice the man he ever was."

"Didn't take it as a criticism. Sometimes it just feels like I'll spend my whole life trying to catch up with all the things he didn't do."

"You've already caught up and run past him," I say, earning a smile. "Here's how my daddy taught me: the long end is a rabbit being chased by a fox, and the short end is a log. The rabbit goes over the log . . . under the log . . . around the log . . . and through the rabbit hole." I make the motions as I talk, tying the knot for him. "Then you slide it up tight, and you're done.

Don't pull on the rabbit; that'll make it too tight. Just slide the knot up like this."

"So the rabbit gets away?"

"Daddy was the type to always pity the frightened rabbit over the hungry fox."

"Tonight we need to be a rabbit who thinks like a fox."

"Or a fox who looks like a rabbit," I say, standing back. "That looks . . ." Sudden shyness hitches my words. "You . . . Jefferson McCauley Kingfisher, I don't mind saying you're the finest-looking young man west of the Mississippi."

He blinks, a little stunned. "And you're beautiful."

I shrug. "The best thing about this dress is it's freshly washed." It's an unremarkable calico, blue to match Becky and Henry, the fabric a little faded. "But I don't mind being a bit ordinary tonight."

"Lee, there's nothing *ordinary* about you," Jefferson says.

Before I can reply, we're interrupted by an overly dramatic sigh. Everyone is staring at us. Mary mimes a huge yawn.

"I offer my enthusiastic support for young love," Becky says. "But can I beg you to hold off on your explorations until tomorrow?"

The Major sits on one of the benches, adjusting the straps that hold his wooden leg—a newer, bulkier design he just finished making. "I think the job that never gets started never gets finished. So let's get started."

Becky says, "Exactly my point. Do you have the invitation?"

I grab it from the table and hold in the air. My hand trembles. "Right here."

The Major hefts Baby Girl Joyner. "Then off we go."

We are solemn and silent as we exit the *Charlotte* and close the door behind us—as if we're still at Jim's funeral. So much hinges on tonight. There are so many things that must go exactly right.

My hand goes to the locket at my throat, but of course it's gone. If all goes according to plan, I'll never see it again, which puts a little ache in my chest. The locket will be nearby for a short while longer, and I reach out with my gold sense toward the Major and discover where he's hidden it. The steady step-*thump* of the Major's gait feels like it could be my own heartbeat.

"I can carry the baby for a spell," Mary says.

The Major gives her up gratefully. He puts on a brave face, but I reckon walking long distances is hard on him, especially with a new leg he's not quite used to yet. I take the lead, with Jefferson walking beside me and everyone else at my back. At the very end of the line, I'm aware of Olive and Andy quietly tagging behind.

Even if I hadn't been to Hardwick's house once already, I'd know which direction to go. Hardwick must have the contents of nearly a dozen gold-filled safes at his house, because it's like a toothache throbbing in my jaw. Blindfold me and bind my hands, and I could still find my way.

But even without my powers, there's no mistaking our path.

First we follow carriages as they rattle past. Then the carriages stop, jamming together at an intersection, waiting in what is only the slightest semblance of a line. We maneuver through the traffic to the place where impatient guests disembark from their assorted rides and join small throngs flowing along the margins of the street. Lanterns light the street and the gardens beyond the wall. Music swells, a Mexican band playing waltzes in the son jalisciense style, with violins, harps, and guitars. Laughter and shouts of delight rise above the music and float toward us.

A line of people awaits entry at the garden gate. Becky takes the baby from Mary.

"I don't mind holding her," Mary says, maybe a little bit wistfully.

"I need something to do right now," Becky replies, clutching the nameless girl to her chest like a shield.

Ahead of us, several people are turned away—first a group of drunken miners, and soon after, a white man and his Indian wife.

"What if they don't let us in?" Becky whispers.

"Then we give up this life of crime and get a good night's sleep?" the Major says.

I glare at him before realizing he's joking.

"They'll let us in," Jefferson says confidently.

"I know the fellows at the gate," I assure them, indicating Large and Larger. But the baby, sensing Becky's anxiety, fusses in her arms, so the Major leans over and sings softly to her.

"There was an old woman tossed up in a basket
Seventeen times as high as the moon
Where she was going, I could not but ask it,
For in her hand she carried a broom

'Old woman, old woman, old woman,' quoth I,
'Oh wither, oh wither, oh wither so high?'
'To sweep the cobwebs from the sky,
But I'll be with you by and by.'"

The baby giggles and grabs at the Major's beard; he leans down farther to let her take hold of it. "That's a silly song," Becky says, and though her words are judgmental, her tone is soft and her gaze fast on his face.

"My father sang it to me," the Major says.

He smiles and Becky smiles back, and I don't say a word, because they are the unlikeliest pair ever, but it seems that slowly and surely they have turned into a pair.

"Hello again," says Large, as we reach the wide iron gate that provides the only entrance into the estate.

"Did you know you would be working here when I inquired about the party last night?" I ask.

They ignore my question. "Do you have your invitation?" asks Larger.

I hand it over.

"We were told to expect eight," Large says, checking a list of names.

Larger looks over our heads. "Counting the young ones and the infant, I see eight."

"I thought the young ones were much younger," Large says as he considers Olive and Andy.

"Children have to grow up fast in California," Becky says smoothly.

"That's the truth," Larger says, waving us in.

We hurry inside before they can change their minds or get a closer look, and then we all stop short, a little over-whelmed. To our left is a lush garden with creeping vines and spired yucca flowers and a single sprawling oak. Beside the oak, the band plays gaily from a temporary stage as couples waltz nearby. Fires glow inside clay ovens, radiating warmth and inviting guests to gather. Lanterns hang from branches and posts, illuminating gaming tables where people are play-ing Spanish monte and rolling dice. To the right, the doors are thrown open to the rambling wings of the house. Violin music and laughter flow from the windows.

It's a wonderland. A place where magic might happen.

And the thing I notice most, that thing that lights me up from all sides, is my sense of gold. I feel like a fly caught in a spiderweb of golden strands. The center of the web is inside the house, where the safes must be stored. But strands shoot out in all directions: at the gambling tables, in every purse and pocket, even near the stage, where the band keeps a col-lection bag.

A young man in a white shirt and a thin black tie approaches with a tray of drinks. Henry snatches up a glass.

"Dancing and games are to your left," the young man says, which we can see very well for ourselves. Then he gestures toward the right. "Food and drink are inside the house."

I follow the direction of his hand. The open double doors frame a familiar profile. The face turns toward us, and the man strides in our direction.

"Frank Dilley," I whisper in warning.

"That's my cue to disappear," Mary says, and she steps away, blending into the swirl of partygoers.

"Olive, Andy," Becky says quickly, "it's time to run and play."

The two of them peel off, their faces hidden by their hats, and disappear into the crowd.

"If you don't mind, I'll follow them," Henry adds, downing his drink in a single gulp and putting the empty glass back on the server's tray.

I glance around for Helena Russell. She is surely in attendance. We all have a job to do here tonight, and right now, my job is to make sure Hardwick and his crew are looking at me. It's the only thing I should be thinking about.

My hand goes to clutch Mama's locket, but of course it's gone. I stride toward Frank as if my knees aren't suddenly wobbling and my heart suddenly pounding. "Thank you for the invitation," I say brightly. "Lovely party."

Frank pretends I don't exist and approaches the Major, glaring down his nose at him. Like he regrets not killing him after the buffalo stampede. Like he might go ahead and correct that mistake right now.

"You showed up," Frank says glumly.

"I thought you'd be glad to see me," the Major replies. "After all, the invitation was delivered by your own hand."

"I can't figure out what drives you, Wally. I guess an old cripple like you is only good for doing women's work and watching children. I'd kill myself before I'd ever do a skirt's job."

The Major smiles at Frank, but the corners of his eyes are as serious as a gunshot. "Dilley, you're neither strong enough nor smart enough to do a skirt's job."

"The Major is the cleverest carpenter in all of California," Becky says. "And he does the work of ten men. We couldn't get by without him."

Frank ignores her too. "We never would have made it across the desert if you were in charge of the wagon train," he says.

The Major's smile disappears. "If I'd stayed in charge, we *all* would have made it across."

Becky opens her mouth but changes her mind about whatever she was going to say. Frank is one of those men who can't feel big unless he's making somebody else smaller. And suddenly, it's like a click in my mind, the way everything settles into place. Frank is lonely. He wanted us here. He needed familiar faces, people he could put down so he could feel better about himself.

"I'm sorry for you, Frank." The words rush out of my mouth before I can stop them, but I decide I don't want to stop them. "You were in charge of the wagon train, and you couldn't keep it together. You worked for my uncle Hiram's mine, and we know how that went. Now you're working for Hardwick, and he's going to leave you behind when he goes to New York. You aren't good enough for anything or anybody."

He puts his hand on his gun. "I was good enough to put your friend Jim in the ground."

And just like that, my pity turns to anger. In fact, I'm so angry now that tears start leaking from my eyes, but a show of tears is probably a good thing.

Jefferson steps forward before I can reply. "You're a murderer, Frank Dilley. Plain and simple."

Frank opens his mouth, taking a menacing step toward us, but he's interrupted by a cheerful greeting.

Hardwick approaches, arm in arm with Helena, who is resplendent in a blue velvet gown. With her auburn hair and pale white skin, she's the colors of the American flag. I focus hard on my anger at Frank, then the scents of beeswax candles and spiced cider, the flickering lanterns and the swirling people.

"Miss Westfall. I was hoping I would get the chance to see you toni—" Hardwick notices Frank's fuming gaze and the hand on his gun. "Go on, Dilley, get out of here."

Frank practically snarls, but he shoots one more angry glance at our group, then strides casually away toward the house, as if that was his plan all along.

"Some dogs you have to keep on a leash," Hardwick says.

"And when the dog bites people anyway?" I ask.

He shrugs. "In one more day, that dog won't be my problem." Hardwick indicates his companion. "You remember my associate, Miss Helena Russell."

We exchange wary nods. Her eyes glitter in the lantern light—merely blue right now. "Pleased to see you again," I lie. "May I introduce my friends . . ." I look around, but Jefferson and the Major have wisely made themselves scarce. "My friend, Mrs. Rebecca Joyner."

Becky curtsies. "We've had the pleasure of meeting once before, Mr. Hardwick, Miss Russell. In the law offices on Portsmouth Square. I was trying to recover possession of my house."

"And did it all work out?" Hardwick asks.

"That remains to be seen," she says.

Hardwick reaches into his pocket and pulls out a pair of solid gold dice. He rolls them in the palm of his hand. I can sense their weight and balance. They are perfect. Beautiful.

"I had them made especially for this evening's festivities," Hardwick says. "Can I persuade you to try your hand at hazard?"

I eye the golden dice. It would be an interesting test of my skills. But I tamp that thought down as soon as it occurs to me. "Hazard? No, thank you, I've faced enough hazards on the road from Georgia to California, and a few more since I arrived."

He has such a patronizing smile. Very like my uncle's when he was eager to explain the world to me. "Hazard is the name of a dice game. I think the origin of our common use of the word comes from the game, and not the other way around."

It's a trap. I'm sure of it. The trap is even called "hazard," which ought to be a warning sign, like the church bells ringing when there's a big fire. But my job tonight is to keep as much attention on me as possible, especially from Hardwick and Helena.

I glance around. Jefferson, the Major, Olive, and Andy are nowhere to be seen. Henry sits at a monte table with the governor and other high rollers. Becky and I are alone. "What do you think, Becky?"

"I think Mr. Joyner loved gambling even though he was never any good at it, and lost far more often than he won."

"But he did love it, right?" I turn back to Hardwick. "I'll give it a try. But you'll have to teach me how."

Something about Hardwick's triumphant smile sets my belly to squirming. He tosses the golden dice in his hand. Helena's eyes gleam; does she already know how this will end?

Chapter Twenty-One

*H*ardwick leads us over to a table shaped like a tub, long and narrow with high sides and lined with green felt. We watch players tossing dice into the tub, and he explains the rules to me—something about a main, a chance, a nick, and so on—but I'm not paying close attention because a tapestry hanging on the wall behind the table catches my eye.

It's the new seal of California that's been proposed, hastily embroidered but clear enough to parse. In the background is the sprawling San Francisco Bay. Miners work in the hills around it, hefting their pickaxes. But what really catches my attention is the woman in the foreground. She wears flowing robes and a helmet, and holds a spear in one hand. Like she's ready for war.

"That's Minerva," Becky whispers in my ear. "The Roman goddess of wisdom." I hear the grin in her voice when she adds, "It's appropriate they'd choose a woman for the seal, don't you think? I hope it gets approved."

I sense Hardwick hovering at my back. The gentlemen around the table shift to make room for us. He greets everyone, waving his golden dice, as more gather around. It's a split second before I realize he's started talking about me.

"A young woman lost all her family back home in Georgia and decided to pack up with some of her friends and come west to California to find gold. And she found it! She and all of her friends found gold and established the prosperous town of Glory, one of the jewels of our new state. And this town, with all of its miners and prominent new residents, chose her as its representative. This young lady right here."

The room grows quiet. Everyone is listening to Hardwick.

"Last Christmas," he continues, "she came to me in Sacramento and asked for my help establishing a charter for their town, to protect their claims and their community."

Every eye is on me. I sense disbelief in several, so I lock gazes with them and try to stare them down, each and every one individually. *That's right, folks, eyes right here.*

"Now, what can *I* do to help with a town charter?" Hardwick asks disingenuously. "Yes, I know many of our politicians, but I'm not one myself. But it made me think, maybe I *should* be. If I really want to help people like this little lady right here, I ought to consider politics. I don't mean to cast any aspersions on our local leaders. I think they're the best in the whole United States."

This brings forth murmurs of "Hear, hear!" and "Right you are!"

"But what America needs right now is not another general,

not another tired old politician from the cities back east. What America needs is a true pioneer to lead them. Someone who's been in the wilderness and knows how things work out here in the West, for a change. So I'm not making any promises, gentlemen—leave that to the professional politicians!"

This earns some laughter.

"But I'm going to head east, and if you see my name on a ballot come the next election, I hope you will give your fellow Californian due consideration."

Men cheer and clap. Several promise to support Hardwick on the spot, while a few others hint at all the help his new administration will need. If they're all cut from the same cloth as Hardwick, it promises to be a government of thieves, by thieves, and for thieves.

"That brings me back to our guest here," he says. "The Golden Goddess. That's what the miners called her."

My cheeks flush. Why bring that up? What's he trying to do? Maybe it's a warning. _He knows what I_ . . . I shove the thought away as soon as it pops up, concentrating instead on the generously oiled mustache of the gentleman closest to me.

"She represents the opportunity that California provides for all of us—to take our chance, to strike it rich, to make something different of ourselves. I had these golden dice made in her honor." He rattles them in his hand and tosses them on the table so everyone can see them, then snatches them up again. "And now we're all going to teach her to play the game of hazard."

He's using me as a symbol, a way to further his own ends.

It's disgusting. The worst violation. And yet, every single eye is on me, exactly as I need. "I've never played before," I say sweetly. "So I'll need everyone's help."

Various middle-aged men shout advice, telling me exactly what to do. One fellow with long sideburns and a garish red cravat slides in and slips an arm around me, but I wriggle away like a snake, and Becky steps in before he can try again. I give her a glance of gratitude.

Hardwick pulls out a stack of gold coins and places it between himself and the gentleman acting as the bank. He declares lucky number seven as his main and rolls the dice. The golden cubes bounce off the back wall of the tub—almost too fast to track with my gold sense—and land upright, with three pips and four. A seven. The dealer doubles Hardwick's money, and there's a flurry of bets as the viewers wager on his next roll.

This time the dice roll up two single pips.

"Snake eyes," says the dealer, and Hardwick loses.

The banker collects money and pays out a variety of bets while Hardwick gathers up the dice and rattles them in the cup of his hand.

Manipulating the dice will take a lot of concentration. And maybe I shouldn't do it with Helena Russell so nearby. But the dice sing to me, so perfect and clear, that I can't resist. Hardwick rolls them again. I pinch my tongue between my teeth to help myself focus. The dice bounce off the far wall of the table and roll across the velvet. They're going to stop . . . *now!* One lands on five, and I take the tiniest split second to continue the roll, pushing it toward the six.

It plops over to a four. I need to be more delicate.

Everyone cheers Hardwick's success. I force myself to smile.

When my turn comes, I reach into my pocket for my last gold coins. I hesitate before putting them on the table. To keep Hardwick occupied as long as possible, I have to win. I pick a number and rattle the dice in my hand. I'm concentrating so hard on the dice themselves, readying myself to flip them over, that I don't throw them hard enough, and they never reach the wall of the table to bounce back.

"Can I try again?" I beg, and most folks are for giving the little lady a second chance, so the dealer gathers the dice and hands them back to me for another throw. I hold them up to the baby in Becky's arms and make a kissing noise. "For newborn luck," I say.

The baby opens her mouth and tries to eat them, which I take for a good sign.

This time my throw goes better. After the dice bounce, I beckon with my fingers, one on each hand, tugging the dice toward me until I get the nick and double my money.

Feeling nervous, I grab my original coins and pull them back to me, leaving only my winnings. A future stake. If I'm going to bet, from now on it will only be with Hardwick's money.

As Hardwick and I go back and forth, my world shrinks to the volume of two golden dice. At first I make a lot of mistakes, lucky to move the dice at all and make it look natural. But as we take turns, my skills improve, and not coincidentally with it, my luck. Hardwick loses more money than he wins, and I win more than I lose. My focus is razor sharp. Maybe too sharp. Surely Helena can sense what I'm doing.

Becky becomes very tense every time I throw the dice. "I start to see why Mr. Joyner enjoyed the thrill of gambling," she confides to me in a whisper.

"Henry, too," I say. "Sometimes it feels good to take a chance on something."

Though I'm doing my best to make sure no chance is involved. Hardwick has been betting on my throws, and I start betting on his. Even when he wins, I win more. Which deflects attention away from my control of the dice.

After a long winning streak, when I've amassed a large stack of coins, Helena Russell says, "I marvel at how lucky the young lady has been. I don't know that I've ever seen someone so lucky."

Her blue eyes are flecked with violet. Just flecks. What does that mean?

Maybe it means I've pushed it too far. Or lost control of my thoughts. I should lose the next round on purpose.

Hardwick pauses before throwing the dice. "Come on, Miss Westfall," he cajoles. "Bet big. Bet like a grown woman and a true Californian. Give me a chance to win back some portion of the money I've lost tonight."

The crowd is all for this. The bigger the stakes, the more they cheer.

I'm in control of this game now. I push all the coins that I've won toward the banker. "Will that do?" I ask.

"Surely the Golden Goddess has something else to add to the pot?" Hardwick says.

I hold up my empty hands. "That's everything." Except for my original stake, which I'll need for the journey back to Glory.

"You must have something more."

"I'm sorry, but I don't—"

"What about the deed to the *Charlotte*?"

My heart stops. "I couldn't."

"Surely you don't plan to stay in San Francisco anyway. You're going back to Glory soon, right? That's why you wanted the town charter. You'll have no need for the *Charlotte* if you're not here."

"Don't do it," whispers Becky. "I don't trust him."

She's right. This was his endgame all along.

"But the *Charlotte* is my home here in San Francisco," I say, loudly so everyone can hear. "I'll stay there every time I'm in town. I've grown fond of it."

"Yes," Becky says. "It's not Glory, but it's a home of sorts."

If I knew, for sure and certain, that I had provided enough of a distraction already, I would walk away right now. But I don't know, and we won't get another chance. I have to keep playing.

Besides, my head buzzes with the power I've used. The dice are my servants, doing whatever I ask. The crowd is cheering for me to take the risk. "You're on a winning streak!" someone says. "You can't lose!" says another. He's right. With my power, I can't lose.

"I've got this," I whisper to Becky. And louder, for everyone's benefit: "I put my whole stake into the *Charlotte*! What would the good Lord say if I gambled it away?" If I'm going to do this, I have to make a spectacle of it.

"Lee!" Becky pleads.

The governor himself saunters over. "I confess, I'm curious to see the Golden Goddess in action," he says. *In action?* My heart takes a tumble.

I glance over at Helena Russell, whose eyes are suddenly the bright, rich purple of royalty. Something is very not right here.

"Dear governor, don't tell me you believe miners' tall tales!" Becky says with a laugh, and suddenly all eyes are on her. She spreads her smile around, bestowing it graciously on each besotted businessman. More than me, maybe even more than Hardwick, Becky is suited to this atmosphere, this world. She's the one who practically glows in the golden lantern light, and I'm grateful for it. It gives me a chance to catch my breath, to calm my nerves.

Which is a good thing, because the governor's sudden interest, along with Becky's charm, has magnified everyone's enthusiasm, and I hear cries of "Golden Goddess!" and "Minerva!" and "It's your lucky night!"

"But what are *you* wagering?" I ask Hardwick. "What are you putting at risk?"

"Besides my reputation?" he asks, drawing a laugh from the crowd. "I mean, I'm taking a big risk being seen losing to a little lady, even one as charming as yourself."

I grit my teeth. "Toughen up, Hardwick. Put something on the table, or I'll take my winnings and walk."

This electrifies the crowd. Cheers of "No!" and "Do it!" and "Place a wager!" sound all around us. The crowd presses in tight, waiting to see what happens.

I start to gather my coins.

"Hold on," he says. He waves over the crowd to one of his servants, who runs off and returns almost immediately with a rosewood cigar box full of gold coins—I don't need to count it to know it's twice what I have on the table, worth more than I paid for the _Charlotte_. Hardwick starts to unload the coins.

He had this box prepared ahead of time, for it to turn up so fast.

"Throw in the box too," I tell him, my voice shaking a little. "I like that silver inlay."

"Very well." He smiles, puts the coins back inside, closes the lid, and sets it on the table. The same servant returns with a piece of paper, and pen and ink. I scrawl out "Deed for the _Charlotte_," and sign my name, and now everyone knows what a disgrace my penmanship is. I toss the paper onto the table.

"Will that do?" I ask.

"Not usually," Hardwick says. With a sweep of his hand, he adds, "But with all these fine Californians to witness, it'll do just fine."

Echoes of "Hear, hear!" rise around us.

"This is a mistake," Becky whispers anxiously. The baby fusses in her arms.

"Maybe," I whisper back. I'm flexing my fingers under the

table, and focusing my thoughts on the gold dice in Hardwick's hand. "But I'm feeling lucky."

Hardwick rattles the dice in his hand and then pauses. He glances over his shoulder, beckoning for someone. Helena.

Who is there, as always, watching. She squeezes through the crowd to reach him, and he holds out his fist with the dice. "For luck," he says.

She leans in, smiles, and—keeping those shining violet eyes on me—blows on the dice.

Ice cracks down my spine.

Everyone is cheering. Hardwick draws back his arm, and I concentrate, waiting for the moment the dice bounce off the back wall of the table. He flings them hard, and—

One die goes flying over the edge of the table, bounces off the banker, and falls on the ground. The banker ducks down quickly and comes up with it. He starts to hand it back, and then pauses.

"One of the corners is smashed," he says, almost apologetically. "It won't roll evenly."

He switched it. I can sense a third die still near the floor, maybe stuffed into his shoe. Or maybe I'm imagining it. There's so much gold in this room, and none of it as familiar as my locket. I could accuse him of cheating, but if I'm wrong, or if I can't prove it, I'll be in even worse trouble. The banker hands the die around the table, so everyone can see that it's ruined.

"Alas, gold is so much softer than bone," Hardwick says. "I guess we'll have to retire these dice and replace them with an ordinary pair."

My pulse jumps in my throat. "Sure."

Becky grabs my hand and gives it a squeeze.

Hardwick pockets the damaged die, and the banker retrieves a conventional pair. They're passed around for inspection, but I can't focus enough to look at them. My stomach is churning, enough that I might throw up. I've played right into Hardwick's hands again. Hardwick's and Russell's. They've been steps ahead of me the whole time. Hardwick knows what I can do after all, and he knew I'd use my power to cheat.

He makes a show of shaking the dice again, and pauses to hold out his fist for Helena. When she leans in to blow on the dice, he snatches his fist away, making everybody in the crowd laugh.

He pauses to look at me. "I'll make my own luck this time."

I smile, but I'm sure it looks sickly. The dice are undoubtedly weighted to favor his call. There's not a man in the crowd that would admit to it, though.

Hardwick tosses the dice. Perfectly this time.

I close my eyes as they bounce off the back of the table.

They thump along the felt, rumbling to a stop.

Half the crowd cheers. Half the crowd groans in disappointment.

When I open my eyes again, the banker is pushing the stack of coins towards Hardwick. He picks up the deed for the *Charlotte*, snapping the corners.

"Oh," Becky breathes. "This is not good at all."

"You win some, you lose some," Hardwick says, waving the

makeshift deed, taunting me with my own signature. "Let me give this to the source of all my good fortune this year, the woman who deserves it most."

With a flourish, he hands it to Helena. She smiles with gratitude, but there's a tremor at the corner of her mouth, and after she folds the sheet of paper and tucks it into her bodice, she lets her hand linger over her heart for a moment, as if assuring herself the deed is actually there.

"That's all for me here," Hardwick says, with a wave of his hand. "If you gentlemen will excuse me, I need to be a good host and visit with the other guests at my party. I return you all to your previous amusements."

As he turns to go, the governor at his heels, I push through the crowd to follow them. Becky grabs my arm and pulls me back. "Let him go," she says.

"He played me. He played me perfectly."

"He knew exactly what you were going to do," she says.

"Because of his Irish woman," I growl.

"No," Becky says, circling around to stand in front of me and block my view. "No, he knew because the two of you were dancing, and you followed his every lead. You let him dictate the tempo and the steps, every step of the way, right up to the end when . . . why are you grinning like a cat that caught the cream?"

"I . . . I can't say. Or even think it. Not yet."

Becky's eyes narrow. "I see."

Quickly she guides me away from the crowds at the gaming tables to a quieter spot beneath a tree hung with lanterns. From here we have a perfect view through the double door of the proposed seal of California, and Becky stares at it, rocking the baby back and forth.

She says, "In that case, you have to calm down, control your thoughts, keep your eye on the horizon." The baby yawns, which is the most adorable thing I've ever seen. "We still have a ways to go."

"I know." I glance around the garden, trying to reorient myself. Hardwick is giving another speech to a different crowd. Henry is still seated at one of the card tables, laughing like he's winning, or at least having a good time. I see glimpses of Olive and Andy—or rather their hats—in the crowd around the band and dance floor. Maybe Becky should pretend to be more concerned about them.

But Jefferson and the Major are nowhere to be seen. When I turn toward the house looking for them, Helena is walking toward us.

Becky sees her at the same time. Taking hold of my arm, she steers me the other direction. "Let's go. I prefer to be in polite company."

"Wait," Helena says. "I just want a quick word."

I hesitate. Becky gives me a stern look, then hugs the baby closer as the other woman approaches. "Be careful," forms on Becky's lips as she hurries away. "Mind your mind."

I think hard about grief. Over losing the _Charlotte_, Jim getting shot, the loss of my parents, now a year gone. Even the empty space at my chest where my locket used to be. Grief is an easy thing to think about. It fills me up, leaving room for nothing else.

Helena stops a few feet away, near yet wary. An infuriating half smile plays about her lips, as if she's pondering hidden knowledge. Her gown and jewelry sparkle, her red hair stuns. You almost can't tell she's a hardworking mountain girl, just like me.

That's what centers me.

I don't want to be anything like her. I don't want to be the special *associate* of some man. A trophy to be shown off at all the balls and parties. I just want Jefferson, a few friends, and work that makes me happy.

That's the difference between me and Hardwick, I suppose, and people like him, too. No matter how much they have, it'll never be enough. They'll never be satisfied. I don't want to always want.

"Thank you for the ship," she says for an opening sally.

I open my mouth to say something possibly rude and insulting, but Mary catches my eye from across the courtyard. She holds up two fingers. The signal that all is ready.

I laugh.

Helena's eyes—mere blue—flare slightly, the only indication of her shaken confidence. I nod toward her bosom, where she slipped the hastily scrawled deed. "Enjoy your slip of paper."

Her next words are cold as ice. "What are you talking about?"

I can't stop my grin, and I don't want to. "I don't legally own that ship. I never did. It's in a man's name. Even if I did own the ship, I couldn't sign away the deed." I bat my eyelashes. "I'm just a little lady. You see, it's a matter of coverture—"

"Hardwick will testify," she snaps.

"No, he's leaving for New York tomorrow. Going to take his millions and buy his way into a political career. The businessman-become-president. He doesn't care about the *Charlotte*. Or you. Unless he's taking you with him?"

For the first time since I've met her, I see panic in her eyes. "I . . . turned down his offer to accompany him to New York."

"And I don't own the ship."

She pauses, sizing me up. "You're too honorable. You wouldn't use the same laws that are unfair to you to treat another woman unfairly."

"Not usually. But I don't care if you were a poor girl down on her luck who found a way to escape some nasty problems. You allied yourself with a monster, so you don't get concessions."

It could be a trick of the flickering lantern light, but I might see tears shining in her eyes. "Seems I backed the wrong horse," she says.

"Do you see that with your power, or are you just guessing?"

"Neither. I knew justice mattered to you, even before I saw into your mind."

And there it is at last. All our cards on the table, with not a bluff left between us. She does see our thoughts. I suspected it, acted on that suspicion as if it was fact, and yet her admission still chills me. "You can't own the *Charlotte* either, as a woman," I point out. "You'd have to find a man to hold the deed for you. Someone you trust as much as you trusted Hardwick."

She shakes her head. "Oh, I don't trust him at all. I'd never go to New York with him. But you're right. To do business here, I'll have to find someone I trust." She taps a lip thoughtfully.

I admit, it warms my heart a little to know Helena doesn't trust Hardwick either. Maybe we have more in common than I thought. "I had several people to choose from," I say. "It was no problem at all, finding someone to hold the deed for me. Trust is a great benefit of having real friends. I highly recommend trying it."

She glares. "Don't act so holier-than-thou with me. People like us don't have real friends."

This poor woman. "They've proven themselves over and over. Whenever I've had trouble that my own abilities couldn't solve, my friends have been there to help me."

"Your abilities." She raises an eyebrow. "Power is more like it. Your *power* is amazing. Like no gift I've ever seen."

I glance around, making sure no one is near enough to hear our conversation. The music of the band provides perfect cover. "And . . . you've seen a lot of gifts?" My question is tentative, even though I want with all my heart to know the answer.

"Not a lot. People like us are very rare. Always women, though. I knew a water dowser who could call water. And I've heard tell of others. Menders, who could fix things with the touch of their hand. Storytellers who could make you believe any lie was true. Weather witches, who knew a storm was coming even with a clear horizon, or pull a few drops of water from a cloudless sky. I once heard about a healer who could call on her powers to save a mother and baby in a childbirth gone bad. But I've never known of any power in the world like yours."

My breath stumbles. Other women with amazing gifts, people who can change the world around them for the better. "But you can see the future! Read thoughts!"

She shakes her head. "I glimpse them, at best. My mother called them the second sight. Claimed they came from the old country, way back. Mother to daughter. That's why she packed up the family and came to the States before the potato famine. She saw nothing but death if she stayed."

"You must have been young." I need to know more.

"Born on the boat over. Mother said being born on water gave my powers extra strength. Said I drew on a deep well."

"She's gone?"

"I saw her death coming, and so did she. We couldn't stop it."

My own mama passed before my very eyes. She always hinted about a childhood gone wrong, got angry whenever I used the word "witch." Now I know she was hiding powers of her own, and something awful must have happened to her in Boston, something I'll probably never know.

Helena's eyes darken with memory—whether hers or mine, I can't know. She turns as if to leave, but I grab her sleeve. "Wait! I have to know . . . how do your powers work?"

She stares down at my hand on her sleeve, and I let go, my face reddening.

"Why should I tell you anything more? We've played nice long enough."

"I'm sorry. It's just . . . I've never met anyone else who . . ."

She turns to go.

"Helena, I will give you the *Charlotte*."

She whirls back around.

"Well, I'll give *half* of it to you," I quickly amend. "If you tell me everything you know, and if you stop helping Hardwick right this instant."

"I thought it wasn't yours to give," she snaps. But she can't hide the sudden hope in her eyes.

"The gentleman who holds it in trust for me would give it away on my word, no questions asked. Look into my mind and know it to be true."

She is silent a long moment, studying me, considering. Her eyes glow violet, and I wish I could see what she was seeing.

"I even know someone who could hold it in trust for you," I coax. "Someone who would never go behind your back."

At last she says, "I believe you."

"Do we have a deal?"

She glances over her shoulder, as if Hardwick might suddenly appear in the gardens. Then she says, "We have a deal."

All the air leaves my body in a rush. "So," I say, grinning. "Tell me how your power works!"

She shrugs, seeming more resigned than happy with our new arrangement. "Let's say a fellow, like your friend Henry, comes into Hardwick's gambling den to win some money. I get glimpses of him—his intent, his need, a direct thought if it's strong enough, sometimes a peek of him at the end of the night. Maybe he's got all the chips, maybe he's about even, or maybe he's flat broke and crying into his mead."

"How does that help Hardwick?"

"I steer him toward the tables with the losers and away from the winners."

I think back to the first time I met her, with Becky in the law offices. "You saw Mrs. Joyner coming with Henry in disguise to claim her house? That's why Frank Dilley was waiting for us."

She smiles. "Yes. One of my clearer visions."

"But you can't change the future, even when you see it?"

"I tried. My mother and I both tried." Bitterness tinges her voice. "I've learned to accept what I see, work *with* it instead of against it. Good men or bad, it doesn't matter—luck flows downhill. There's no point in fighting upstream against it."

The *Charlotte* notwithstanding, she's giving everything away more freely than I expected. Maybe she's lonely. Maybe she's as eager as I am to talk to someone else with witchy gifts. I nod toward the gambling tables. "So what do you see for my friend Henry tonight?"

"Oh, Henry's going away broke, but you don't need to buy him a drink. He'll be perfectly happy." She pauses. "And I'm not sure why."

"Because he's always happy. It's his nature." I glance over my shoulder to look at Henry and smile.

And freeze instead.

Tom is strolling through the tables with an arm around Mr. Keys, who staggers drunkenly. Together, they are singing loud enough to drown out the band.

Henry laughs out loud, delighted to see Tom in his cups. He stands to say hello.

But this is *my* cue. Henry doesn't know this part of the plan. He could ruin everything. I need to reach Tom before Henry does.

I pick up my skirts and run. "Tom! Thomas Bigler!" Becky once used some choice words, and I mine my memory for them. "Thomas Bigler, you no-good, rotten, pusillanimous snake!"

The shocked crowd parts to make way for me. Henry sinks back down to his seat. I reach Tom and shove him in the chest.

"Hello, Lee," Tom says. Mr. Keys shrinks away from us both, eyes wide.

"Don't 'Hello, Lee' to me," I shout. "I can't believe you work for that scoundrel Hardwick. Not after everything he did to us. He just took the roof right from over our heads. Becky lost her house because of *you*! Jim got shot because of *you*!"

I keep advancing on him as I talk, grabbing and pushing, grabbing and pushing, until he has to grab me in return just to keep his balance.

I can't stop now. "You sold us out. You told Hardwick that Becky and Henry were going to pick up her house from the customs officer!"

"Don't blame any of those things on me," he says. "A man has to earn a living."

Party guests gather to watch the show, and a few good Samaritans try to intervene, gently coaxing us apart. Tom and I elbow them back.

"You don't have to work for *him*," I snap.

We're all tangled up, and I'm right in his face, close enough to feel his breath on me. But it's the last thing I get to say. Hands pry us apart, and rough knuckles on my collar drag me back and fling me to the ground.

Frank Dilley looms over me, Mr. Keys at his side. Tom stands beside them like a brother-in-arms, yanking down his vest and checking his pockets.

"You can't talk to Mr. Hardwick's employees that way," Dilley says. "Now get to your feet, so I can throw you out on the street where you belong."

First I smooth my dress and pat my pocket, noticing that all my coins are gone—even the original stake I painstakingly preserved. I take my time rising as the crowd presses in, every eye on us.

A baby's cry penetrates the din. Becky appears, angry infant in her arms, and stands over me like a shelter in a storm. "You can't treat a young lady that way," she says.

"Lee Westfall ain't no lady," Dilley says. "Way I remember it, she prefers to wear pants."

"You're just steamed because I wear them better than you." Dilley raises his hand as if to strike me, but Hardwick arrives, giving Dilley pause. Becky helps me to my feet.

"There's no need for trouble here," Hardwick says.

I back into the crowd, until there's no room to back away farther. Several hands reach out to steady me, and I'm not sure if they're trying to be helpful or just looking for an excuse to lay hands on a young woman. I glare at Hardwick. "You're not content to rob me, you have to threaten me, too! You're a lowdown thief."

"Miss Westfall, you can't be a guest in my home and impugn me with that kind of language," Hardwick says very reasonably.

"It's not impugning if it's the truth," I shout. "You're a thief! You sell land that isn't yours. You kick people out of houses they paid for. You steal people's most treasured possessions, the things they shipped to San Francisco, and then sell them at auction."

"Miss Westfall," Hardwick says. "I've done nothing illegal."

And that's the crux of it, isn't it? The law is always on Hardwick's side.

I glance at Tom, who gives a barely discernable nod. He has dealt with my stash of coins, and it's finally time to play my final card. I say, "You're a thief just the same. And you invited all these people here tonight"—I swing my arm around to indicate every judge, businessman, and politician in the crowd—"to rob them one last time before you leave town. Did you think no one would notice?" There. I've planted the seed. It will be up to Henry to water it and make it grow.

"Friends, friends, I apologize," Hardwick says, addressing the crowd. "Clearly she has had too much to drink. A little beer and little gambling are too much for any lady to handle."

People laugh politely, even though anyone nearby can tell I'm sober as a funeral. "I haven't touched a drop of your cheap watered-down booze."

"Clearly you brought your own," Hardwick says, getting a

few more laughs. He's so slick, nothing sticks to him. It's like watching water slide off a duck. "One of the great things I love about California is its egalitarian promise. Everyone who wants to work hard and earn their way can rise to the top. It will make this the greatest state in the Union. Unfortunately," he pauses to give me a pitying look, "some people try to gamble their way to riches instead, and end up losing everything." He beckons Frank with a wave of his hand. "Please escort the two ladies to the gate. Round up their other friends as you find them, and see them out as well."

Frank grins, reaching out like he means to take us by the collar, but I slap his hand away. "We'll go quietly. Don't you dare touch us."

"I was growing tired of this party anyway," Becky says, rocking the baby against her shoulder. "It's hard to find common interests with such low company as yourself."

"If you want low company, I can put you both in the ground," Dilley says, resting a hand on his gun.

"You might get away with shooting a man at an auction," I say. "But not even Mr. Hardwick will protect you if you shoot a woman in his garden." Henry sure is taking his time. I trust him to know the exact perfect moment, but waiting is nerve-wracking, nonetheless.

"Don't try me," Dilley says. The music and chatter have stopped. Everyone watches as he escorts us to the gates at gunpoint. Large and Larger guard the entrance, and as usual, they appear to be suffering from an excess of boredom, at least until they see us coming. Not that they move, or rise from their chairs, but I think, in the light of the lantern, that I see their eyebrows go up.

"Where are your brats?" Frank asks Becky.

"I'm sure I don't know what you're talking about," she says.

"Your children. The guest log says they came with you."

"Well, they're not here," she says.

"They're very curious children," I say, just to stall. "They could have wandered anywhere. You should probably go look for them."

Finally, a high, operatic tenor rises loud and clear over the garden, from the direction of the gaming tables. "I've been robbed! Help!" the voice sings. "My gold is gone, stolen right out of my pockets! Check your pockets, everyone."

Henry is overdoing it somewhat, but before I can worry, his cry is followed by a second, unfamiliar voice. "My watch is gone!"

There's a sudden babble. Frank Dilley turns to Large and Larger. "Lock the gates. No one leaves until we've got this solved. Especially not these two troublemakers."

Frank takes off to investigate.

"So, are you enjoying the party?" I ask Large and Larger as the commotion in the garden grows louder.

"It's starting to get interesting," says Large.

"But I don't expect it to last," says Larger.

"Somebody would have to be really stupid to steal anything at one of Mr. Hardwick's parties," Large says.

"They'd be sure to get caught," Larger agrees.

I lock eyes with Becky, but I decide not to say a thing. I try to clutch my locket for comfort, but of course it's not there anymore.

One of the waiters runs up to the gate, a young man with his collar undone and his tie loose. "Are you all right, young man?" Becky asks.

"One of those nights," he answers. To the two guards, he says, "Mr. Hardwick says you must run and fetch the sheriff. There's been a theft, and he wants it solved and the thief punished."

Large looks at Larger.

"Do you feel like running?"

"I don't get paid enough to run."

"Me neither."

Larger stands and opens the gate. "You better go and fetch the sheriff," he tells the waiter. "You know all the details anyway."

The young man starts to protest, but Larger put his hand on his Colt revolver. "Sure," the waiter says quickly. "I can do that."

After he dashes through the gate, they drag it closed and lock it again. I ask, "Do you mind if we go see what's happening?"

"Just don't try to leave through this gate," Larger says.

"Because then we'd have to stop you," Large says.

"And it feels like that could take some effort," Larger adds.

Becky and I stroll back toward the crowd, which has gathered around Hardwick's porch. The general sentiment seems to be anger and suspicion, with everyone giving the side-eye to everyone else. Hardwick himself stands in the doorway, backlit by a fire in the hearth of the room behind him, while various prominent men deliver complaints. The governor points to the missing pocket watch at the end of his gold chain. The wife of a senator complains about her absent necklace and bracelets. A judge wants Hardwick to know that his pocket has been picked clean of golden eagles.

Hardwick is doing his best to calm everyone down when Mr. Keys appears at his shoulder to whisper something in his ear.

"I can't hear you," Hardwick says.

The whole crowd falls silent just as Mr. Keys, still clearly tipsy, shouts, "We have a problem inside—someone broke into one of our safes!"

The timing could not be better, and it's hard to resist clapping. For once, luck is with us.

Hardwick follows Mr. Keys into the house, and the crowd surges forward. I make sure I'm near the front as we push in and chase him through the house to a large storeroom behind the kitchen. Eleven safes stand neatly in two rows against the wall. Being this close to that much gold is nearly enough to make my knees buckle.

The largest safe, from Owen and Son, Bankers, stands with its door wide open and its shelves completely empty. Almost two hundred thousand dollars in gold was held in that safe. An unimaginable amount. And now it's all gone.

I grin in spite of myself.

"Is there something amusing about this?" Hardwick asks me. His voice cracks, which widens my grin. He's finally losing his composure.

"I told you to stay by the gate," Frank yells when he spots me.

"You didn't, actually. You just said we couldn't leave—"

An unfamiliar voice hollers, "Look at all those safes! If Hardwick has so much money, why'd he steal from us?"

"Thief!" someone else shouts.

"Yeah, thief!" I chime in.

Hardwick raises his hands. "Hold on, friends. The sheriff will be here any moment, and we'll sort this out. Now, please, please, all of you go back to the parlor. We have wine, whiskey, hors d'oeuvres . . ."

California is still too new and wild for people to ignore free food. A bit mollified, we all wait, crowded inside and around the front of his mansion, until Sheriff Purcell storms in, accompanied by several deputies.

Somehow, I thought he'd be larger. Imposing. Instead, the sheriff is of medium height and weight, with curly light brown hair turning to gray. He has a hornet's-nest-poked-with-a-stick kind of look about him, thanks to his unkempt hair and beard, which bodes either very well or very ill.

"You have some nerve, hauling me down here," Purcell says to Hardwick.

A puzzled look flits across Hardwick's face. "Perhaps we should discuss the situation in private."

Purcell glances around, noting all the familiar faces in the crowd. "No, I think I'm fine discussing it in front of witnesses."

"Something has upset you," Hardwick observes.

"You left me with a colossal mess after the auction yesterday. I'm still sorting out all the complaints!"

"What complaints?" Hardwick seems truly baffled, and I'm not ashamed to say I don't feel sorry for him in the least.

"Theirs and mine," Purcell says. "Their complaints are that you sold a bunch of property that was already owned by other people. I've got two sets of owners for all these different plots of land lined up in my office, wanting a resolution."

"Thief!" someone shouts behind me. Jefferson's voice, unless I miss my guess. Whispered echoes of "thief" ripple through the crowd.

"That's not what I . . . that's not right," Hardwick says.

"No, James, it's not right at all. *My* complaint is that you set the prices for the last auction so low that my office's cut of the proceeds is just a fraction of what we need this month. I'm going to have to let deputies go, because I can't afford to pay them, and that's on you." Purcell sticks a finger in Hardwick's chest.

"That's a lie," Hardwick says furiously. "I chose those prices myself."

"So you admit it's your fault," Purcell says.

"I admit nothing," Hardwick says. "But if you help me figure out who the thief is tonight, I promise I'll make it right with you."

"Your promises are worth squat," the sheriff says.

This is working out far better than I had hoped or dreamed.

The governor steps forward and rests a hand on Purcell's shoulder. "What about *my* promises? Help us find the culprit tonight, resolve this situation, and *I* will make it right with you."

The sheriff's outrage melts away like a spring snowfall. "Yes, sir," Purcell says. He waves over some deputies. "Make a list of everything that's been stolen, and then start searching everyone."

This process moves quickly, more quickly than I expected, because the party is no longer any fun, the whiskey is no longer flowing, and people are eager to wrap up this problem and leave. When my turn comes, I report that I've lost a few five-dollar pieces, and a quick search of my pockets and purse turn up empty. I'm herded toward a group of folks who have already been searched.

"Miss Westfall?" asks a voice.

I look up to see the governor again. "Hello, sir," I say, wondering if the sheriff really had the gumption to search the governor, or if it was all a pretense. "This is a terrible situation." I hope my face matches the solemnity of my voice.

"I'm sure you remember when we first met," he says.

"In Sacramento, at the Christmas ball," I offer.

"You were already the Golden Goddess, but a goddess without a realm. Did you receive a happy resolution to your problem that day?"

"No, sir, I did not," I answer. "Me and the miners of Glory, we raised all the gold we had, and gave it to Mr. Hardwick, who promised to make sure we had a town charter. Something that would protect our claims, and protect our right to govern ourselves. Only it turned out he made a promise he couldn't deliver."

"I'm getting the impression that he has made many promises he's incapable of delivering," the governor says, his face grave.

Everyone is jumping ship now, even Hardwick's closest associates.

The governor's scrutiny becomes intense, making me fidget. "You're still interested in that town charter, I presume?" he says.

My breath catches. "Yes, sir. Naturally, sir."

"Good to know," he says noncommittally.

Frank Dilley drags two small forms by the scruffs of their necks, and throws them to the ground at the sheriff's feet. It's Sonia, the pickpocket, and her little towheaded companion, Billy. Naturally, I'm shocked to see them.

"I caught these two lingering near the gate," Frank says. "I recognized them for cutpurses who hang around the docks. If anyone is guilty of theft, it's them."

People in the crowd draw back from the two as if they're infected with measles. Sonia looks up at the sheriff, eyes wide with innocence. "That's not true, sir. We just came for the music and the food."

"I was hungry," Billy adds, with his sad puppy-dog eyes.

"Search us, sir," Sonia says, holding up her arms. "You won't find anything."

"Well," Billy says. "I've got a couple sausages in my pocket. But they're small sausages. And some cheese."

"Billy!"

"Search them," the sheriff tells his deputies, but their careful patting down, including a search for any hidden pockets, turns up only lint-covered sausages, smooshed cheese, and a slice of dried apple.

"They're clean," the deputy reports. He wrinkles his nose. "Well, not clean, but they don't have any valuables on them."

"How'd you get into the party?" the sheriff asks. "Climb over a wall? Sneak in?"

"We came right in through the front gate," Billy says earnestly, as he sticks the cheese and sausages back in his pockets, and shoves the browned apple slice into his mouth.

"That's the honest truth, sir," Sonia says. "We came with an invitation from Mr. Dilley, here."

"Frank?" Hardwick says, his voice hard.

"That's a damn lie!" Frank answers.

"We've searched all the guests and the grounds," one of the deputies reports to the sheriff. "The stolen items are nowhere to be found."

"Then maybe we should search inside the house," the sheriff says.

Helena sidles up to him. "You won't find anything in there," she says to him. "Nobody's been in the private quarters, except Hardwick and his staff."

She must have sussed out part of our plan. I give Helena a grateful look. All I demanded was that she stop helping Hardwick, not that she help us instead. But I'll take it.

"It's true," Hardwick says. "No one has been inside the private wing."

"You'd swear to that?" the sheriff answers.

Hardwick opens his mouth. Closes it. The trap has been set, and he has no answer.

The sheriff and deputies go from room to room. After only a few minutes, a cry reaches us from one of the bedrooms. Footsteps hurry to investigate. The sheriff and his men return carrying the governor's gold watch, the senator's wife's ruby bracelet, and a handful of other items.

"We found the jewelry under the mattress," he says. "It's all there."

They lay out everything on a long serving table. The last two items are an iron key, which I would bet money fits the open safe in the storeroom, and the burned fragment of a safe ledger, still smoking, as though just rescued from the cinders.

"Whose room is along the west wall?" the sheriff asks. "The one with red velvet curtains and the beehive fireplace?"

Hardwick stares at Frank. "Where's the gold, Dilley? Where's the gold from the safe?"

"I don't know what you're talking about," Frank says.

"That was Frank Dilley's room," Hardwick says. "And the key and ledger match a very specific safe. I want to know where he put my two hundred thousand dollars."

"I never stole anything you didn't tell me to steal," Frank sneers as the deputies close around him.

"So you're saying it wasn't your fault?" the sheriff prompts. "Hardwick ordered you to steal the jewelry?"

Silence. Frank looks back and forth between Hardwick and the sheriff.

"Don't take the fall for Hardwick," I tell him.

Everyone in the room is listening closely. It's so quiet you could hear a flea sneeze.

I see the exact moment Frank makes his decision. "Yes. Hardwick made me do it."

"That's a lie!" Hardwick yells.

Quicker than a blink, Frank draws his gun and aims it at Hardwick. Someone shouts a warning. The deputies tackle Frank, and the gun fires into the ceiling, raining plaster onto Hardwick's head.

Hardwick's face goes from terrified to controlled in the space of a breath. He has the poise and presence of a leader. A president. "Please claim your items, people," Hardwick says, his face white from plaster dust, but just as composed as you please. "I'm very sorry for the problem here tonight."

"You're only sorry you got caught," I say. There's no proof Hardwick did it, just the confession of a desperate man. But my words are bound to be repeated.

We gather at the gate. Becky is there waiting, along with a couple of droopy heads hiding under Olive's and Andy's hats. The Major stands beside them, rocking the baby in his arms. She's sleeping hard, with one hand tangled in his beard, and a thumb jammed firmly into her mouth. Jefferson and Henry show up just as I do. I scan the crowd for Mary and spot her clearing empty platters from a refreshment table, making herself useful as always.

Guests stream past us, muttering that the only thing Hardwick is sorry for is finally getting caught.

"It's just as well Hardwick is leaving," the governor tells

someone. "He won't be our problem anymore."

Jefferson and I exchange a grin.

"Well, for once, we had a spot of luck," Jefferson says.

"Yep," I agree. "Thanks to Helena and Frank."

"Could it have gone any better?" Becky adds, and she can't keep the glee from her voice.

The sheriff and his deputies come by, dragging a kicking and protesting Frank Dilley by his elbows.

"So it was him?" asks Larger.

"What's going to happen to Dilley?" asks Large.

"He'll be treated the way we treat any other thief," the sheriff says. "After he tells us where he hid all the gold coins from Mr. Hardwick's safe."

I can't help thinking about the gallows standing in Portsmouth Square. Or the way they cast a shadow over the spot where Jim was shot, where he lay bleeding in the mud. "He has legitimately earned anything this city can dish out," I say. "Right?"

The Major says, "If Frank swings, I won't be shedding any tears."

"If he had swung earlier, a whole lot of good folks would still be alive," Jefferson says.

"This is a good night," Henry assures me. "We did a good thing."

But there are ten full safes sitting in Hardwick's storeroom, holding close to two million dollars' worth of gold. And he has a ship chartered to take him to New York, along with his fortune. "We aren't done," I say. "Not quite yet."

Chapter Twenty-Two

We return to the *Charlotte*, but I hardly sleep at all, and I wake too early. The *Argos* won't leave until the evening tide, so I have plenty of time. I force myself to enjoy a leisurely breakfast, but I don't taste a single bite. Finally I can't take it anymore, and I pop up from the table, don a wool coat, and climb down to the stable to saddle Peony.

She's so excited to see me grab her bridle that she tosses her head, whinnying and stomping her hooves. I can hardly hold her still enough to cinch the saddle. I lead her from the hold, up the ramp, and into the street, and by the time I mount her she's almost shaking with anticipation.

The tiniest nudge with my heels sends her into a fast trot, and together we head uphill. People gape as we pass, and I soak up their attention. Peony is the most beautiful horse I ever knew, with her caramel-sugar coat and her mane and tail blond like spun sunshine. I'm proud to ride her, and after everything we've done here in San Francisco, it's finally okay to draw a little attention.

Together we crest a green hill near the Soldier's Cemetery and Jim's grave, where I'm certain to have the very best view. I dismount and turn her loose to graze on fresh grass for a change.

The bay is a wonder—fog sends opaque fingers through the Golden Gate into the bay, and the eastern sunrise sets it all on fire. The fog makes my view of the *Argos* blurry, but I can see enough. Crews are already loading Hardwick's fortune on board. A safe dangles from a boom, wrapped in ropes. The boom lifts it away from the dock and swings it over the deck toward the open hold. It's a slow, careful, dangerous process.

I stretch out my hand. It would be so easy to call that gold to me, to make it snap the ropes and drop through the dock or even the deck of the ship. But what good would that do? Not enough, that's for sure.

If a single safe broke open, Hardwick's men would just gather the coins and start over. He could hire another ship. Repair the damage. It would slow him down, but not stop him.

I sit for hours, watching. As they raise and swivel each safe into place, I wrap my head around the shape and weight of its contents. When they lower it belowdecks, out of my sight, I can still sense it down in the hold. I can tell where they place the first one, right along the keel line. The second one is lashed against it so tight that the two volumes become one. A voice, a voice, and then a harmony.

By the time they're lowering the third safe, Jefferson appears, riding Sorry. He dismounts and retrieves a canteen and a bit of hardtack from his saddlebag. The water feels good sliding down my throat. "Thanks."

"I figured I'd find you here."

"One thing left to do," I say.

"You should have told me you were going."

"I didn't want to wake you."

"Which would have been no big deal at all. Lee. We're going to be *married*. You're not alone anymore. You have to stop thinking like an alone person."

"I . . . you're right. I'm sorry."

"You've been through a lot. I understand."

And I believe he really does. "Keep reminding me," I say. "Keep lecturing. I agree with you. It's just that, like with the gold, I need practice."

He wraps an arm around my shoulders and plants a kiss on the top of my head.

I watch every safe swing into the ship. I stretch out my hand, close my eyes, and get the shape and feel of it all. So much gold. All in one place. My practice must be paying off, because a year ago, maybe even a month ago, so much gold nearby would have rendered me senseless.

The fog is burning away, and the breeze is picking up when one of the safes clangs like a cymbal in my head. I gasp.

"Lee? What's wrong?"

"I . . . nothing." My breath comes in pants. "It's *the* safe. The one I was waiting for."

His face breaks into a grin. "So it worked! You can sense that one just fine, then?"

"Oh, yes. Oh, my. It's . . . intense." I close my eyes and follow the safe and its contents as it's lowered into place. It's near the keel line now, lashed to the other safes. Perfect.

"Are you going to be okay?"

"Yes."

"You've given up so much already, Lee. I hate to see you lose this, too."

I yawn and rub my eyes. Those golden dice were small, but it took so much effort and concentration to control them last night that I'm exhausted. Like I climbed the Rockies again instead of just playing a few hands of cards. "It will be worth it," I tell him. "I started my journey with that locket. It's only fitting I end with it." *It will be worth it,* I repeat silently to myself.

Jefferson collects Sorry, and they leave to refill his canteen and fetch more food.

I'm glad, because I need this moment alone to say good-bye. After today, the very last tangible memory of my mother will be gone. *Thank you, Mama,* I say, hoping she can hear me from wherever she is.

The ship is almost fully loaded by the time Jefferson and Sorry return. He carries a basket of still-warm biscuits, but I only take a few bites. I don't want nature calling me away. I don't want to miss a thing.

As gold fills the hold of the ship, the temptation to do something grows stronger, but I have to wait a little longer.

Hardwick arrives with a wagon carrying the last pair of safes. Mr. Keys is with him, slumped over as though half drunk and twice as miserable as the night before. As the penultimate safe swings into the air, I stretch out my hand and think about how easy it would be. Just push and pull, get the rope swinging back and forth in the right direction, then yank it off so it lands right on Hardwick's head.

But I'm not a murderer. I'm not that coldhearted. Am I?

Plenty of folks have gotten hurt around me. Daddy and Mama, gunned down like animals in their own home. Poor Mr. Joyner, crushed when the wagon rolled down the mountainside. Therese, dying in the desert, giving up her life to save her family. Her brother Martin, killed by my uncle's men. All of Muskrat's people, dying in the mining camp—maybe even Muskrat himself, since no one has seen him since that terrible night. Jim, shot before my very eyes, bleeding in the mud at my feet. And Frank Dilley, who even now might be hanging at Portsmouth Square.

The last safe swings over the ship and gradually lowers into the hold, and I let it. I don't do a thing about it.

Beside me, Jefferson uses his pocketknife to slide a bit of cheese from a wedge. "Want some?" he asks.

"Not just yet."

This is my last chance to fix that final safe full of gold in my mind, to feel where it fits with the others in the hold of the ship. The ship rocks on the waves, but the safes are tied down tightly. I sense them moving with the flow of water, but their weights don't shift one bit relative to one another. In the center of it all is the familiar chest, containing a stack of gold bars, all wrapped tight with rope around the centerpiece of my mama's locket.

I know from Melancthon that the captain wants to take the ship out with the ebb tide, as the moon rises late this afternoon. I feel hollow inside, from all the gold I moved yesterday, from the lack of sleep and food, from the final choice I know I'm about to make.

Hardwick stands on the deck, with only Mr. Keys at his side. Hardwick is smaller than a toy soldier, but I still recognize him. Two days ago, he was arguably the most powerful man in California. Today, no one shows up to wish him farewell.

But it's not enough to sully his reputation and cast suspicion. The people of New York don't know him like we do. When he shows up with all the gold he's collected in California, they'll fall all over themselves to make him feel at home.

A few loyal underlings wander the deck. I recognize the fellow who was guarding the bank the night they caught the robber. But I'm glad Large and Larger are not among them. I never saw them do anything cruel.

The captain calls out to the crew, and they cast off from the dock. A boat with long oars tugs them out of the harbor and into the bay.

I stand as the ship goes by. "I need to keep my eyes on it," I tell Jefferson. "Time to mount up."

Jefferson shoves leftovers back into his saddlebag, and we both return to our saddles. I direct Peony so I can follow the ship around the bay line, always keeping it in sight, never releasing my mental grip on all that gold. As the ship rounds the mouth of the bay, I coax Peony into a trot. Sorry's hooves clatter behind me.

The air turns cold with the evening, and the bellies of the clouds are burnished red gold with the setting sun. The lighthouse at Alcatraz Island winks on, and behind it stretch the green hills of Rancho Saucelito. The sea is choppy. The waves rock the ship back and forth as it sails toward the Golden Gate and the Pacific Ocean.

I pull Peony up, to give her a quick rest and to reach out with my gold sense. The ship is moving faster than we are, stretching the distance between us, but I can still feel its golden cargo, especially Mama's precious locket. It's like a song wafting toward me from a great distance, through a valley in the mountains.

"It's not far enough," I whisper to myself.

"What's not far enough?" Jefferson asks.

"The ship. There are islands. Like Alcatraz. Places it can put into shore."

"That's a good thing, right? We don't want anyone to die."

"Melancthon took care of that," I assure him. "The *Argos* needs to be close enough to shore that lifeboats can reach safety, but far enough away that the ship itself can't."

"I suppose you're right."

"I—we—have to get to the fort at the Presidio," I tell him. "We have to see her through the Golden Gate."

"Then we'd better move. Fast."

But I'm already urging Peony forward, and Jefferson quickly falls in behind. It's almost a mile from here to the army fort at the Presidio, but we're on land and the ship is going with the tide. Thank goodness it's sailing directly into a west wind.

I give Peony a light kick with my heels, and she eagerly stretches into a full gallop. She is a wonder, game to run and giving it her all in spite of being cooped up for so long. I lean forward onto her withers, where my weight will be easiest to bear. She recognizes the weight shift and what it means. Without any further coaxing, she lowers her head like a thoroughbred and runs even faster.

Still, it's going to be a close thing.

Wind chaps my face, and my hair loosens from its braid. People stare as we fly by, and we must be a sight—two people breezing their horses through the San Francisco streets, dodging carts and amblers and puddles. Sorry begins to fall a little behind, but I don't dare slow down so she and Jeff can catch up.

If we do get there in time, what if my gold sense isn't up to the task? I've done some amazing things with it, for sure and certain. I found a lost boy in the middle of the night on the wide-open prairie. I collapsed my uncle's mine. Of course, that mine was only a stone's throw away, and my gold sense was aided by a liberal application of gunpowder. By the time I reach the fort, the *Argos* will be halfway to the setting sun.

I just don't know if my second sight, or whatever it is, will be enough.

The white walls of the Presidio rise before us. The flagpoles fly the banners of California and the United States.

"Whoa," I say, pulling back on the reins. Peony slows, and I dismount. Her coat is damp now. She'll need a good rubdown as soon as I get a chance.

The flags snap in the wind, which is changing direction to favor the *Argos*.

But I can still see her. She's in the middle of the Golden Gate now, pinched between two peninsulas, a quarter mile away. From here, at last, I can see the Pacific, and the sight catches my breath, makes me feel like we've run a hundred miles instead of one.

"Have you ever seen its like?" Jefferson says breathlessly, riding up on Sorry. The sun is setting over the ocean, skipping coins of gleaming light across the waves. The watery horizon stretches forever, slightly curved, and finally I understand how big the world is.

The ebb tide runs rough, and the waves are high, tossing the ship back and forth as it doggedly pushes for the open sea. Seabirds circle and dart. A few have landed on the mast, but they are barely more than black dots at this distance.

I close my eyes and stretch out my right hand, find the shape of the gold. It's easy. Mama's locket jumps out at me in particular. Even through the haze of gold surrounding it, I feel its gentle curve, its tiny latch, its flower etching.

I squeeze my fist around the heart shape, and I pull it toward me.

Nothing happens.

I concentrate again, and push it away with all my power.

Still nothing.

I've waited too long. My plan was never going to work.

"Don't give up, Lee," Jefferson says. He has dismounted and now stands at my side.

I grab the gold and pull it toward me with all my strength. I hold my fist up tight against my chest, then I fling it away, as hard as I can.

The ship slips past us, toward open water.

There's nothing complex about this part of my plan. It should be as simple as sensing a broken coin in someone's pocket, and pulling and pushing it, back and forth, until the coin rips the seam. As easy as pushing a saddlebag full of gold back and forth across a bedroom floor. As easy as flipping over a pair of golden dice.

I reach out with both hands, close my eyes. Ten safes. Almost two million dollars in gold coins. More money than I ever imagined. All tied down around the heart of my mama's final gift to me. And using that final gift as a focus, I pull my hands against my chest and squeeze, like I'm giving all that gold the fiercest bear hug of my life.

To anyone watching, I must appear to have taken leave of my sense, but I don't care. I punch my fists out, like I'm trying to knock an attacker down to save my life.

Something moves.

My eyes shoot open. The ship is farther away, heading toward deep water.

I stretch out my arms again, and pull the gold toward me. I feel it skew, unevenly, as something breaks. I shove it away again, and the mass lurches hard.

The cargo is no longer tied down, and the ship rolls in the waves.

I remember what Melancthon told me about the capsized ship: the waves and the cargo together were what sank it. So I wait—just a moment—until the ship is listing toward my shore, and I pull with all my strength, working with the waves instead of against. I release it, and when the hull begins to tip back in the other direction, I push as hard as I can.

Now the loose cargo is doing half the work, sliding on its own as the ship tosses in the rough tide.

"Lee," Jefferson whispers. "Your nose is bleeding."

"Tell me if my eyes start bleeding," I snap. But I lick my lips and taste raw copper on my tongue, thinking of the story Becky told me, about the man who moved the tree and caused his heart to burst.

But I can't quit now, with the job half done. If I do, the crew will just go down into the hold and secure the cargo.

So I stand here, pushing and pulling, one way and then the other, as the ship rides off into the distance. My legs start to wobble. I'm vaguely aware when Jefferson closes the gap between our bodies, and suddenly I realize I'm no longer standing on my own strength, that his arm is wrapped around my waist.

The *Argos* is rolling so violently now that the masts nearly kiss the waves. Dark specks flee the tossing ship—the crew has managed to launch several of the lifeboats.

The ship is so far away now, I can barely sense the locket at all. It feels like a nugget, lost in a rushing creek, beneath gravel and ice. It's going to get away.

My luck changes. The ship slows. The captain, either in a

panic, or under orders from Hardwick, is trying to turn the ship back. To put to shore before all is lost.

It gives me a chance. A large wave hits it nearly broadside. I grab the gold and pull it as hard as I can. The ship rolls right over. The mast breaks as it hits the water. A split second after I see it, I hear the sharp snap of cracking wood.

I sink to my knees.

"Lee," Jefferson says. "Lee . . . Lee, are you *all right?*"

I reach out one last time with both fists, and yank down as hard as I can, hurling that gold down to the bottom of the ocean. I hope the water is a mile deep. Or at least too deep for any divers to reach it.

"Lee!"

Bloods gushes out of my nose and runs down over my lips and chin.

"I . . ."

I don't remember falling over, but I'm lying sideways, and my head hurts where it hit the ground. Gravel presses tiny dots of pain into my cheek.

"Lee!"

Jefferson's hands grasp me, but they feel faraway, almost like they're touching someone else. So tired. Hollowed out. Sun fading away.

"S'okay," I tell him, from a distance. "Trust you . . . help me home?" Arms wrap me tight, bolster me. I'm barely conscious as he helps me into my saddle. Fortunately, riding Peony is something I can almost do in my sleep, and we start a slow, careful trek back toward the *Charlotte*.

Chapter Twenty-Three

$\mathcal{I}$'m feeling better by the time we return, but I still fall into my cot and sleep like the dead. When I wake, morning shines bright through the window Melancthon made for me. I scratch my itchy upper lip and discover that more blood caked there overnight. The bleeding seems to have stopped for good, though, so I force myself out of bed, wash quickly, and fetch Jefferson, who is hugely relieved to see me awake and hale. Everyone else has left already; Jefferson convinced them to let me sleep.

Dawn chills the air as we return to the cemetery on Peony and Sorry, following the same road we galloped along just hours before. The horses are delighted to be out again so soon. Peony kicks up her heels and tosses her head at every bird and bug. I'm glad one of us has some spunk; I'm so tired I could die.

"I don't think you should be up and about," Jefferson says. "In fact, maybe you should stay in bed for a week. Possibly a month."

"After the meeting," I promise. "I'll sleep then."

To be fair to him and his concerns, my head is throbbing, like there's an arrastra inside my skull, and a mule is dragging a grindstone around and around in a circle. My knees are weak, and my arms feel twisted and limp as a hen's wry neck.

"If I'm this exhausted," Jefferson says, "you must be about to faint."

"I promise I won't try to roll over any ships today," I say.

Jefferson shakes his head. "If I hadn't been there to see it, I wouldn't believe it."

"I hope everyone is all right."

"Saw Melancthon at breakfast," Jefferson says. "He said the crew got safely ashore. The ebb tide carried the smaller boats out to sea, but other ships were there to pick them up. Hardwick's pinnace made it into shore this morning, right before we left."

"But the *Argos* did sink, right?" I'd hate to hear it was all for naught, that the ship somehow survived.

"The officer said they expect some light wreckage to drift ashore, but I don't reckon it will include any gold-filled safes. The water in that part of the bay is more than fifty fathoms deep."

"Is fifty fathoms deep?"

"Deep enough to sink Hardwick's fortune."

Sorry shakes her ruddy head, jangling her bridle, as if putting an end to the matter. As the sun rises across the bay, I feel a little warmer and a lot more whole again.

"We really did it, didn't we?" Jefferson says.

"Yep. Nobody in California will trust Hardwick again. And

he'll find it a lot harder to start rebuilding his fortune from scratch."

"Looks like almost everyone is here already," Jefferson says.

The Sailor's Cemetery stretches before us, green as an emerald with all the recent rain. A small crowd gathers around Jim's grave. A final chance to say good-bye. The wagon is here, and it looks like it's carrying a full load of lumber—Becky's house, if I don't miss my guess. Breath rises like fog from the carthorses' nostrils.

"There you are!" Becky says when she sees us.

"I needed a little extra sleep," I admit.

"See, Wally?" Becky says to the Major. "Just a touch of lethargy. She's always that way after using her gift."

He reaches out and quietly squeezes her hand. She squeezes back like she has no intention of letting go.

Mary steps forward, wearing her traveling dress. I hope that means she's planning to return with us.

I smile at her. "Thank you for coming. And for working so hard."

"Glad to see you didn't kill yourself," she says.

Henry leans against the wagon. He's wearing another new suit, this one a brown tweed, a little plainer and more practical than the one he wore to Hardwick's party. "The news around the city this morning is that the *Argos* capsized on its way out of the bay last night. All of Hardwick's gold sank to the bottom of the ocean."

"We might have heard a thing or two about that," Jefferson said.

Melancthon reaches up to calm one of the carthorses. "A shipwreck is a bad business," he says. "And capsizing is one of the worst."

I nod solemnly. "I was glad to learn the crew survived."

"Still," he says. "Makes a fellow glad he didn't accept that job."

"Other ships will be headed east soon enough," I tell him.

"True enough. But I might find a reason to stay."

Two figures enter the cemetery and walk toward us through the fog. It's Tom, along with Hampton.

Andy runs forward, arms outstretched. "Hampton! You're back!"

Hampton lifts the boy into his arms. "I missed you too, my friend." Hampton is thin and haggard, but he grins like it's Christmas. Everyone rushes forward to clap him on the back or shake his hand.

"It does my heart good to see you safe," Becky says.

"Here come the last of the stragglers," I say.

Jasper approaches, hands in the pockets of his waistcoat, while his companion makes his way with the help of a crutch. I've never been so happy to see anyone in my whole life.

"Jim!" I say, running to greet him. At his warning look, I stop short of wrapping him in a hug.

"I'm still prone to toppling over," Jim cautions.

I settle for grasping his shoulder and grinning like a fool.

"He's lucky to be alive and walking at all," Jasper says. "I'd hate to see him fall down and undo all the amazing surgery

I did to save his life. My recommendation was that he stay in bed today."

"I told *her* the same thing," Jefferson said, jerking his thumb at me.

"Some folks make the worst patients," Jasper says.

"All right, now that everybody's here, let's be quick," I say. Henry is already grabbing shovels from the wagon and handing them out. I take one, eager to get started.

"Wait a second," says Hampton. "Boisclair . . . you're alive?" His eyes are as wide as saucers.

"Alive and kicking," Jim says. "Well, I'll be kicking in a few weeks, I'm sure."

"Not that I'm complaining, but . . . could someone explain this, please?" Hampton says. Relief and anger do battle across his face. I hate that we caused him any more suffering, and I wouldn't blame him one bit if he decided to be mad as a wet cat.

"I'm pretty sure none of us knows the whole story," Jefferson says. He yanks the shovel out of my hand and gives me a stay-put-or-else look.

"Then this is a good time to put it together," I say, and everyone nods agreement.

"First," Becky says, "I want to know how Hardwick was able to set a trap for us that day at the Custom House. How did he know I'd try to reclaim my house? Was it that mind reader of his?"

Henry stops digging long enough to wipe sweat from his forehead. "I've wondered the same thing."

"Wait," Hampton says. "Mind reader?"

I nod. "Miss Helena Russell. When she sees people, she gets glimpses of the future, sometimes the thoughts in their heads. So when she met us in the law offices, she got a picture in her head of Becky returning with Henry in tow. She warned Hardwick, who sent his guards."

"Is that what she told you at the party?" Becky asks.

"I asked her outright, and she admitted it. After our failed attempt to reclaim the house, Hardwick's men kidnapped Hampton." I nod toward my friend.

"That's when we decided to ruin Hardwick," Mary says smugly.

"I knew you were up to something big, something that involved Hardwick," Melancthon says. "But . . . this is a lot for a fellow to swallow. A mind reader?"

I'm so glad we decided to trust the sailor. He ended up playing an important role. I say, "That was the hardest part—deciding how to act when Hardwick had someone who could pluck our thoughts right out of our heads. We had to divide the plan into parts, and give each person a single part to figure out on their own."

Tom says, "I pretended to be at odds with everyone, and I went to work for Hardwick."

"In the meantime," I say, "we spied on the banks where he kept his money."

"I loitered around the docks to spread word about how much money he had," Jefferson says. He's standing knee-deep in a hole, with his jacket off and his shirtsleeves rolled to his elbows.

"I helped with that!" Henry says. "I spread the word at gambling houses throughout the city."

"I even suggested that some people might be planning to steal it," Jefferson adds. "The idea was to have the rumors get back to Hardwick, so we could see what protection measures he'd put in place. But that part backfired a little. When we went to the bank that night to check it out, a couple of ambitious knuckleheads got there first."

"We did find out exactly how his money was guarded," I say. "But I couldn't let the robbers get away with the safe—we needed that safe intact." The shadow of the gallows passes across my thoughts.

"In the meantime," Tom says, "I learned everything I could about the sheriff's auctions. Hardwick managed them, and Sheriff Purcell took a cut of the money. I soon discovered that Purcell felt he wasn't getting his fair share."

"So Jefferson sabotaged the auction," I say. "All the prices were too low, only a fraction of what Hardwick wanted. And every single lot he had sold at the last auction was listed again. But, Jefferson . . ." I turn toward him. Sweat runs down his neck. "How did you do it?"

His self-satisfied grin is the best thing I've seen in days. "I paid a printer to run off phony auction sheets," he says. "Billy, the pickpocket, was already working at the auctions, handing out price sheets every month. So Hardwick's printer handed him the real price sheets, and then we replaced them with fake ones we commissioned, and Billy distributed them, just like always."

"Custom House lot twenty-three!" Becky says.

"Huh?" I say.

"Custom House lot twenty-three, that was the other thing you changed. The original bid sheet said 'one house, from Tennessee, complete with furnishings and ready for assembly.' But the fake one said 'one small load of wood, somewhat water damaged.'"

I grin. "That probably made it easier to buy."

"We were the only bidders," Henry says, looking up from the hole again, which is now almost waist-deep. "Imagine that!"

"My job was to create a distraction," Jim says. "To keep the auctioneer from paying close attention to the false bid sheets, and to put the crowd on edge." He winces. "That proved to be an even better distraction than anticipated."

"You mean *worse*," I say, glaring.

"After Jim was shot," Becky says, "Henry and I stuck around for a while, sowing discord."

"We put on a fine bit of theater, if you ask me," Henry says. "We didn't know what kind of shape Jim was in, but we soldiered on."

"Ideally, the plan should have worked either way," I say. "If they didn't catch the substitution, then the sale proceeded and the sheriff would think Hardwick was trying to cheat him. If the auctioneer did notice something wrong and called off the auction, then both Hardwick and the sheriff would come up empty-handed." I turn to Jim and say, "But neither one was worth your life. If Frank Dilley had killed you, I don't know what I would have done."

"I didn't come all the way out to California just to die," Jim says. He stretches out his crutch and taps the name on the grave marker. "But since everyone thinks I did, I might try being someone else for a while."

"Well, you're welcome in Glory, Mr. Boisclair," says the Major.

"But why?" Hampton says. "Why let people go on thinking Jim was dead? I'm still so confused."

"We're getting to that," Mary assures him.

Hampton's frown deepens. I open my mouth to assure him, to explain, but he jumps into the muddy hole and takes Jefferson's shovel. "I have no idea what's going on here, but let me spell you a bit."

"Thanks, Hampton." Jeff wipes his forehead with his sleeve and climbs out.

Following Hampton's lead, Jasper rolls up his sleeves and jumps in to spell Henry.

"The best thing about the auction," Tom says, "is that it made Sheriff Purcell steaming mad at Hardwick, even before he got called out to the party."

"Party?" says Hampton. He pauses midshovel, and dirt clods topple back into the hole.

"I bet the sheriff expected to confiscate all the money Frank Dilley stole," the Major says.

"Frank Dilley stole a bunch of money?" Jasper asks, exchanging a baffled look with Hampton.

"Don't stop digging!" Mary says. "We have to get this done before anyone comes along."

As they resume their attack on the hole, I say, "*We* stole the money. But we made it look like Frank Dilley did it."

"That's the best news I've heard all month," Hampton says.

"Tell me how you did it," Jasper demands.

"Well, we needed your help for that," Henry says.

"Ah," Jasper says. "That's what all the fuss with Jim was about."

"Yep," I say. "After Jim was shot, Mary had the *best* idea."

Mary grins. "It turned out pretty well, if I do say so myself. Once we had the keys for Hardwick's safes—"

"Hold on, hold on, hold on," Tom interrupts. "How did you get the keys to Hardwick's safes? I've been dying to know how you managed it. They were never out of Ichabod's hands."

"Ichabod?" I ask.

"His accountant."

"Mr. Keys!" Jefferson says. He's leaning against the wagon now, taking a breather. "That was a tough one. He checked those keys every time he sat down and again the second he stood up. So I paid Sonia to help us. One day when Mr. Keys . . . Ichabod . . . stopped for lunch, she lifted his key ring. We had wax trays ready so she could make impressions of all the keys in just a few minutes."

"Like the locksmith who worked on the *Charlotte*," Melancthon says.

Jefferson nods. "By the time his food was served, the ring was back on his belt; he never noticed it was gone."

"Once we had the keys for Hardwick's safes," the Major continues, "we needed a way to get the gold out quickly and efficiently, and then transport it without it being noticed."

"Aha!" Melancthon interjects. "That's what you needed that bilge hose for. They're heavy when full, but easy to move."

"We were going fill the hose with gold coins, and then store them all in the *Charlotte* in a barrel," the Major says. "But it's a good thing we didn't. After he was arrested, Frank Dilley told the sheriff that *we* stole the money, and Purcell came and searched the *Charlotte* from stem to stern yesterday. If we'd had a single coin hidden aboard the ship, he would have found it."

"I still don't understand how you got the money out of the bank," Jasper says.

"That was me, too," Jefferson says. "The bank has a tile roof. I climbed up, removed a few tiles, and slipped directly into the cage. Took me a minute to figure out which key opened the safe. Then I stuffed the gold coins into the bilge hose."

"Which was why Major Craven had me line it with cotton padding," Melancthon says, running a hand through his whisk-broom hair. "To muffle the sound."

"Exactly," the Major says.

"My job was to talk to the guards," I say. "Keep them from walking around the back of the building or paying too much attention to any odd noises." I helped in another way, too, by giving all that gold a little push, making the bilge hose easier to handle. But I'm not sure I should say so aloud. Melancthon doesn't need to know *all* our secrets.

"I thought for sure they were going to catch me when they opened the door," Jefferson says. "There was just enough time to close the safe door and crouch behind it. If it hadn't been cloudy and dark, he might have noticed the hole in the roof." He looks at me. "You did a great job distracting them."

I shrug. "Those fellows weren't too bad."

"Once the safe was empty," Jefferson continues. "I climbed back up to the roof, holding one end of the hose. I pulled it over the edge and loaded it onto the wagon. Then I replaced the roof tiles, and it was like I'd never been there."

Mary is all grins. "The next day, I paid Hardwick's Chinese workers—the ones who moved all his safes—to pretend that one safe was just as heavy as the others, even though it was empty."

"He never suspected a thing," Tom says. "*I* never suspected a thing."

"So, back to Jim," I say, "Once he was shot, Mary recognized an opportunity. A way to hide all the gold we planned to steal."

Jasper says, "So *that's* why she told me to keep Jim hidden."

"She made all the arrangements," Henry adds. "She organized everything."

"I came to San Francisco alone," Mary says. "So I didn't think Hardwick would realize I was part of the group. I had to keep out of sight around the *Charlotte*, though, sneaking in and out through the hold. I was afraid Frank Dilley would recognize me from Hiram's Gulch."

"It worked out," I say. "Mary was able to get things done without Hardwick ever catching wind."

Becky stares at Mary. "I thought . . . I thought you were avoiding me."

Mary stares back, not answering.

"So that's why we're digging," Jasper says, attacking the hole with renewed enthusiasm.

"Because you did bury something here," Hampton agrees. "But it's not Jim."

A sharp crack sounds. Hampton and Jasper use their shovels to scrape dirt away, revealing a muddy wooden casket.

"Go ahead, Hampton," I say. "You do the honors."

He shoves the tip of his shovel beneath the lid and levers it off.

We all crowd around and peer down into the hole. About four thousand coins sit piled inside the casket, all fifty-dollar pieces. There's a moment of silence, as if someone has died and we're all showing respect. It's not inappropriate, I think. People probably did die to collect this gold. The Indians who had their land stolen. The forty-niners who died on the wagon trail west. The miners who worked themselves sick. The people Hardwick kicked out of their homes to live in the cold, wet San Francisco streets.

Jim gives a low, appreciative whistle.

"Hampton, I'm so sorry we lied to you," I say. "It was meant to protect Jim from any further reprisals, and we weren't sure how to get the real information to you."

"I have to admit," Hampton says, "after getting my freedom papers, then having my freedom taken away again . . . more bad news was awful hard to take in." He takes a good long gander at all that gold. "But it also gave you a casket and a reason to bury it," he adds graciously.

Becky says, "It comes to about three hundred and thirty coins per portion. We'd better get them counted out quick."

"Already on it," Jefferson says. He climbs back into the hole with a dozen bags, and he and Hampton start counting out the coins.

"So what happened at the party last night?" Jasper asks. "You know, the one I missed so Mary could go in my place?" He says it with mock effrontery, as if he was the type of fellow to actually care about a party.

"All I know is that I was supposed to debauch Ichabod yesterday," Tom says. "If anyone was going to sense something amiss, it was going to be him. I was successful, and I hesitate to share all the details, although I confess that we opened the first bottle of wine before lunch. He's a decent enough fellow. I was glad to hear he escaped the sinking of the *Argos*."

"At the party, we had to get inside one of the safes *and* frame Frank Dilley," I say. "But I don't know this part. The Major took care of that." I turn to him. "Please tell me how you did it!"

"We needed to use those copied keys again," the Major says. "So many people are abandoning steady employment and running for the golden hills that the caterers were understaffed. They were thrilled when Mary and I volunteered to help out."

"It took a long time for us to figure out which room was Frank's," Mary says.

"Almost too long," the Major says. "By the way, this crutch

is noisy as all get-out. I stepped on rugs whenever possible, but I don't mind saying that getting in and out of Frank's room is one of the most hair-raising things I've ever done."

Becky pats his arm. "You're a brave man."

"So we found the safes first. We opened one and put Lee's little bundle inside, then I marked it with a bit of chalk so the dockhands would know which one to put in the center of the hold."

"Huh?" says Melancthon. "'Little bundle?'"

"Just a keepsake," I hurry to say. "A locket I carried west with me. It belonged to my mother. I wanted to give it a ceremonial burial at sea, in her honor."

Henry gives me an admiring look, and Mary coughs to cover a laugh.

"Then we found Frank's room," the Major continues, "and we left the key there, along with some other incriminating evidence."

"Where did you hide the duplicate key?" Tom asks. "Everyone at the party was searched closely, and staff was searched _twice_."

The Major hands the baby to Becky and sits down on the edge of the wagon. He pops open a small door on his wooden leg to reveal a secret compartment within. "I carried it here, along with everything else. They searched my pockets, and the seams of my clothes, but they didn't even want to touch my wooden leg."

"You're so clever," Becky says.

"I manage."

Jefferson and Hampton finish dividing the last of the coins. They stack the bags beside the grave and climb out of the hole. Jeff offers the first bag to Hampton. "For all your trouble," he says.

"I've had a lot more trouble than this in my life," Hampton says. "But I'll take some of that gold, I'm not ashamed to say."

Jefferson hands the second bag to Tom.

"As an officer of the court, who may have to testify under oath at some point in the future, I cannot in good conscience accept stolen property." Jefferson starts to withdraw the bag, but Tom grabs it. "I can, however, with a clear heart, give it to someone who should never have been treated as property in the first place, as a first step toward making things right. So I shall hold it in trust for Adelaide."

Hampton beams. "Any word of her while I was gone?" he says.

Tom's smile is sympathetic. "You know it's too early, Hampton. It takes months for these things to happen."

"Well, this ought to help me open that general store," Jim says, taking his bag.

Jasper says it'll help him start his own practice and provide services to the people of California who can't afford a doctor. Mary, Melancthon, the Major, and Henry all accept their shares.

When it's Becky's turn, she opens the bag, removes a few coins, and then hands it back. Holding up the coins, she says, "This is reimbursement from Mr. Hardwick, to repay the cost of recovering my house at auction. But otherwise, I don't feel comfortable stealing from anyone, not even a man as terrible as he was. He's been ruined, and that's enough for me."

Jefferson hesitates, glancing at me uncertainly.

The Major reaches out and grabs the bag. "I'll take it and invest it for the children. We'll plant it like a seed and let it grow, so that they have something to inherit when they're older."

"Wally!"

"Don't try to talk me out of it. My old man left me nothing but a bunch of debt and some bad memories. I figure these little ones already have good memories of their father, all except for the babe here. But there's no reason they can't have a little money. It's what your husband would do if he was still here."

"I'm pretty sure he would gamble it all away," Becky says.

I'm pretty sure she's right.

"So, I think I understand the whole story now," Jasper says. "Except for one thing. How did you steal all those jewels? The pocket watches and gold coins?"

"It was us," says a sulky voice.

"Sonia!" She has arrived with Billy, which I expected, and with Helena, who I wasn't sure would show up.

Jefferson, Hampton, and Jasper clamber out of the hole, and they work fast to shovel all the dirt back in. Everyone gives Helena a wide berth, even though she's here at my invitation.

"These are our new friends, Sonia and Billy," I say. "They helped us all along, mostly by working with Jefferson and

Mary. They also joined us at Hardwick's party, disguised as Becky's children."

"That's why the children stayed with me all night on the *Charlotte*," Melancthon says.

"They were supposed to be us?" Olive asks, running up to Sonia. "You're so big!"

"You'll be big soon enough," Sonia says, chucking her under the chin. "Don't rush it."

"Nobody but Frank Dilley knew what Becky's children looked like," I explain. "So we were able to sneak them in."

"Which I might have foreseen," Helena says. "But I don't think you ever really looked at them."

"I tried to think of them as Olive and Andy," I say. "It was hard."

"But it worked."

"So you're the mind reader," Melancthon says to Helena.

Helena just smiles at him.

"You've counted out all the portions," Sonia says, her voice suddenly cracking with anger. "And you weren't going to leave any for us."

"A promise is a promise," I say, bending over to pick up one of the remaining bags. "I trust you'll use it to look after Billy."

The fight melts out of her. "And maybe a few other kids," she says, cradling the gold to her chest, a shy smile forming.

"It'd help if you had a decent roof over your heads and some honest work," I say.

Her smile disappears. "It'd help if someone would give us honest work."

"We'll see," I say, and I glance over at Helena. "I think the *Charlotte* would make a fine hotel. It already has a good carpenter, who is also an excellent cook, but he needs someone who can manage the business side of things. Someone who is good at working with people, and who can see trouble coming before it arrives."

"You gave *him* the deed for the *Charlotte*," Helena says fiercely.

"No. I gave it to my good friend Wally Craven."

The Major steps forward, pulling a bit of paper from his pocket. "And I'd like to give it to our new friends, Helena Russell and Melancthon Jones," he says. "Miss Russell, you need a man to hold the deed in trust for you, and I can't think of a more trustworthy fellow than Mr. Jones."

"Either one of you can buy the other out at any time, of course," Tom adds.

Helena snatches the deed from the Major's hand. Melancthon and Helena regard each other like a pair of alley cats who discover themselves in a corner.

After a moment, Helena says, "I can see myself working with him," and I wonder if she means it literally or figuratively. "Mr. Jones, it looks like we're going into business together."

Melancthon's eyes are wide with amazement. "I can hardly believe it."

"You've been such a help, sir," I tell him. "We couldn't have done this without you. You worked hard getting the *Charlotte* into livable shape. You watched the children during the party.

Most importantly, you convinced the crew of the *Argos* to have plenty of lifeboats ready."

"I . . . yes . . . I mean, sailors are a superstitious lot. All I had to say was I'd heard omens about it being a bad day for sailing and . . . really? You're giving us the ship?"

With a glance at Jefferson, I say, "I can't own property, being a woman. And my future husband can't own property either, being half Cherokee."

"And I have no use for a ship," the Major says, staring at Becky. "My home is in Glory."

I say, "So the *Charlotte* belongs to Melancthon and Helena now. If you rent out rooms, you'll need someone to clean them, run errands, and the like. May I introduce you to my friends Sonia and Billy? They are currently in possession of their own means of support, but could use some stability and a future."

The four of them regard one another uncertainly.

"Lee," Jefferson says, pausing to toss his shovels back on the wagon. "It's time to be on our way."

I turn toward my mare.

"Wait," Melancthon says. "I have one more big question."

All of us wait expectantly.

"How did you sink the *Argos*?"

The air is suddenly taut. Everyone stares at me, wondering what I'll tell him. The wind is picking up, clearing the morning fog. A sea hawk screeches overhead.

I smile. "Melancthon," I say, "I'm afraid that's one secret we're not willing to share."

Before he can press, Jasper says, "I need to get back to work. But I'll be in Glory for the wedding, don't think I won't."

Tom and Henry take their leave, insisting that this is "not a real good-bye," promising to be in touch soon. Jim declares that he's fetching his things and heading for Glory, that staying in this city might be bad for his health, and Hampton offers to help him along.

Becky and the Major are on the wagon bench, the children in the back, all waiting for Jefferson and me to finish up. Mary stands beside the wagon, looking a little lost.

"If the *Charlotte* makes a successful hotel," Melancthon says, "there might be funds waiting for you. I could hold them in escrow—"

I wave my hand at him. "The deed is in your name. The ship is yours."

He gapes at me. "But—"

Helena puts a hand on his arm. "She has resources," she says. "The girl will be just fine."

Jefferson puts our gold into Peony's saddlebags. He hefts the bag, gauging its weight. "This is less than we had when we arrived in San Francisco."

"But still more than we need." I put a foot in the stirrup and swing myself up onto Peony's back. "Mary, are you staying in the city or coming home with us?"

She hesitates.

"Mary?" I say.

Mary and Becky are staring at each other. Becky's jaw twitches.

Finally Becky says, "Mary, don't be daft. You know I can't run that restaurant without you." She lifts her chin. "You're the *third best* employee I've ever had, and I've grown fond of y— your company." After another too-long pause, Becky adds, "And fine. I'll raise your wages."

Mary's smile could light up the bay. "Glory is my home."

"Oh, Mary, I'm so glad," I tell her, nudging Peony forward. "Jefferson, are you ready to go home?"

Jefferson climbs onto Sorry's back, and I swear the horse sighs. "More than ready."

APRIL 1850

Chapter Twenty-Four

Our first spring in California is glorious. It's like the sun dropped dollops of its very own self all over our claims, because the land bursts with yellow mustard and bright orange poppies. The oaks grow heavy with soft gray-green leaves, and everywhere the air is filled with the sounds of birdsong and trickling water. Truly, we have come to the promised land.

The morning before our wedding, a small letter-shaped parcel reaches me from San Francisco. It's made of beautiful, thick parchment, sealed with a splotch of red wax, stamped with the words OFFICE OF THE GOVERNOR OF CALIFORNIA.

I'm serving coffee in the Worst Tavern. It's another busy day, because a group of Chinese miners are traveling through again, and the whole lot of them decided to stop for biscuits and gravy. Letters aren't too uncommon since the weather turned; it seems the peddler or some other traveler stops by with a bundle at least twice a week now. So Mary is the only one paying attention as I break the seal with my fingernail and open it.

I gasp.

"What?" Mary says. "What is it?"

"It's . . ." Two pieces of paper. One is a letter from the governor himself, which I quickly skim. The other . . . "Mary, I think this is a town charter."

"What? Let me see." She snatches the charter from my hand.

Becky sidles over to find out why we've stopped working.

"That sure is a fancy seal," Mary says, gazing down at the charter. "And look at all those signatures!"

Becky snatches the letter from my other hand, so I'm holding nothing.

"The governor thanks you for ridding California of the problem of James Henry Hardwick," she says, reading quickly. "He doesn't know what you did exactly, but he knows where credit is due. It's his pleasure to do you this favor, blah, blah, flattery and more flattery, and he hopes you will remember him in the first election after California attains statehood. . . ." She looks up at me, grinning ear to ear. "He did this to cultivate you as an ally," she says. "He thinks you're *important*."

"I'm happy to not dissuade him," I say, and I'm grinning ear to ear, too. A town charter. Signed by the governor himself and several others, probably delegates from California's constitutional convention, which is what passes for a government in these lawless lands.

Becky takes it from Mary's hand. "After the breakfast rush, I'll frame it and post it in the tavern so everyone can see it," she says brightly. She tucks the charter and letter into her apron pocket. "Now, get back to work, both of you. These miners won't feed themselves."

We've barely served a handful of people before Jefferson arrives, looking more proper and well-groomed than he usually does before a hard day of prospecting. I'm about to tell him about our shiny new charter, but he preempts me in an overly loud voice. "Leah Elizabeth Westfall!"

I'm so startled that I almost drop the coffeepot.

He grins. "Maybe you should set that down."

I do, slowly, as the sound of scraping forks ceases and everyone—Becky, the Buckeyes, the Chinese, and Mary—all turn to stare.

"Um. Good morning, Jeff?"

Still grinning, he reaches into his pocket while dropping to one knee. "I know you already proposed to me, and I know we're getting hitched tomorrow, one way or the other. But I still reckon it's right and proper to give you this." He reaches up, and my gold sense knows what he holds in his hand even before my eyes take it in. A gold band, shiny and new.

I pinch it between thumb and forefinger, holding it up to the light. "Jeff," I say. "You know I don't need fancies. Or any more gold."

"I know. But that ring is special, see. Remember that nugget you gave me? Seems like a long time ago now. You tracked a wounded deer onto our homestead and chanced upon that nugget in a stream. And you gave it to me the day your mama and daddy died, said it wasn't yours by right."

"I remember."

"Well, this is me, giving it back to you."

I blink at him, my knees suddenly quivery. I knew he had kept it. I found it in a box of his things the night Frank Dilley set our camp on fire, but I'd had no idea *why* he kept it. Tears prick at my eyes. "Jefferson, this is the nicest thing. Making that nugget into a ring . . ."

"Put it on."

I do, and it slips onto my finger and sends tingling warmth through my whole hand, like it was meant to be there all along. I hold it up, admiring the way it shines in the light. A little piece of home, a bit of shared history, tying us together as powerfully as any wedding vow.

"Thank you."

"So does this mean you'll marry me after all?"

As if there was any question. I lean down and throw my arms around him, almost knocking him back. Everyone around us cheers like it was a proper proposal, even the Chinese miners.

Jefferson gets to his feet and hugs me back, his face nuzzling my hair. Reluctantly, I disentangle myself. There's a lot to do before our wedding tomorrow, and I need to get back to work.

Someone clears his throat. It's Old Tug, standing from the table, hat crumpled tight in his hand. His friends give him nods of encouragement. "You can do it, Tug," says one, as another slaps him on the back.

"I guess this is as fine a moment as any," he says. For once, he wears a clean shirt and pressed trousers, and he's obviously made an attempt at combing his thistly hair. He takes a deep breath.

Jefferson and I exchange a puzzled glance and sit on the nearest bench, glad to cede the stage to someone else.

"Miss Mary," Tug begins, and he starts twisting that hat in his hand.

Mary freezes, like a rabbit who's sighted a fox. Slowly, carefully, she sets her basket of biscuits on the table and folds her hands together over her apron.

Twist, twist, twist, goes Tug's hat. "I know I'm not a fancy man. And even though I'm mighty fine looking, I concede that I am but the fourth best-looking fellow in this town."

Fourth? At least he doesn't lack optimism.

"But I work hard, and I'm healthy and strong," Tug continues. "A catch for any woman. But, see, I don't want any woman. I want you, Miss Mary. To be my wife. You're the nicest, handsomest, uppittiest woman I ever knew, and it'd make me the happiest man in the world if you said yes."

And then, Tug shocks us all by clearing his throat again and letting loose a long string of Chinese. No one gapes more than Mary.

Tug grins. "Been practicing that for months, with the help of some of my friends here. You'll always be smarter than me, and I'm sure I bungled that a fair piece, but . . . maybe you can teach me true?"

Silence reigns in the tavern.

I lean toward Jefferson and whisper, "He's never proposed like that before. He must really love her."

Jefferson whispers back, "Mary is the only thing he's been talking about for the last two months."

Finally Mary unclenches her hands, lifts her chin, and says, "Mr. Tuggle, I would be honored to become your wife."

Tears brim over in Tug's eyes, and suddenly all the Buckeyes are whooping and hollering like it's the Fourth of July.

"Two weddings in Glory this year!" I say, delighted.

"Three," says a voice at my ear. It's the Major, slipping onto the bench beside Jeff and me. "Becky said yes," he explains. "But we prefer to keep things quiet for now. We'll wait until her husband has been gone from us a whole year, God rest his soul."

Jefferson claps him on the back, as I reach out to take his hand. "That's wonderful news, Major," I tell him.

From her place at the stove, Becky bangs a pair of tongs against a kettle, creating enough racket that everyone falls silent again.

She announces, "In honor of the upcoming nuptials of my dearest friends, everyone gets free seconds today!"

And once again, the miners cheer wildly. I get to my feet. "Becky is going to need my help," I say to Jefferson.

"And mine," Jefferson says. "Just put me to work."

The next afternoon, Becky helps me don my ridiculous spun-sugar wedding gown. We're getting ready inside her brand-new house—well, old house, I suppose—which has a porch, two rooms, a loft, and three windows. Her honeymoon cottage, shipped all the way from Tennessee.

We stand before a long floor mirror in a silver frame, and I can hardly believe such a fragile, frivolous thing made it to California unscathed.

"You sure you don't mind?" I ask Becky as she cinches my waist so tight I can hardly breathe.

"Of course not. This is the nicest house in all of Glory. You and Jefferson should enjoy it as newlyweds for at least a week." She works the ribbons in back, forming a perfect bow. "I'll take the house back soon enough, don't you worry. But Wally and Wilhelm and the Buckeyes worked so hard putting this place together; I reckon the whole town will want to see it put to good use right away."

I stare at my reflection in the mirror. It seems as though Mama is looking back at me—those same golden-brown eyes, the same golden-brown hair, that strong, stubborn chin. My hand goes toward my throat, reaching for a locket that's no longer there. I don't imagine that I'll ever get used to its absence.

Olive steps forward with a bouquet of wildflowers— mustard, poppies, blue lupine, and purple paintbrush. "I made this for you," she says shyly.

"Olive, this is beautiful. The best wedding bouquet I've ever seen."

The girl's cheeks blush rosy. "I made a littler one for Minnie, too," she says.

"Minnie?" I give Becky a questioning look.

Becky frowns at her oldest, but it's empty of true vexation. "I was going to wait until after the wedding to tell you," she says. "I've named my daughter."

I can hardly believe it. After all this time. "Becky, that's wonderful. Minnie, is it?"

"Minerva."

"From the California seal."

"Exactly. I wanted a strong name for her."

"Minerva is the Roman goddess of wisdom," Olive informs me solemnly. "I'm the big sister, so I have to teach her to be wise."

"I can't think of a better teacher."

The dinner bell rings, even though no meal is being served right now.

"It's time!" Becky says. "You look lovely. Ready to go?"

"I've kept that boy waiting long enough." I just hope I don't drown in lace before I can get myself properly hitched.

Becky leads me from the house, Olive following behind. Mary meets me at the door, dressed in a pretty gown of soft yellow. We are the four women of Glory, and we make a brightly colored but careful procession toward the Worst Tavern.

All the people I love in the world are already seated—Jim Boisclair, who has opened up a new general store right here in Glory, the Major with his future stepdaughter in his arms, Hampton, even Wilhelm and the Buckeyes. The college men have returned: Henry and Tom for a visit, but Jasper is here to stay. Tom waits at the front beneath the awning. He is licensed to perform wedding ceremonies now, and I'll have no one else. Henry gazes up at him adoringly from the first row.

Beside Tom stands Jefferson, and my heart tumbles a little. His straight black hair is fresh from a wash, his skin bronzed from working outside so much, his eyes bright with anticipation. I hate to admit it, but Becky and Henry were right. Plum is the perfect color for him, and I etch this moment in my mind, so that later I'll be able to pull it from my memory and treasure it.

Nailed to the wall behind Tom is our town charter, neatly framed. At Jeff's feet sit Nugget and Coney. I can safely say I've never attended a wedding with dogs before, but everything is different in California.

As I reach the front, Jefferson whispers, "You're right. You look like a pastry."

I grin up at him, wondering if any moment could be more golden than this one.

"I mean, you look really pretty, Lee. The prettiest girl in the land." He would know. He's seen a whole continent.

Tom begins. "Dearly beloved . . ."

It's going to be a quick ceremony, because Jefferson and I aren't fancy people. It's not the wedding that's important to us, it's the marriage. It's working together for the rest of our lives. It's knowing someone so deeply that facing the unknown together isn't dark and dangerous, but instead beautiful and bright.

I place my hand in Jefferson's, mouthing the words I hardly ever say, even though I feel them with my whole heart, for him, for my friends, for my home.

Author's Note

The descriptions of San Francisco owe much to the careful attention of journalist Bayard Taylor and his book *Eldorado*, originally published in 1850. Taylor traveled from New York to California in 1849 to report for the *New York Tribune*. I relied on the annotated edition, *Eldorado: Adventures in the Path of Empire*, published in 2000 by Santa Clara University and Heydey Books.

Coverture, the legal doctrine whereby a married woman's legal rights were entirely subsumed by her husband, was a real part of American history, though the specific laws varied by state and over time, in more complicated ways than I can cover here. One of the first goals of early feminists was to eliminate the doctrine of coverture. The Supreme Court finally struck down the last state law based on coverture in 1981, when I was eight years old.

Hampton's kidnapping was inspired by several historical instances, in particular, the account of Stephen Hill, a free black man kidnapped by slave catchers, whose freedom papers were destroyed. Delilah Beasley's *The Negro Trail Blazers of California,* originally published in 1919, is one of the earliest books to describe the many instances of free blacks who were held by slave catchers, as well as the black community's efforts to free them. She also described former slaves, like Hampton, who mined gold to buy family members out of slavery.

The *Charlotte*, run aground and converted into a residence, is loosely based on accounts of the whaling ship *Niantic*, one of the finest hotels in the early days of San Francisco. The Apollo saloon was a real saloon in San Francisco that also started out as a grounded ship.

The land-fraud schemes attributed to Hardwick all took place in San Francisco during the Gold Rush. In particular, several fortunes were built by selling titles to "water lots" in the bay. The practice of sinking ships to claim lots and begin the landfill process was very common, especially during 1851 and 1852, and was more mechanized than I've described in this book.

Sheriff Purcell was inspired by two early sheriffs in San Francisco, William Landers and John C. Pulis, both of who came west during the Mexican War as part of the New York Volunteers military unit.

The attempted bank robbery and the hanging that followed was inspired by a contemporary account of John Jenkins, an Australian who stole an entire safe from a bank and was captured during his escape and executed by a vigilance committee without a trial.

I hope the reader can forgive me, because the hymn "O Sleepless Nights, O Cheerless Days," from which the book's title is taken, was not published until well after the Gold Rush. It was written by Helen Smith Arnold, who was born in 1849. Arnold wrote two other hymns, and died in 1873 at the age of twenty-three.

James Boisclair is one of the few historical figures to appear in these novels. After buying his freedom and opening a successful general store in Dahlonega, Georgia, Boisclair packed up and joined the Gold Rush to California. Very little is known about what happened after he arrived, only that he was shot and killed. One of the best historical accounts of Boisclair is found in "Georgia's Forgotten Miners: African Americans and the Georgia Gold Rush of 1829," by David Williams, published in _Appalachians and Race: The Mountain South from Slavery to Segregation_, edited by John C. Inscoe (University Press of Kentucky, 2001).

A special thank-you goes to Dr. Shirley Ann Wilson Moore, Professor Emerita of History at California State University, Sacramento, who reviewed this manuscript and applied her vast knowledge to the text. For further reading on this time period, I recommend her outstanding book, _Sweet Freedom's Plains: African Americans on the Overland Trails 1841–1869_ (University of Oklahoma Press, 2016).

In telling Mary's story, I was influenced by the historical accounts of Polly Bemis, a Chinese immigrant who came to San Francisco as a concubine, lived in the gold-mining camps of Idaho, and wedded Charlie Bemis, a white saloonkeeper, in a marriage of convenience. Her story can be found in *The Poker Bride: The First Chinese in the Wild West,* by Christopher Corbett (Atlantic Monthly Press, 2010). Mrs. Bemis remained independent throughout her life, controlling her own destiny. Though I didn't use specific details about Mrs. Bemis's life, I wanted Mary's story to illustrate both the opportunities briefly available to nonwhite women during the early Gold Rush period, as well as the challenges they encountered that forced them to make hard choices.

Books are hard to write. Trilogies are harder. I couldn't have written this one without my team, which includes my husband and researcher, C. C. Finlay; my indefatigable editor, Martha Mihalick; and my agent-cheerleader, Holly Root. I also owe a huge debt to my readers. Thank you for your tweets, your emails, your Facebook messages, and most of all for hanging out with me at events all over the country. You make this job the best in the world.